UNHINGED
BOOK 3 OF THE "WHAT HAPPENED TO MIA DAVIS?" SERIES

K.T. CARLISLE

Copyright © 2024 by K.T. Carlisle

All rights reserved.

No part of this publication may be reproduced, distributed, or transmitted in any form or by any means, including photocopying, recording, or other electronic or mechanical methods, without the prior written permission of the publisher, except as permitted by U.S. copyright law. For permission requests, visit www.ktcarlisle.com.

The story, all names, characters, and incidents portrayed in this production are fictitious. No identification with actual persons (living or deceased), places, buildings, and products is intended or should be inferred.

CONTENTS

Prologue — 1

Part 1
Michael

    Chapter 1 — 13

    Chapter 2 — 29

    Chapter 3 — 43

    Chapter 4 — 67

    Chapter 5 — 87

    Chapter 6 — 105

    Chapter 7 — 131

    Chapter 8 — 155

    Chapter 9 — 185

    Chapter 10 — 213

    Chapter 11 — 241

    Chapter 12 — 267

Part 2
Evan
    Chapter 13   295
Part 3
Rachel
    Chapter 14   307
Epilogue   319

For Sara,

You are the reason this book exists. Thank you for making this series what it is.

I love you.

PROLOGUE

June 5, 1996

Michael leaned his head against the window of his mother's old station wagon as he watched the world pass by from the backseat. He tried to focus his attention on the way the car's vibrations rattled through his skull as it rolled over the pavement rather than the mounting dread building in his ribcage, but he could feel his mother's eyes on him. Like two swollen water balloons staring at him through the rearview mirror, threatening to burst.

"It's only for a little while," she reminded him for what seemed like the hundredth time that day. Her voice was tight, fragile—even Michael's eight-year-old mind could deduce that his mother was close to tears. But he didn't care. He was tired of hearing her excuses. Rather than answer her, he folded his arms across his chest in defiance and kicked the back of the passenger's seat.

"I want to go *home!*" he shouted, kicking the seat again for emphasis as he formed the final word. His mother jumped, startled by her son's anger. She tucked a strand of sandy hair behind her ear before gripping the steering wheel with white knuckles. Her fingernails dug into the leather, as close to breaking as the woman they belonged to. A slow, staggered sigh escaped her red-painted lips.

"I told you already, honey, Grandpa's house is gonna be your new home." She peered into the rearview mirror, catching her son's eyes in the reflection. They were beautiful eyes—an exact match for her own, the color of a blizzard streaking across powder blue skies. On any other day, she might have admired how her son managed to inherit what she deemed to be the most attractive of her physical attributes. But as they held each other's stare, an icy sensation began to creep into her heart, hardening in the hidden chambers of her chest.

"I hate you." Michael's words landed with the force of a dagger on his mother's ears. He turned away from her reflection in the mirror, anger puckering his flesh with a trail of hot goosebumps as he resumed looking out the window.

A silent tear glided down his mother's cheek as she tore her eyes away from her son and refocused her attention on the road. It wasn't the first time that the two had fought since she broke the news that he would have to go and live with his grandfather. But that didn't make it any easier to be on the receiving end of her firstborn's wrath. She sighed, removing a hand from the steering wheel and resting it on her pregnant belly.

You'd better be worth all the trouble you're causing this family, she joked with her unborn child. As soon as the thought left her brain, guilt took its place. *That's no way to talk to your son, Carolyn*, she reprimanded herself. *It's not his fault you're too broke to keep his brother.*

Carolyn bit down on her lip to keep from sobbing, the taste of blood blooming over her tongue. She didn't want to go through with this, didn't want to rip her son away from everything that he knew. It wasn't fair to either of them. But with an overdrawn bank account, a dilapidated mobile home, a job that paid minimum wage, and a baby on the way, what choice did she have? She and her boyfriend could barely afford to feed themselves and Michael as it was. Adding diapers and formula and doctor's visits to their mountain of debt would seal their fates to the poorhouse sooner than they could say "government cheese."

She couldn't do that to her children. At least with Michael at her father's house, she could have some peace of mind knowing he'd be well-fed and with family. Besides, the cattle ranch in Red Rock was just a short drive away from the trailer park in Sudbury where she lived. She could visit Michael whenever she wanted. It wasn't as though she were abandoning him there forever. It was just temporary. Until she got on her feet. A few months. Maybe a year, tops.

While his mother wrestled with herself in the driver's seat, Michael remained tangled in a knot of quiet contemplation. His mind was a dark cloud illuminated only by lightning bolts of rage. He couldn't understand why any of this was happening. All he knew for certain was that it meant he would have to go to a new school in a new town full of new faces. There would be no more Sudbury Elementary School. No more Friday night fast food and movie marathons with his mom. But most importantly, no more Mia Davis.

His heart pinched at the realization, saltwater stinging his eyes as the tears came, blurring his vision until the world beyond the car window became nothing more than a kaleidoscope of greens and blues. It had never been easy for Michael to make friends.

He was shy, soft-spoken, timid—not at all like the other boys in school who had fathers at home who loved them, role models who were eager to help mold them into men. His mother's boyfriend had only recently entered the picture, not that it had made any difference in terms of bolstering Michael's self-esteem or sense of masculinity. Steve wasn't an abusive addition to the household, but his indifference toward establishing a meaningful relationship with his girlfriend's son did not go unnoticed—not in Michael's eyes, at least.

Without a paternal figure of his own to guide him through the nuances of boyhood, Michael lacked a sense of confidence that seemed to radiate off the flesh of his peers, and they could sense it. Like a shiver of sharks circling their prey, the children pointed and laughed, their gleaming teeth framed around shrill cackles that seemed to call attention to every shortcoming with pinpoint accuracy. Whether it was his unkempt blonde locks, his clearance rack clothing, or his absent athleticism, there seemed to be no shortage of reasons for Michael to be on the receiving end of fresh ridicule. But not from Mia. Never from Mia.

"Leave him alone!" Her battle cry came one day during recess as one of Michael's many bullies taunted him mercilessly on the blacktop.

"Make me!" the boy had sneered, sticking out his tongue. Though they were only in kindergarten at the time, the child seemed to tower above his fellow students, blocking out the sun with his mane of thick, dark curls. Michael cowered in the boy's shadow, lip quivering around the words he didn't have the courage to produce. But Mia was undeterred by the bully's size. Rather than shrink away, she scrunched up her button nose, narrowed her eyes, and sent the full force of her foot careening into the boy's shin. He doubled over in pain, gripping at his leg as he hobbled over to the nearest teacher.

"C'mon!" Mia slipped her hand around Michael's, her eyes imploring him to follow her so they wouldn't get into trouble with their teacher. She didn't need to ask him twice.

From that moment onward, the two were inseparable. And even though the other kids at school still didn't want anything to do with Michael, winning the affection of the most popular girl in class was enough to spare him from further torment. He was grateful for Mia's friendship. More than grateful, he was enamored with her. The infectious twist of her lips as they curled up into her rosy cheeks. The delicate trill of laughter that followed, like windchimes swimming through a summer breeze. The softness of her skin as she wrapped her dainty fingers around his. Everything about her seemed to hold him hostage, his heart a fragile prisoner and she his whimsical warden. Now, Michael would be forced to endure a new kind of captivity—one that made the butterflies in his stomach flap with fear rather than infatuation.

He had been to his grandfather's cattle ranch a few times over the years, each visit spawning pinpricks of panic deep within Michael's intestines. Of course, there were the normal aversions that children often felt when faced with the inevitable passage of time. Like the way his grandfather's wrinkled skin reminded him of a Halloween mask—grotesque and repulsive. There was also the nauseating smell of manure that clung to the back of Michael's throat, stealing the air from his lungs in an instant whenever his mother's station wagon turned off the dirt road and onto the long stretch of gravel driveway that led to the farmhouse.

But there was something else, too.

An ominous undercurrent that tiptoed in the shadowy creases of his grandfather's eyes whenever they landed on Michael. As hard as he tried to be a good boy, nothing he did seemed satisfactory enough to wipe the look of disgust from his grandfather's face. He couldn't understand why, but Michael got the distinct sensation that he was unwanted in that house. As his mother's car bumped along the familiar path to the rickety structure that haunted the end of the driveway, that feeling of being unwelcome pulsated through Michael's tiny body.

"Here we are," Carolyn announced, a thin smile ghosting across her lips while she parked the car. She hoisted herself out of the driver's seat with a grunt, her swollen belly making an otherwise simple action daunting and laborious. Michael remained glued to the backseat, unyielding, unmoving.

If she wants me to get out, he thought in bitter silence, *she's gonna have to drag me out.*

Carolyn removed a single rolling luggage from the trunk of her station wagon before walking over to open the back door on the passenger's side of the car. A thick, hot fog of humidity invaded the cabin, still cool from having the air conditioning on full blast for the duration of their drive. The sticky air was as oppressive and offensive to Michael as the idea of living under the A-framed roof of his grandfather's log cabin masquerading as a farmhouse.

"C'mon, sweetheart," Carolyn begged. "Time to get out of the car."

"No!" Michael crossed his arms and pouted. "I wanna go home! I wanna go home!"

"Honey, *please!*" Exasperation mounted in his mother's voice as she bent over Michael to unbuckle his seatbelt. Panic and outrage swelled inside his chest, the imminence of his removal striking fresh fear into Michael's heart. He wriggled away, thrashing his head against the car seat, his limbs flailing with the wild abandon of a plastic bag dancing in the wind. In the heat of his tantrum, one of Michael's skinny kneecaps connected with his mother's gut, forcing the breath from her lungs.

Carolyn staggered backward, hands clutching the space above her navel where her son's knee had made contact with her pregnant belly. A deep cramp tugged at her insides, sending icy tendrils of anxiety down her inner thighs as she contemplated the wellbeing of her unborn child. She let out a low groan, grimacing slightly as she rubbed her stomach and gauged whether the blow had caused any significant damage or had simply caught her off guard. Just as she opened her mouth to reprimand her son for his unruly behavior, the crack of the screen door slamming against her father's house stunned her speechless. No sooner had the sound jolted her into silence than the old man was upon her.

Though he was well into his sixties, Michael Davies, Sr. was a storm of a man, with a square set jaw and strong arms that bulged in testament to the decades spent working the fields of his farm. He shared the same arctic blue irises as his daughter and grandson, but as he marched over to the station wagon, his eyes were like two lumps of coal embedded in a blanket of leathery skin.

"Daddy, I'm fine," Carolyn stammered. "It was an accident. He didn't mean to—"

"Quiet," he barked. "He's at my house now, and I won't tolerate this kind of nonsense. It's best he learn that now."

Carolyn cast her gaze down to the dirt beneath her feet. She knew better than to argue with her father. If she continued to protest, and made him angry, he might go back on his promise to watch over her son. Sucking in slow, even breaths, she pretended not to hear the thunderclap of her father's open palm across young Michael's face or the wail of pain that erupted from her son's lips.

"Quit your cryin', boy," Michael cowered away from his grandfather's nicotine-stained breath as the old man leaned into the backseat and ripped the seatbelt out of its buckle. Michael Sr. snaked a callused hand around the back of the young boy's neck, grabbed a fistful of his shirt collar, and yanked him out of the station wagon.

"So long as you're under my roof, you'll abide by my rules." His eyes simmered with icy fire as he reprimanded his namesake. "Rule number one: Respect your elders. Now, apologize to your mother."

Michael's throat constricted around the urge to scream, tears and snot streaming down his face, which was still stinging from the slap he had endured. He had never been hit before—not by an adult, at least. Was this what life would be like at his grandfather's house? The thought made his legs feel like liquid as he inched closer to his mother's shadow. Gulping down mouthfuls of humid air in an effort to calm himself, Michael sniffled and rubbed his eyes with the back of his hand.

"I'm sorry, Mama," he whimpered. Carolyn's heart went numb with remorse at the sight of the palmprint emblazoned across her child's cheek. She had suffered the same fate on more than one occasion. After all, the only way her father knew how to keep the children under his care from misbehaving was with the back of his hand.

Part of her wanted to gather Michael into her arms, stuff him back into the station wagon, and bring him back to her mobile home. But, the protrusion of her stomach reminded her that there were far worse circumstances that would await her son in Sudbury than a stinging face. Michael was a good boy. He would learn from this mistake. But there was nothing to be learned from a starving stomach or sleeping on the floor.

Carolyn ran her thin fingers through Michael's sandy hair, sliding her hand down the side of his face to rest on his burning cheek. As she bent down to meet him at eye level, she placed a gentle kiss on the red, swollen mark imprinted on her son's face, fighting back tears as she whispered in his ear.

"It's okay, baby," she cooed. "Mama loves you."

PART 1
MICHAEL

CHAPTER I

May 13, 2023

Have you ever just... snapped? Like your skin is made of glass and all the blood in your body is a river of tiny hammers chiseling away at your flesh until finally, you explode into a thousand pieces? Shards of yourself scatter into the abyss. Deep down, you know that you're a whole person. You can feel where the jagged edges of your fractured parts are supposed to fit together, but they can't connect. And you don't want them to. Because the moment you lose control is the freest you've ever been in your entire life.

That's how I felt that day. It's how I felt for most of my existence—like a rabid dog tethered to a tree, snarling and lunging with all its might until, inevitably, the rope frays, the tension loosens, and the beast is released. I loved that feeling. Loved how the velvety edges of the shadows in my mind would turn blacker than black, drowning me in a darkness so complete, it was like dying. No, it was better than dying. It was *becoming* death. A total transformation from mortal to god in the blink of an eye.

It wasn't a foreign feeling. I was practiced in navigating the ebb and flow of the darkness inside of me. We had an understanding, my demons and I. They'd tell me their secrets, and I'd let their whispers eat my ear until their hushed voices reached a terrible crescendo too loud, too powerful to ignore. They'd demand sustenance, and I'd feed them. Over and over again, I'd feed them. It became somewhat predictable, manageable even. But that day was different. That day, the hunger came without warning.

And I wanted to devour everything.

I'd like to pretend that if I had stayed home from the office that day, things would have turned out differently, but that would be a lie. The malignance inside of me had become ravenous, insatiable despite its many recent feedings. I knew it was inevitable that I would need to nourish it again, but there hadn't been enough time since the last feast to prepare for another. The cyclical pattern had been broken, the need to eat increasing in urgency, demanding attention that I wasn't yet ready to provide. I had already leveraged the student housing project in Charlotte to satisfy my cravings twice in two months, and I never indulged in the same city more than once. But I was starving. And when Evan walked into my office that afternoon, his words carved a new emptiness into my stomach unlike anything I had felt before.

I liked Evan. He was smaller than me, with spindly arms that I often dreamed about breaking. His quickness to anger meant that he was both irrational and easy to manipulate, which made him even less of a threat than his waiflike appearance would suggest. But what I liked the most about Evan was how others seemed to perceive these same qualities. Where I observed malleability and weakness, others saw violence and intimidation. It was almost comical the way others feared him, as though there were anything remotely frightening about a hopelessly predictable, borderline anorexic alcoholic. I needed someone like that. Someone who could absorb whatever shadowy suspicions might otherwise have landed squarely on my shoulders in the aftermath of all my feasts.

It was nice to have him around as a useful idiot of sorts. He had been the perfect scapegoat for me the first time my hunger had grown too strong to stomach. Though I found nearly every one of his attributes to be fundamentally repugnant, I grew to think of him as somewhat of a friend as the years passed. That is, until I learned that he was fucking my wife. Or at least, that's what Elaine had led me to believe.

Goddamn Elaine. She had come to my hotel room drunk and sniveling during that first trip to Charlotte back in March, bursting to tell me all about the secret sex lives of our spouses. Well, *my* spouse. She and Evan had been divorced for a long time by that point. The revelation had been infuriating to me, partly because on some level, I loved Cat, and her betrayal cut deeper than a jagged pane of glass wedging itself inside my forearm. But what angered me the most was how the unwanted discovery had disrupted my ritual. No sooner had I completed my most recent feeding than Elaine was knocking down my door, demanding to be let inside with the same persistence as the voices within my mind, longing for sustenance. A killing as sublime as the one from which I had returned would normally have quelled my hunger to a dull ache for at least a year's time. But once Elaine told me about the affair, it was as though I had been starved all over again. The need to satiate the darkness inside me became pervasive. Unavoidable.

Inescapable.

It wasn't the infidelity that bothered me so much as it was the overwhelming desire to drown in Evan's blood. Containing my need to watch the light fade from another's eyes was challenging enough as it was without adding the sting of a cheating spouse to the equation. It was even more difficult to keep a lid on my fury when both my wife and the man she was screwing behind my back were also my business partners. We co-owned an interior design firm together, which meant I was forced to be in their presence each day.

I didn't appreciate the way their affair made my insides quake with yearning, the demand for flesh so all-consuming, it rendered me as weak and pitiful as the very man who had stolen what was mine. But the visceral rage that ravaged my soul as I obsessed over the thought of them being together paled in comparison to the emptiness that threatened to swallow me after I learned that the entire thing had been an illusion. A fallacy imagined by a combination of Elaine's assumptive idiocy and some nosy detective's need to destroy everything that I had worked so hard to build. Part of me feared that the deceit would unravel me, make it impossible to keep my composure, plan ahead, be methodical. The hungry part of me wanted to become undone. Maybe that's why I didn't simply walk away when Evan entered my office looking for a fight.

"Elaine still shopping around for a gun?" He scowled at me from the doorway, arms folded across his scrawny chest like a pair of twigs begging to be snapped in half. I wondered what it would sound like to hear his bones crack. Would it be as loud as a tree branch splintering away from its trunk in the wake of a hurricane? Or would the satisfying pop of his elbow separating at the joint get muted beneath the muscles and skin surrounding his skeleton? If I listened close enough, I swore I could hear the—

"Hello? Asshole?" It appeared Evan wasn't in the mood to tolerate my private musings. "What're you talking about?" I sighed. I tore my gaze away from his arms, trying to ignore the fact that we were alone in the office. That there was no one around to hear him scream. That I was so, so hungry, and he was looking more like a country buffet with each passing second.

"Elaine," he said. The sound of his ex-wife's name sent shivers of indignation down my spine the moment it left Evan's lips and reached my ears. "You'd better fucking watch her."

I gestured toward the parking lot through my office window, devoid of any vehicles aside from my silver Altima and Evan's bright-red Wrangler.

"In case you haven't noticed, she's not around. Hasn't been all week." It was an unfortunate observation—one that had already set my mind on edge. I had thought about hunting her down since the moment I let her walk out the door of our shared home the previous week, but I couldn't risk it. Not when I knew who was watching in the background.

"Do you know where she is?" Evan's growing impatience was wearing thin on my already frayed nerves. I squinted into the rat-like features of his pointed face, imagining what it would be like to cross the room and drive my fist between his teeth, feel the crunch of his jaw as it collided with my knuckles.

Do it, Michael. We've already shown you how good it feels to deviate. What's one more body?

I shook the voices from my mind. *Quiet!* I reprimanded them. *Not here.*

"She's staying with her parents," I muttered. Evan scoffed at this, his throat strangled around a strange guffawing noise that made my teeth grind together.

"Her *parents?*" He raised a dubious eyebrow that disappeared behind the ridiculous mane of shaggy, black tresses dangling in a haphazard mess from his puny skull. "You're sure about that?"

I was getting irritated by the unwanted conversation, but the tone of his voice as he posed the question gave me the odd sensation that he knew something I didn't. My insides hardened at the thought.

What could this imbecile possibly know that I don't? I doubled down.

"That's where she said she was going last Friday," I told him. A curiously cocky expression consumed Evan's features, his lips twitching upward in a satisfied smirk. The sight of it made my fingers itch with the desire to rip the flesh from his face.

"Oh yeah?" he taunted. "Did she also mention that she'd be making a stop at my apartment on the way?"

Flames licked at the walls of my stomach.

"What do you mean?" The words crackled in my throat like embers sparking from a fire pit.

"I mean that whatever bullshit you started by cheating on your wife with her best friend is getting out of hand," Evan answered. "Elaine's completely out of her mind."

Somewhere inside my chest, I could feel the demons stirring, sinking their claws into my sternum as anxiety swelled within.

"Why was she at your apartment?" I growled.

"From the sound of it, she wanted to kill Cat," Evan replied. "She came barreling into my place, screaming about Holiday Inn receipts and fake IDs, demanding that I give her a gun!"

His words swirled around in my head like a tornado, vacuuming up every poisonous thought in the darkest recesses of my brain.

For one glorious moment, my mind went blank. Everything was still. There were no voices. No demons demanding to be fed. No daydreams of death and destruction. All was quiet. Tranquil.

Then the hunger came. The dinner bell chimed. I could taste blood.

"Get out." I could feel the words scrape against my vocal cords but couldn't hear them over the crazed chorus cackling through my mind. *Kill him. Kill her. Kill them.* I wanted nothing more than to give the voices what they demanded. Judging from the way he remained stationed in my doorway, Evan seemed unaware of how dangerously close he was to becoming my next victim. Rather than retreat, he took a step closer—a child at the zoo wiggling a set of tasty fingers through a tiger's cage, daring me to take a bite.

"Keep your bitch in check," he snarled. "I don't know what she's scheming, but I won't let her or you continue to hurt the woman I—"

I sprang from my seat without warning, the clatter of my chair as it crashed against the hardwood causing Evan to jump back in fear before he could complete his sentence. We locked eyes with one another, the words he left unsaid pulsating in the air around us, making me nauseous with rage. He swallowed nervously.

"Just keep her away from Cat," he croaked. "Especially today."

My fists clenched, fingernails embedded deep into my palms. The edges of my vision began to melt away. I was slipping fast. If I didn't get out of there soon, I wasn't certain that I'd be able to keep myself from painting the walls with his blood. I'd give the demons what they craved. But not there. It was too risky. I needed to think. I needed a plan.

As I exited the tiny concrete building that contained our office space and stepped into the parking lot, the sun blared violently overhead. My long-sleeved button-down clung to my skin, the day's humidity creeping up my arms, plastering the polyester fabric to my body like papier-mâché. Heat waves lunged forward from my sedan as I flung the car door open and sank into the driver's seat. My flesh boiled, and it wasn't just because the late afternoon sun had transformed the inside of my Altima into an oven. It was the unadulterated rage coursing through my veins as Evan's words continued to pound against my eardrum.

Holiday Inn receipts and fake IDs.

My pulse was racing, teeth grinding back and forth until an electric current tore through my enamel, telling me I had cracked a molar. I slammed my fist into the top of my steering wheel.

"FUCK!" Flecks of spit projected from my mouth as I continued to spew profanities into the stifling sauna my car had become. I could feel myself bursting at the seams, fragments of my fury disintegrating into the ether as waves of realization continued to crash down on me. The world as I knew it—the world I had worked meticulously to create—was ending. And it was all because of that fucking bitch. Her assumptions, her stubbornness, her outright stupidity—all of it had led me down a path of self-destruction. There was no turning back. She knew too much.

And I had allowed it to happen.

My eyes drifted to the rearview, catching a glimpse of the dark blue sedan that was parked across the street. Watching. I had noticed the detective's presence looming in the shadows long before Elaine's frantic confession to me the previous week regarding their encounter. Anyone whose extracurricular interests were as incriminating as mine would take notice of these kinds of things. But I wasn't worried about it. I was confident that my years of careful misdirection would lead anyone to believe Evan was to blame for all of my horrific handiwork. Even Elaine seemed convinced of her ex-husband's involvement in whatever crimes Detective Rachel McGowen had alluded to during their talk.

I suspected that the investigator was likely still nurturing the seeds of doubt that I had planted in her impressionable little mind after what I did to her roommate all those years ago. It was Evan she was after, not me. But as I peered into the reflection at her unassuming Honda Civic, my self-assurance on the matter began to wane. If Elaine had gone behind my back to confront Evan about *Holiday Inn hotel rooms and fake IDs* as he suggested, then she would have left his apartment knowing that her fears had been unfounded. How long would it have taken her afterward to connect the rest of the dots? To realize who the real monster was? To convey her findings to her newfound confidante?

You have to kill her, Michael. It's the only way to keep us safe. To keep us fed. You have to—

"Shut up!" I screamed, grabbing fistfuls of sandy hair between my fingers. "Shut up, shut up, shut up! Let me *think*, goddamn it!"

I tried to steady my breathing, focus my attention on slowing my heart rate, but my gaze kept falling back on that sedan. Each time my eyes landed on that shitty car, all I could think about was how much longer it would be before the detective within would make her inevitable arrest. The thought made the pores of my skin slick with sweat. No, wait. That was just the oppressive heat baking into my bones. I jammed my car keys into the ignition and waited for the air conditioning to kick on. Maybe the cool air would help clear my mind, allow me a moment's peace so I could come up with a plan.

The voices were right, after all. If I wanted to avoid spending my life behind bars—or worse—then I would need to make sure that what Elaine knew never reached another's ears. She needed to be dealt with. Permanently. And so did Evan. I didn't think he was smart enough to piece together the significance of what Elaine had gone to his apartment to discuss, but I couldn't get his parting words out of my head.

I won't let her or you continue to hurt the woman I—

Not even while alone in my car could I bring myself to complete his thought, the implication of his unspoken sentiment enough to make me want to storm right back inside the office building and tear him limb from limb. I wasn't going to let another man steal what was mine. Not again. I needed to eliminate him. But I also needed to be rational. After all, I couldn't just kill him in broad daylight with Rachel watching across the street. And murdering the man whom I had planned would take my fall when the time came would only make matters worse for me. Still, the demons demanded action. They were ravenous, clawing at my mind in ways that made it difficult to concentrate on anything other than the instant gratification I would feel from giving them what they craved.

You could get away with it, they urged. *You're a smart boy, Michael. You've gotten away with more difficult things before.*

"This is different," I grumbled. "I need more time."

Steven.

"Don't," I begged.

Jimmy.

"Stop," I pled.

Mia, Laura, Sylvie, Joan, Kayla, Brittany, Hannah, Tina, Stacy—

"SHUT UP!" I threw the car into reverse and peeled out of the parking lot, my eyes locked on Detective McGowen's sedan as I turned onto the road. As I continued down the street, I kept my gaze fixed on the rearview mirror, watching for any sign that the Honda was following.

See? She doesn't know a thing. The voices laughed with renewed confidence, but I remained unconvinced of my safety. *You're too tense, Michael. Here... let us help you.*

"I don't need your—" But it was too late. The decision had been made for me.

I was no longer in control.

***

The first thing I noticed when I regained my senses was the familiar fog of rusted metal nestled in my nostrils, followed by the taste of copper on my tongue. I was dizzy and disoriented, a sensation I had grown accustomed to whenever the demons grew weary of my resistance and seized power over my body. As I waited for the initial confusion to subside, I realized that my hands were coated in a thick layer of warmth that felt somehow slick and sticky all at once.

The metallic odor coupled with the syrupy substance stuck to my skin reminded me of Sir's cattle ranch, how the stench of iron and death lingered in the barn long after the final cow was brought to slaughter. I could almost hear their panicked moos right before the bolt was shot into their brains, piercing and pervasive. Unnatural. But I didn't just hear them. I felt the grit of their anguish stinging at the back of my throat, burning through my esophagus like hot bile. Because the sounds weren't just the product of a vivid daydream manifested through the power of olfactory memory. They were real. They were palpable.

They were coming from me.

My agony rattled in my ears, sharpening my vision with each guttural scream that erupted from me. As my eyes adjusted to the darkness, fresh torment surged from deep within my abdomen, hot embers exploding through my vocal cords and into the face of the woman I loved. The one who had abandoned me. The one who had forgotten me. The one who had created me.

My chest quivered around deep, gasping breaths as I peered into the moonlight trapped inside her unblinking blue eyes. I hated the way they seemed to look straight through me, as though I were nothing but a shadow. A fragment from a memory that she couldn't place. Flower stems wrapped around tiny fingers. Stalks of sun-scorched weeds towering above tiny bodies. Promises of forever stretched across pink lips. It wasn't supposed to be this way. Maybe in another life, it could have been different. I could have had her. Could have kept her. Alive.

"Mia!" I cried into the night. "I'm so sorry, Mia. I had to do it. I *had* to. You promised me. You *promised!* And now look what you've made me do..."

She said nothing. She never said *anything*. Just looked through me with that cold, indifferent stare. And still, I loved her. I craved her. More than anything in the world, I hungered for her. A shock of cold ran through my fingertips as I brushed the golden tresses away from her vacant face. Even in death—or maybe it was especially in death—she was beautiful. She was perfect.

My Mia Davis.

I lowered my lips onto hers, savoring the sweetness of her skin. It was the only redemption I could afford, the only peace I was proffered until the next time we met. As I pulled away, I wiped the excess blood from my hand across my jeans and draped my fingers over her eyes, laying her to rest as I had done so many times before.

"I love you, Mia," I whispered. "We'll be together soon."

The instant the words left my mouth, the illusion was shattered. My spine stiffened, hyperawareness shooting into overdrive as I realized where I was. What I had done. Who I had done it to. Why I had lost control.

I was kneeling on the marble floor of Cat's kitchen. Elaine's bloody body was blooming fluid across the tile, soaking into my knees. My hand was still wrapped around the kitchen knife that I had apparently used to drain her, though I had no recollection of having done so. This was common for me—minutes, sometimes hours of my life gone missing from my mind, only for awareness to return in time for me to have my moment with Mia. Those seconds in her presence, though imagined and often painful, had been the only nourishment for my tormented soul. A second chance at a life that always should have been, enough to fill the cavity that her apathy had left behind. But as I surveyed the gory aftermath of what happened while I had been lost somewhere in the ether, the usual feelings of bliss that a fresh kill provided were nowhere to be found.

What did you make me do? I scolded the entities within that I knew had been responsible for the carnage.

What needed to be done, they answered. *Time to clean up.*

Clean up? I balked at the pool of deep red liquid oozing from Elaine's many open wounds. *This isn't like the others. I can't just clean this up.*

Turn around, the demons commanded. My head snapped back in the opposite direction. Across the bloodstained marble floors, I could see the silhouette of my wife's body lying in a crumpled mass beside the kitchen island. A flood of icy panic drenched my insides until the shadows stopped dancing around her figure long enough for me to realize that she was still breathing. I hadn't killed her.

Get up.

Again, I obeyed the orders. In all my years of symbiosis with the creatures haunting my mind, I had learned it was always best to listen to their commands in the moments immediately following our gruesome escapades. They had a calmness about them, a structured discipline that kept us both out of harm's way.

Go to her.

With the butcher's blade still glued to my right hand like an extra appendage, I cautiously traversed the blood-soaked tile, careful not to leave my footprints behind as I stopped beside Cat's unconscious form.

Place the knife in her hand.

I hesitated for a moment, nudged Cat with the tip of my shoe until she rolled over on her back and I could see her face. She wasn't as beautiful as my Mia, with wild ringlets of black hair framed around an angular face that was every bit as feline as her name. But she was still mine. I still loved her. After all, if it hadn't been for her, I wouldn't have been able to accomplish half of the things I had done over the years. Our marriage had enabled me to maintain an illusion of normalcy, to operate in the shadows undetected, to appease my demons. If it hadn't been for Elaine's meddling, I could have continued with the charade, could have played the part of happy husband with Cat as my supporting actress, none the wiser to my ruse than any other unsuspecting person. But that possibility had been stolen from me, and now I was faced with an impossible decision—one that would destroy the only woman who had ever shown me any mercy.

Do it, now! The voices grew impatient the longer I stood there. I sank onto the floor, folding myself over Cat's body to steal a final embrace as I prepared to place the knife in her hand and seal her fate to a jail cell. Pulling away from her, I placed a kiss on her cheek, stroking her porcelain skin with the back of my hand as I raised myself into a seated position on the floor.

"Thank you," I murmured. Though I knew she was out cold, I hoped that my gratitude had somehow worked its way into her subconscious. Using her tee shirt, I wiped the knife handle clean of my fingerprints and placed the blade into her right hand. With the incriminating picture complete, I stood up and headed toward the back door. Before I could place my hand on the doorknob, the voices stopped me in my tracks.

Call the police, they instructed. *They have to find her before she wakes up.*

In a daze, I reached for the corded phone bolted to the wall beside the back door and dialed 911. The operator answered within moments, her nasally voice absent of urgency as she inquired about the nature of my emergency.

"There's been a murder at 29 Fieldstone Avenue." The words left my body like smoke from a campfire curling up toward a star-studded sky. "Hurry."

Rather than wait to hear the woman's response, I let the phone clatter against the wall as it dropped from my hands, and I slipped through the back door into the blackness beyond.

CHAPTER 2

October 21, 1998

The cows weren't visible from my bedroom window—they had already been ushered into the barn for the night—but their distressed braying penetrated the glass. As though they, too, could feel the obsidian umbra of hurt threatening to overtake me. As though they could already detect a shift in the wind, the unmistakable reek of change mingling together with the thick cloud of manure steaming along the horizon. I tried to drown them out, shove a pillow over my head, pretend they didn't know better. But deep down, I knew they were right.

Everything was different now—and it was only going to get worse.

It didn't happen overnight. Sometimes I wondered if it even happened at all, or if I had simply imagined it. I guess that's the trouble with losing your mind. You spend so much time drifting in waves of uncertainty, oscillating between possibilities, convincing yourself everything is fine, everything is *normal*, that when you finally look in the mirror and fail to recognize your reflection, it's already too late.

You're gone. And someone else has taken your place.

Maybe it doesn't happen that way with everyone, but that's how it felt for me. One day, I was an ordinary, happy eleven-year-old boy (or at least, I was trying to be). But the more time I spent on Sir's ranch, the murkier that image became until I finally had to admit to myself that I was neither happy nor ordinary.

I was nothing.

I was no one.

Though I was aware that a physical form existed, it was as though my body belonged to someone else. A mirage lulling those around me into a sense of false security only for them to discover nothing more than a burning, barren wasteland hidden just beneath the surface.

**

September 13, 1998

The process was slow, gradual. But, if I had to pinpoint the precise moment when the emptiness inside devoured me, it was probably during the weeks leading up to my twelfth birthday. It was the beginning of fifth grade, which meant it was the third consecutive year that I had spent living in isolation on Sir's ranch. Excited chatter swarmed around my head like a colony of bees as my peers gossiped about summer vacations and sleepovers and Fourth of July celebrations—all of which sounded too good to be true. None of which I had been invited to experience firsthand. Why would I have been? Even though it had been years since I was enrolled in Red Rock Elementary, I was still considered the new kid. The loser. The freak that nobody wanted to befriend. Even if

I hadn't been perceived as a social outcast, Sir never would have let me go off and have any fun.

"Please, Grampa," I had begged him once during that first, dreadful summer. "It's so hot, and I already finished refilling all the feed. Can't I just play in the hose for a little?"

He glowered at me through pale gray eyes, sweat gathering in the creases of his leathery skin. I should have known better than to complain about the day's work, but it was early on in my imprisonment; I hadn't yet learned the importance of remaining quiet. Obedient. It didn't take me long to commit the lesson to memory. Before I knew what had happened, the back of his hand connected with my jaw so hard, I could see constellations emblazoned across the sky in the middle of high noon.

"There's no such thing as playtime, you stupid little faggot," he barked. "And I'm not your pappy, boy. So long as you're on this ranch, you call me Sir—you understand?"

I nodded in stunned disbelief, blood swishing around in my mouth from the puncture pierced through my tongue that Sir's strike had caused. For the remainder of that afternoon, I swallowed mouthfuls of metallic-tasting saliva along with whatever foolish requests for rest dared to enter my mind.

In the years that followed, I never so much as asked for a sip of water to quench my unyielding thirst as we worked the land, let alone a day off to ride bicycles with the neighborhood kids. Not that I had a bicycle. Or children nearby who were interested in doing such things with me. I didn't even have a grandmother to serve as a buffer or break up the monotony of farm chores with something less physically demanding, like baking pies or dusting windows. Sir's wife died years before I was born—a fact that was never confirmed through discussion but rather deduced merely by observing her absence. The same way a child understands that the grass is green or a cow says "moo." There's no conversation about why. It simply is. And there's nothing you can do to change it.

That was the way I understood most of my life on Sir's ranch: A series of simple facts that were as unshakeable as they were irrefutable. Grandma was dead. Sir was mean. Michael was lonely. I didn't think it would ever change. But when fifth grade started and our teacher mentioned a field trip to the Sudbury Cider Mill, I couldn't contain my excitement.

"It's going to be a full day of apple-picking fun," Mrs. Donavan chirped as she passed out permission slips to each student. "There will be a hayride, a picnic lunch, and you'll even get to learn how apple cider is made."

She gave me a warm wink as she placed a pink sheet of paper on my desk, as though the palpable anticipation on my face was at all related to whatever drivel was spewing out of her overly-painted lips. Apples, cattle—it made no difference to me what the farm's purpose was. I had spent enough time on Sir's ranch to become disgusted by the prospect of spending a single moment longer in any field, no matter what it had growing or grazing along its horizon. But the name of the orchard in question had caught my attention.

Sudbury Cider Mill.

As soon as Mrs. Donavan resumed her place at the front of the class, my hand shot up in the air.

"Yes, um... Michael?" She called on me after referencing her class roster, still struggling to remember the names of her new students.

"Will other schools be joining us on the field trip?" My voice wavered around the question, crackling with hope. From my peripheral, I could see a few students snickering.

"What a stupid question!" One of them mocked. The echoes of laughter that followed caused my cheeks to burn as red as the hair that sat in a severe bun atop my teacher's head. Mrs. Donavan spotted the source of the outburst, fixing the student with a fiery glare that warned of dire repercussions should they dare to continue.

"There's no such thing as a stupid question," she said pointedly before turning kinder eyes in my direction. "I suppose it's possible that other schools may be at the orchard on that day."

It's possible.

Those were the only words I needed to hear for my mind to become alive with visions of Mia Davis. Then again, it never took much more than a glimpse of blonde hair in a crowded hallway to get my imagination going. My stomach somersaulted whenever I was fooled by the sweet southern twang of a schoolgirl whose voice even remotely resembled that of the one who had stolen my heart. But those were just fantasies. Delusions brought on by sheer desire and loneliness. This was a field trip in the town that I had been forced to leave behind. The same town where I had last seen her. It wasn't just a daydream. It was a *real* possibility. A chance to see my precious, perfect Mia Davis.

I peered down at the pink paper on my desk as though it held psychic knowledge, a degree of certainty about the future that my clown-faced teacher did not possess. As I combed the page for answers, my eyes fell on the date of the trip: My birthday. October 21. If I had any lingering doubt in my mind about this trip being some form of divine intervention meant to reunite me with the only friend that I had ever known, it was smothered the moment I saw that date. There was no question about it—I was going on that field trip.

The only thing I needed to figure out was how.

Of course, when I approached Sir with the permission slip that very night, his wheezy, whistling laughter ripped a hole through my chest in response. Though I understood the chances were slim that he would allow me to go, it still eviscerated me to have such a simple request so swiftly denied.

"Oh, he wants to go *pick apples*." Sir slapped his knee with open derision, whooping and hollering as though he were at a comedy club. It was the first time that I had seen him appear anywhere close to joyful in the two long, miserable years that I had suffered under his care. With a final swipe of his filthy index finger to flick away the tears of laughter that my apparently *hilarious* question had caused, the usual storm of disgust and disappointment clouded his features once more.

"The answer is no, boy. Get this garbage out of my sight. I don't want to hear another word about it."

"But, Sir—"

Smack!

The force of his hand on the back of my skull sent my forehead careening into the corner of the wooden dining table. I could feel my skin begin to stretch as it made room for the throbbing welt that my disobedience had earned me.

"Don't you fucking talk back to me, boy!" Sir warned. I didn't speak another word. Didn't dare rub the pulsing contusion that was threatening to burst through my skin, blinding me with pain as

I silently shuffled peas across my plate. I simply pocketed the pink piece of paper and waited for Sir to finish his dinner so I could wash the dishes and go to my room where I would spend the remainder of the night screaming and weeping into my pillow, wishing I was anywhere on earth but that godforsaken ranch.

That was the first night it happened.

I was curled up in my twin bed—the only piece of furniture in my closet-sized room—my tongue dry and sticky from hours of stifling sobs with my tattered pillowcase, when I heard them call to me.

Michael.

At first, I thought that I was imagining things. Perhaps the bruise on my forehead had caused some sort of concussion, or maybe I had already cried myself to sleep and what I heard was just a dream. Then an even more terrifying thought: Maybe it was Sir's sinister voice that was creeping through my darkened bedroom. But that couldn't be. He only ever referred to me as "boy" or "faggot" or "pussy." Never—

Michael!

I shot up in the bed, snot rolling over my upper lip like two slugs sliding out of my nostrils. My heart thumped against my ribcage as I squinted around the empty room, nothing but shadows staring back at me. I sniffed, wiped my face with my sleeve, and started to lower myself back down when it came again—louder this time. As though it were right on top of me. As though it were *inside* of me.

MICHAEL!

A tingling sensation stung somewhere in my underpants as all of the blood drained from my body and the urge to urinate threatened to overtake me. No, I wasn't dreaming. I wasn't imagining things. I was wide awake.

And I was not alone.

"Wh–who are you?" I whispered into the darkness. Fresh tears blurred my vision, no longer evidence of my turmoil but rather a physical manifestation of the fear that was ballooning inside of my abdomen.

Don't be afraid, Michael, the voices soothed. *We're here to help you.*

All at once, my muscles relaxed. Suddenly, it didn't matter to whom the voices belonged—or what. They'd offered to help. There had only ever been one person in my life who offered to help me. Maybe that's what made her so impossible to forget. If these disembodied entities were willing to do the same, who was I to deny their kindness?

"How are you going to help me?" My voice was barely audible through the rush of blood caressing my eardrum with electric adrenaline as I dared to ask the question.

Get up, they answered. *Let us show you.*

As though pulled by a string, my legs swung over the edge of my lumpy mattress, bare feet thwacking against the wooden floorboards with a thud I could hear but could not feel. I rose from the bed in a daze, drifting over to my bedroom door like a ghost gliding through the ether. My hand reached out for the doorknob, gripping the smooth, brass surface in my palm. Though I knew what it should have felt like, the sensation of cool metal against my skin failed to register. Every inch of my body had gone completely numb, as though a surgeon had reached inside me and severed the connection from my nerve endings to my brain.

"What's happening to me?" I tried to speak, but the words were too far away.

We are in control now, the voices replied.

I knew I should have been scared, should have wanted whatever otherness it was that surged inside of me to release me, but I wasn't and I didn't. Normally, the lack of control I felt over every aspect of my life was something that disturbed me, angered me beyond reason. But, as I slipped through the doorway of my bedroom into the sleeping house beyond, I felt oddly comforted by the fact that I was no longer responsible for my actions. I was a meat puppet, a shell, my soul abandoned elsewhere as blackness swallowed my senses, relieving me of the curse that was my existence—if only for a little while.

The sound of Sir's snoring rattled against the wood-paneled walls of the tiny hallway that snaked out to the left of my bedroom. Down the end of the hall was a multi-purpose room that served as the foyer, kitchen, and dining room. Across from my bedroom was the door to the living room—a modest space that overcompensated for its lack of entertainment with a giant stone hearth against the back wall. Though he tolerated my presence in these areas under his supervision, Sir had made it clear that I was not permitted to skulk about the house during sleeping hours. Yet another lesson I had learned from the back of his hand.

"I need to go back to bed," I urged, worried that the slightest disturbance might rouse Sir from his slumber and earn me a fresh beating. The lump on my forehead pulsed with warning as my feet carried me deeper into the darkened hallway.

It's okay, Michael, the voices reassured me. *This won't take long.*

I couldn't explain the reason why, but something about the raspy whispers tickling the inside of my ear told me I should trust them. They had told me they were there to help, after all. And I was in no position to be turning away promises of that magnitude.

Still, uncertainty swelled within me as my zombified body marched on unfeeling legs closer to Sir's bedroom door. I didn't know where the voices planned to take me, but reaching my final destination would almost certainly require me to tiptoe across the creaky floorboards just outside his chamber. Unless, of course, we were headed towards—

"The bathroom?" I voiced my confusion as my body made an unexpected turn through the doorway on the left in between Sir's bedroom and mine. Momentary relief swept over me as I realized that the voices were not carrying me into forbidden territory. Though he had prohibited me from exploring the house after hours, not even Sir was so much of a monster as to deny me the need to use the bathroom in the middle of the night.

Like everything else in the farmhouse, the bathroom was plain and cramped, with dark, wood-paneled walls that absorbed the yellow glow of the single overhead light that was fixed to the ceiling. The toilet was located immediately to the right of the doorway with a drop-in sink next to it, one of the cabinet doors beneath which had been damaged beyond repair and never replaced. Against the back of the room was a walk-in shower barely large enough to contain an adult body. I found myself standing in the center of the stained linoleum tile, my toes almost touching the rusty ring around the shower drain.

Grab the shampoo bottle, the voices demanded. I did as I was told and reached for the container of children's shampoo that was resting in the metal shower caddy which hung around the silver showerhead in place of a built-in niche. Before my fingers grazed the bottle, my hand jerked back involuntarily.

Not yours, the voices corrected. *His.*

I gulped.

"I... I can't." My voice was laden with disappointment at the sound of my own cowardice. What would my new friends think of my inability to comply with their wishes? Would they abandon me there in the shower? Refuse to offer their assistance? I still hadn't learned how it was that they planned to help me. They couldn't disappear on me yet.

I needed them.

It's okay, Michael, their discordant voices washed over me, lulling me into an instant calm. *We're right here. Very soon, it'll all be over, and you can go back to bed.*

I nodded my head as though they could see me, showing them that I was ready to listen. I was ready to be a good boy. I was ready to have their help.

Now, grab the shampoo bottle, they prompted again. This time, I obeyed without hesitation, grasping the thin, plastic container in my hand. *Good boy*, they praised me. *Twist off the cap.*

Again, I submitted to their demands, removing the cap from the bottle and placing it back in the shower caddy as I waited for further instructions.

Take off your pants, they said next. Though my body was still numb, I could sense on some level that my cheeks had grown hot with embarrassment at the request. It felt wrong that my new friends would want me to expose myself.

"I don't want to do that," I complained.

Don't you want our help?

My mind raced at the words. Of course, I wanted their help. But what they had asked had made me uncomfortable. It reminded me of when the policemen came to visit our classroom the year before to warn us about bad touches from grown-ups.

"Never do anything with an adult that feels wrong," they had told us. "And if any adult ever asks you to do something that makes you uncomfortable, find a teacher, a parent, or any adult you trust, and tell them about it immediately."

I stood frozen in the shower stall with the shampoo bottle still clutched in my hand, contemplating my next move. If I did what the voices asked me to do, I might not like it, and I might have to find an adult to tell afterward. The thought of what that might entail frightened me. But, if I didn't do what they said, they might leave me, and I couldn't bear the thought of being left alone again. Of being forgotten. Of having no one to help. I hung my head and allowed my free hand to loosen the drawstring around my pajama bottoms. I mean, *technically*, the voices didn't belong to an adult, so maybe it wasn't the same thing as what the policemen had warned us about. Maybe this would be okay.

My pajama bottoms and boxer shorts dropped to my ankles, and I stood half-naked in the shower, unsure what would come next. Sensation returned to my body as suddenly as I had lost it, and I became painfully aware that I needed to pee. I started to step out of the shower and head for the toilet, but the voices spoke before I could move any further.

The bottle, they said. *Use the bottle.*

Before I could voice my objections, the urge to urinate overpowered me. I stuck myself inside the container and allowed the floodgates to open, waves of euphoria crashing down on me as instantaneous relief blanketed me in a warm embrace. The bottle was half-full before I started, but by the time I was finished, it had been filled to the brim. I looked wide-eyed at the container as the warmth I had released within radiated through the plastic in my hands. My heart raced with excitement, butterflies scraping against the lining of my chest as I struggled to suppress a giggle at the sight of what I had done. I peed in my grandpa's shampoo—what fun!

Then came the icy grip of dread around my intestines.

If asking permission to go on a field trip had secured me a knot on my head, did I even want to know what fresh hell awaited me for urinating in Sir's shampoo bottle? The container was practically overflowing with piss. Surely, he would notice during his shower when the morning arrived.

Pour some out, the voices suggested. *Keep just enough, and dump the rest in the toilet.*

I set the container down on the shower floor so I could bring my pants back up around my waist before stepping out of the stall and creeping toward the toilet, careful not to let the warm liquid trickle over my hands as I drained the bottle into the bowl. When there was nothing more than an inch's worth of my urine left inside, I felt satisfied that what remained would not get me caught. After flushing the toilet, I returned to the shower to place the cap back on the bottle and leave my prize in the metal caddy.

Not so fast, the voices warned as I turned to leave the restroom. *You have to shake it up first so it blends in.*

Once more, I listened to what my new friends told me to do, twisting the cap tighter for good measure to ensure no pee would leak out from the top as I proceeded to shake the bottle with vigor until the contents within were thoroughly mixed. When I was finished, I placed the container back in the caddy, washed my hands, and snuck back to my bedroom, giddy with the unspeakable secret of what I had done.

What the voices had made me do.

"I can't believe I did that," I breathed, lowering my head to the pillow that was still damp from the tears I had shed.

You can do lots of things, Michael, the voices told me. *Would you like us to show you how?*

A smile worked its way across my lips as I lay in bed, staring into the moonlight that shone beyond my window.

"Yes," I whispered. "I'd like that very much."

Good, they answered.

And with that, I fell fast asleep.

CHAPTER 3

October 6, 1998

After that night, I didn't hear the voices again for a long time. Though I was delighted by the prank we had pulled together—even more so by the fact that Sir continued to soak his head in urine without me having to endure a single beating—I was disappointed that they, like everybody else in my life, had abandoned me. They had told me that night they would help me, they would show me how to do more fun things. But when I awoke the next day, I couldn't hear them.

They were gone.

I stayed up way past my bedtime for several nights in a row, waiting for the voices to return, hearing nothing but the sound of Sir's incessant snoring thundering through the hallway. After almost a month of complete silence, I started to wonder if I had imagined the entire thing. Maybe the voices weren't real. Maybe the reason I didn't get in trouble was because I didn't pee in Sir's shampoo bottle at all. Maybe I was all alone, and no one would ever bother to help me.

These were the thoughts that paraded through my mind as Mrs. Donavan's cheerful tenor cut through the air, every bit as intrusive and grating as the trill of the school bell that had just signaled the end of another horrible day.

"Listen up, class!" She hollered over the noise of rowdy pupils preparing to take their leave. "Tomorrow is the final day to hand in your permission slips for the trip to Sudbury Cider Mill. If you haven't done so already, be sure to get a signature from a parent or guardian so you can attend. Those of you who will not be joining us for the trip—" her eyes locked with mine, as though my absence had been predetermined, "—will be spending the day with Mrs. Newbury's class instead.

"Okay, everybody, have a wonderful afternoon! Don't forget to do your reading for tonight. You never know when the next pop quiz will be." A few students groaned at the words, the mere mention of the word *quiz* enough to inspire unfathomable dread. Mrs. Donavan smirked in response, "Now, now. I've got to make sure you're understanding the material somehow! Okay, y'all have a good day now. Oh, and Michael?"

I froze in place at the sound of my name. My skin prickled as twenty pairs of curious eyeballs darted in my direction.

"Hang back for a moment, honey. I need to speak with you." Her gaudy lipstick twitched up in a tight smile that made my stomach as queasy as the chorus of *ooohs* that bleated from the throats of every student in class at her request. She invited the class to settle down, but her reprimands did little to quell their excitement, nor did it ease the anxiety squeezing at my insides as I remained seated at my desk, waiting for the other children to exit the room.

When they were finally gone, Mrs. Donavan beckoned me to join her at her desk at the front of the class. A jackhammer rattled around my chest as I obeyed her command and walked on gelatin legs to the front of the room. She folded her hands on top of a stack of papers and spoke in a stern yet gentle voice.

"Do you know why I asked you to stay, Michael?"

I scuffed my sneaker across the linoleum floor and shrugged, choosing to look at my feet rather than face the inquiring adult before me. She sighed.

"I'm worried about you, honey," she began. The concern in her voice was jarring enough to make me lift my gaze in her direction. I had never been spoken to with so much care before—at least not since the last time I'd seen my mom. She continued, "You seem distracted lately. Is everything alright at home?"

An iceberg formed and melted in my gut, turning my insides to slush. *No,* I wanted to tell her. *Nothing is "alright" at home.* But I couldn't risk telling her the truth. Couldn't even fathom the thought of what my punishment might be for saying such things. So, I lied.

"Yeah," I croaked. "Just tired, I guess."

"Tired?" A scarlet eyebrow ventured toward the fiery strands of hair that decorated her scalp, an invitation for me to explain.

"We live on a ranch," I answered. "I have to get up early and help a lot."

"I see," she nodded and smiled. I detected a note of relief in her voice, as though she had just solved a difficult equation that had been keeping her up for nights on end. "That must be hard work. I bet your grandpa appreciates all the help."

I swallowed hard.

"Yeah," I lied again. "I guess so."

"You're a good boy, Michael," Mrs. Donavan said with a grin. She unfolded her hands and removed the top piece of paper from the pile on her desk, the smile fading from her lips as she pushed the sheet across to me. "But, I'm afraid I have some bad news."

I looked down at the paper she had placed between us, a bright red "F" glaring back at me.

"You failed last week's math test, honey," she stated. "I'm going to have to ask you to get your grandpa's signature on this so he knows you're having a tough time. It's school policy."

My stomach twisted in knots. I couldn't be sure if I was going to puke or have diarrhea. One thing was certain: Sir was not going to like this—not one bit.

"Michael?" Mrs. Donavan's voice called me back to reality. "You understand what I've told you?"

"Yes, ma'am," I mumbled, stuffing the evil test with its mocking red marks into my backpack. She gave me a tight smile, and I headed toward the door so I could make it to the bus loop in time to catch my ride back to the ranch. Before I could place my hand on the doorknob, Mrs. Donavan called to me once more.

"And Michael?" I turned to face her. "If you ever need to talk or need some extra tutoring, you know you can come to me—right, honey?"

"Yes, ma'am," I repeated. She gave me a wink, and I exited the classroom, fighting the urge to cry as I raced to board the school bus that would carry me to my doom.

I decided to wait to break the news to Sir until after we had finished our chores for the evening. It was difficult enough slaving away in the late afternoon sun with the usual threat of his backhand looming heavy on my mind. I didn't want to give him any more of a reason than he had already to "beat the sense into me" as he often proclaimed. Part of me thought about avoiding the subject altogether, throwing the flunked math test in the garbage with our dinner scraps instead of facing Sir's wrath. But Mrs. Donavan had been kind to me. She had called me a good boy. I didn't want her to think less of me for failing to do what she asked.

After I finished clearing the table and washing the dishes, I went to my bedroom to retrieve the test from my backpack and trudged across the hall into the living room where I knew Sir was reading his farmer's almanac in front of the unlit fireplace. I crossed the room on leaden legs and approached him where he sat on the faded, green sofa.

"What do you want?" he snarled without looking up from his book. The paper shook through my trembling, sweaty fingertips as I held it out to him and hung my head low, not brave enough to look into his face. He snatched the test out of my hands with a huff. "What's this?"

"It's my math test, Sir," I shakily explained. "I failed and I... I need you to sign it."

I braced myself for the beating that I was certain was coming my way, flinching away in anticipation of the blow. A few moments passed as I cowered in fear until I realized that nothing was happening. I peeked in Sir's direction and was surprised to see a strange expression on his face. It wasn't love or tenderness, but it was something close. Like sympathy. Or understanding.

"Honesty is what separates the men from the boys," he said in a gruff voice before rising from his seat. He exited the room through the door to the dining area where I could hear him shuffling through the junk drawer beside the sink that I had just used to clean up after dinner. Within a few moments, he returned with a pen and scribbled his name on the test, using the coffee table for leverage. When he was finished, he handed the paper back to me and I reached out to accept it. As I did so, he grabbed me by the wrist with his free hand and pulled me closer, the calluses on his palm scratchy and unsettling against my skin.

"Remember why I spared you, boy. Never lie to me."

"Yes, Sir," I squeaked, and he released me. I darted out of the room in a hurry before he had time to change his mind.

I lay awake in bed that night, listening to the crickets chirp outside my window, and replayed that interaction over and over again, unable to make sense of the foreign tenderness in Sir's stare when I asked him for his signature. It was the most civil conversation that we had ever shared, but I couldn't ignore the warning he had given me.

Never lie to me.

The words seemed almost premonitory—as though he had peered inside my soul and seen that there would come a day when I would forget the grace that he had shown me, and he would be forced to teach me a lesson like none he had ever imparted on me before. I vowed to myself in that moment that I would do everything in my power to stay on his good side. I would be a good boy. I would always tell the truth. I would—

Michael.

The chorus of crickets stopped and a deafening quiet filled the room. I sat up in bed, the lightness in my chest lifting me to a seated position as though it were Santa's sleigh that I had heard clamoring through the night rather than the coarse whisper calling my name in the darkness. An agonizing moment of silence passed and I began to think that, once again, I had imagined it. But the instant my back hit the mattress, I was jolted upright by that soft, scratchy voice purring my name.

Michael.

"You came back," I gasped. "I thought you weren't real."

We're real, Michael, they assured me. *But Sir is not.*

I screwed up my face in confusion.

"What do you mean Sir's not real?"

He will hurt you again, they answered. *Do not trust him.*

"But he didn't hit me tonight," I argued. "He said—"

It doesn't matter what he said, they interrupted. *It only matters what he's done. What he will continue to do. Aren't you tired of living in fear?*

As though a projector screen had fallen in front of my eyes, a highlight reel of my time on the ranch appeared before me. Every beating I had suffered for talking back or moving too slowly or voicing a complaint or not being strong enough—all of it played on repeat, reminding me that no matter how hard I tried to appease him and follow his rules, I would never be good enough for Sir. I was nothing more than a nuisance, a burden placed upon him thanks to his poor, pregnant daughter who was too down on her luck to raise two children.

It wasn't fair. I hadn't asked for a sibling. I hadn't asked to be ripped away from the only friend I had ever known. Mama had promised that it wouldn't be forever. She would come back for me, and I would go home to Sudbury. I would get to have a normal life. I would see Mia again.

Mia.

Just thinking about her made my eyes flood with tears, the emptiness in my chest so cavernous and hollow that it hurt to breathe. Between Sir's punishments and my complete lack of social life at school, the loneliness had been intolerable. Mia had been a beacon of hope, a lighthouse blinking somewhere in the distance, promising an end to the stormy current that had pulled me so far from shore. But the longer I remained on that ranch, the more difficult it became to see the light through the darkness.

You miss her, don't you, Michael? I blinked away tears, nodding my head as though the voices could see my nonverbal response to their question. *So find a way.*

I wiped my face with the back of my hand, a deep crease forming along my forehead as my eyebrows bunched together in confusion.

"What do you mean?" I sniffed.

The trip, they answered. *Go on the trip.*

Through the shadowy bedroom, my gaze landed on my backpack lying in a misshapen heap on the floor. Despite Sir's denial, I still hadn't discarded the permission slip. That pink piece of paper was still tucked away inside my knapsack, waiting for a signature that would never come.

"I can't go," I lamented. "I need Sir's permission. He won't sign it, and tomorrow's the last day to hand it in."

But you already have what you need, the voices countered. Once again, my body seemed to move of its own accord, feet padding against the floor without feeling as I was guided across the room. My fingers fiddled with the zipper on my backpack, numb yet somehow nimble as they extracted both the pink permission slip and my failed math test, Sir's signature scribbled just beneath the giant, red "F." After placing both sheets of paper on the ground, my hands flew back to the bottom of the bag and came out with a ballpoint pen.

"What're we doing?" I whispered as my body rose from the floor and proceeded to turn on the bedroom light.

Getting permission, the voices answered. I watched myself kneel on the floor, placing the math test down first, lining the permission slip down on top of it until the faint outline of Sir's signature was just visible above the empty space that read "Parent/Guardian." Next, I grabbed the pen, a slight tremor working through my hand as it hovered in place above the papers on the ground.

"Wait," I pled with the voices, Sir's warning from earlier still fresh in my mind: *Never lie to me*. "I'll get into trouble. I can't. I—"

Yes, you can, Michael, they insisted. Before I could object any further, the pen connected with the paper, tracing over the chaotic cursive outline of Sir's signature until the name Michael Davies, Sr. materialized on the permission slip, every bit as convincing as the original from which it was copied. It was done. I was going on that trip.

I was going to see Mia again.

***

October 21, 1998

The school bus was full of chatty children, giggling and gorging themselves on juicy bites of the freshly picked apples they had secured on our trip to the orchard. At the back of the bus, a pair of my pigtailed peers chanted together as they clapped each other's hands in perfect rhythm. Even Mrs. Donavan's role as the unargued authoritarian seemed to diminish in the aftermath of what she had referred to as "apple-picking fun." Everyone was in good spirits. Everyone had enjoyed themselves. Everyone, except for me.

It's possible.

Why had I let Mrs. Donavan's words wedge themselves so deeply in my mind? I felt foolish for allowing her to fill me with such hope. Hadn't my time on Sir's ranch taught me anything? There was no such thing as hope. There was no such thing as happiness. There was only hurt. Excruciating, immeasurable hurt. And now I was on my way to what I was certain would be the most painful punishment that I would ever endure with nothing but a bag of lousy apples to show for it.

To say the trip to Sudbury Cider Mill was a disappointment would have been an understatement. I should have known that it was going to be a terrible day from the moment the school bus pulled into the long stretch of gravel driveway that led to the industrial-sized barn where we later learned the cider was made. The big, yellow abomination that transported us there was the only vehicle on-site aside from the tractor that pulled us along for a hayride shortly after our arrival. Though I had kept my head on a swivel, hoping to catch sight of a familiar blonde bob bouncing along through the rows of apple trees, she never appeared. There were no other schools present on the trip.

There was no Mia Davis.

As if her absence hadn't sucked enough of the wind out of my sails, it seemed that my deceit in securing a spot on the trip was destined to be discovered by Sir. In my haste to forge my grandfather's signature in the dead of night, I hadn't bothered to read further about any of the trip's details, so it wasn't until the class was on its way back to Red Rock Elementary that I realized we wouldn't arrive at the school until much later than usual. That meant there would be no bus to take me back to the ranch, and I would be forced to make the three-and-a-half-mile trek from the school back to Sir's farmhouse. Alone.

It was four-thirty in the afternoon by the time we made it back from the orchard, but the walk to Sir's ranch took me another hour and a half. Dirt roads carved through sleepy fields dotted with silage bales tinged orange from the setting sun, their shadows stretching out like black mouths etched into the earth, threatening to swallow me whole as I shuffled past them. The sky was mottled with plumes of indigo by the time I turned into the gravel driveway, dread flooding every fiber of my being as I neared the house at the end of the path. My skin ached in anticipation of Sir's blows; I knew he would not spare me as he had when I presented him with my math test. I expected him to be waiting for me outside his front door, belt in hand, itching to drive the leather into my back. But, when I reached the end of the driveway, I was surprised to see that Sir was not alone.

"Michael!" Mama shrieked as she shoved past a pair of officers who were standing beside a patrol car. "Oh my God, Michael! Where have you been, baby? We've all been so worried about you!"

Before I could answer, she wrapped me in her arms, suffocating me in a cloud of vanilla and chamomile as I breathed her in. Her hands tangled themselves in my hair, pressing my face deeper into her chest until my lungs burned from lack of oxygen. As though she could detect my struggle, she placed her hands on my shoulders and held me at arm's length, peering into my face. Her eyes looked like glass—fragile yet sharp.

"Where have you been?" she repeated. My throat felt hot and swollen as I felt the urge to cry. Even though she had forced me to move away, I still loved my mom. She didn't get to visit often—*Mama's boys make bad ranchers,* Sir had warned her that first summer—but whenever she did come to the farm, I was always glad to see her. Always hopeful that it would be the day she'd rescue me as she had promised. But, as her fingernails dug into my shoulders, blonde hair matted to splotchy, tear-stained cheeks, I felt overwhelmed with sadness knowing that I had caused her pain. Knowing even more that she hadn't come there to save me.

"I'm s–sorry, Mama," I wailed. "I j–just wanted t–to go on the t–trip."

"Trip?" She bunched her brows together in a knot. Before I could explain, her body became enveloped in a long, black shadow as Sir towered over her crouching figure.

"I thought I told you no, boy," he bellowed. "Didn't I warn you never to lie to me? Look at the mess you've caused!"

"Daddy, please," Mama yelled in my defense, but it was no use.

"You hush, Carolyn," Sir snapped, pushing his daughter out of the way until she toppled onto her knees in the dirt. "This is between me and the boy."

I raised my hands to my face, shrinking away behind my palms as I braced myself for what was to come. The earth shook with the weight of his body as he stomped closer in my direction. Suddenly my boxers became damp and warm, a slow, steady trickle of fear working its way down my left leg. Just as I was certain that he would tear the skin right off my body, one of the policemen spoke.

"That your grandson, Mr. Davies?" I watched Sir clench his fists, teeth clamped tight as he delivered a reluctant response.

"Yes," he hissed. The officer joined Sir at his side and gave me a warm smile before crouching down to meet me at eye level. He had a big, porous nose that reminded me of a strawberry and fleshy, round cheeks like overfilled balloons, but his eyes were kind as they bore into mine. I decided I liked him even though he was ugly.

"Your family's been real worried about you, sport," he told me. "Mind if we have a chat?"

I rubbed my eyes with a dirty fist and nodded. Together, the officer and I walked to the squad car where I proceeded to tell him all about my trip to the apple orchard. I told him all about how I had forged Sir's signature, how the class had returned much later than I expected, how I needed to walk all the way home by myself. He made lots of scribbles in his little spiral notebook as he listened to my story.

"You and your grandpa get along alright?" he asked when I was finished, lifting his eyes to meet mine. I busied myself tracing circles in the dirt with my sneaker, actively avoiding his gaze.

"Yeah," I lied. "He's just strict sometimes is all."

"Is that what made you fake your grandpa's signature?" he probed. I wanted to tell him the truth, but something inside me said that I shouldn't mention the voices in my head. So, I lied again.

"Yeah," I said. "He wouldn't let me go, and I really wanted to."

The officer exchanged a glance with his partner, and I thought I caught the slightest hint of a smile sneak across their lips.

"Listen, sport," he knelt down once again so he could face me, "I know it's tough to hear the word 'no' sometimes, but you can't just go around doing whatever you want, okay? You realize what you did is a serious crime?"

I gulped. It had occurred to me that I had lied, but that was the extent of what I thought my wrongdoing had been. I had no idea that what I had done was considered criminal.

"No, sir," I shook my head.

"Well, it is," he assured me. "It's called forgery, son. If you were older, you'd be in a lot of trouble with the law. You could even go to jail for a long time."

My eyes went wide with fear. *Was I going to jail?*

"Don't worry, sport," the officer hooked a strong hand around my shoulder and smiled, "I'm not gonna book ya. But you'd better listen to your grandpa from now on, okay? Next time you break the rules like this, it could be a different story, you understand?"

I nodded my head; I was hyperaware of Sir's presence lurking in the background, watching the entire exchange. Satisfied that he had gotten through to me, the officer rose to a standing position and faced the glowering man behind him.

"Well, I think that about does it," he announced. "We'll let you take it from here."

My heart sank as I watched the officers shake hands with the man who had called them there before piling into their car and driving away. Part of me started to think it would have been better if they had stuffed me in the back and hauled me off to jail. It was a much better option than whatever punishment Sir had in store, of that I was certain.

"Get inside," he ordered once the dust from the tires settled back to the earth. "Go to your room and don't come out 'till morning."

"Daddy—"

"I don't want to hear another word out of you, Carolyn!" Sir hollered. "I told you that so long as this... this *menace* is under my roof, he'll live by my rules. And when he breaks those rules, he'll have consequences."

"But it's his birthday," Mama pled. "Can't you go easy on him just this once?"

"You want to take him home with you? Be my guest," Sir waved his hand in my direction, daring his daughter to call his bluff. My chest pinched with hope. Was it finally happening? Was this how my nightmare would end?

Mama gazed longingly in my direction, as though she were looking at me from miles away rather than the few feet that separated us. She bit her lip and hung her head, the solemn gesture all that was needed to confirm my worst fears.

"That's what I thought," Sir sneered. He whipped his head back in my direction. "What're you still doing here, boy? Go to your room—now!"

My stomach groaned in protest, hunger surging deep within my abdomen. I hadn't eaten since the picnic lunch at the apple orchard, and the long walk home had made me ravenous.

"Please, Sir, can I have some dinner first before I—"

Smack!

Fire scorched my cheek in the place where his palm connected with my face.

"The next time you talk back to me, it'll be my fist in your teeth—you understand me, boy?" he snarled. "Now, get in that fucking house and go to your room!"

My eyes welled with tears as I peered through the twilight, silently begging my mother to save me from this terrible man. But she never looked up from the ground. Just stood there quiet and cowardly, staring at her feet like some overgrown toddler accepting a punishment of her own. With my hand pressed against my cheek, I scurried through the front door, past the dining area, down the narrow hallway on the right, and into my bedroom. I slammed the door shut behind me and flopped down on the bed, burying my face in my pillow. Before long, I heard the distinct sound of tires crunching against gravel and dirt as Mama drove away, leaving me in hell.

I stayed up for hours sobbing, screaming into that filthy pillowcase until my voice went hoarse and the only sound I could produce was a high-pitched whistle that crackled around my vocal cords the way fireworks fizzle into the darkness. When my eyes could no longer produce tears, all that was left to lull me to sleep were the cattle's muffled moos and the sound of my hunger rumbling like thunder through my empty gut.

***

October 22, 1998

"Get up!" Sir jerked me out of slumber early the next morning. I blinked bleary-eyed through the shadows, eyes puffy and painful from all the crying I had done. The sky was still inky, little diamonds twinkling through the blackness, telling me the sun was still hours away from the horizon. Somewhere through the darkness, I heard a strangled wailing that sounded like it was coming from the barn.

"I said, get *up!*" Sir yanked me off the bed, sending me crashing to the floor. I didn't have the energy to cry, could hardly feel the sting in my knees where they had collided with the hardwood.

"What's happening?" I mumbled.

"Heifer's in labor—c'mon, boy, we ain't got all day." Sir pushed me out the door with a firm grip on my shoulder as we shuffled down the hallway to the foyer. I threw on a pair of boots that I had lying by the front door and grabbed a coat off the hook beside it before following Sir into the darkened world beyond.

A crisp autumn breeze crept across the lawn, biting at my cheeks as we stepped into the darkness of the early morning. The air vibrated with the sound of the animal's distress, her anguished cries like a delayed echo of the endless sobs that had filled my bedroom hours earlier. I had helped Sir during the calving process on several occasions, but I had never heard a heifer produce noises like the ones that were coming from the barn that morning. She was in pain, that much was obvious.

"Grab the supplies," Sir commanded as we entered the barn. I stumbled to the workbench at the far end of the structure to retrieve the calving chain, gloves, and lube while he ushered the heifer into a chute to restrain her. Once she was settled, he snatched the gloves away from me and slid his arms inside until they were secured around his biceps. He held out his hands and waited for me to douse them with lubricant so he could ease himself inside and help the poor girl push her baby out. A pair of hoofed feet stuck out from a swath of moist and wrinkled skin, the sight of which made the bile in my empty stomach churn with disgust.

"Don't just stand there gaggin', boy! Loop the chains around," Sir snapped. I swallowed the urge to vomit, placed the chains around the calf's feet, and waited for further direction. Within moments, Sir was elbow-deep in the heifer. I knew not to pull on the chains until he told me it was safe and he could feel her contractions. As soon as he felt the first push squeeze around his arm, he gave me the nod which meant it was time for me to pull with all my might. Though I wasn't very strong, Sir's assistance from the inside made it easier for me to make an impact.

It was slow work, and the sound of the heifer's howling made it feel even slower. Together, the three of us worked in unison—the cow signaling her readiness to Sir, Sir giving me the nod of approval, me yanking on the calf's feet with every ounce of strength I could muster. It seemed as though we might be there until daybreak until finally, at long last, I stumbled back as the tension broke and the newborn fell to the floor.

The moment the calf was out, Sir set to work clearing its airways, inviting it to take its first breath by tickling its little pink nose with a piece of straw from the barn floor. I watched in sickened silence as he cradled it in his arms, oozing levels of adoration and affection that he had never once shown to me.

"C'mon, buddy," he cooed to the animal. "You can do it."

Die, I heard a voice say somewhere in the barn. Before I could register where it had come from, I heard a wet sneeze burst through the air—the official proclamation of life.

"There ya go." Sir laughed with pride, his eyes full of light as he peered into the calf's dampened face. I inched closer to the pair, wishing to insert myself into the magic memory that was unfolding before me. Sensing my approach, Sir's back stiffened. His face darkened as he twisted his head in my direction.

"Don't just stand there like a mongoloid! Prepare the stall."

"Yes, Sir," I murmured.

Hanging on the stall beside the workbench was a shovel, which I retrieved before making my way to the empty stall in the back corner of the barn that remained unoccupied for such occasions. As I prepared a bed of fresh hay, I could hear Sir doting on the calf, his voice soft and gentle—not at all the bone-chilling gravel tone he used when speaking to me.

"You're a good boy, aren't you, little fella?" he purred, a ripple of laughter undulating through the air, twisting my stomach in knots as I worked. My grip tightened around the shovel's wooden handle, the rough surface splintering into my palms.

Kill, the voice spoke again. Somewhere in my gut, I felt a spark—the prickle of combustion stirring like a stoked fire in my intestines. I wanted to burst.

"Get out of the way!" The sound of Sir's impatience snapped me out of my temporary trance as he pushed through the stall, carrying the calf in his arms like a sleeping toddler. He laid the animal down among the straw, giving it a gentle pat on its head as he spoke in a hushed voice, "Happy birthday, little guy. Welcome to the family."

That's when it happened.

My skin turned to lava, embers engulfing every inch of my flesh as though I had been dipped in liquid fire. A loud ringing pierced through my eardrum, dizzying and deafening all at once. Goosebumps prickled from the arches of my feet to the top of my head, enveloping me in a blanket of numbness. I opened my mouth to scream, felt the muted vibration of sound erupting from my throat, but I heard nothing. Before I had time to panic over my diminishing ability to feel or what the noiselessness meant, everything went blurry. Black patches formed at the edge of my vision until I wasn't just deaf or numb anymore.

I was blind with rage.

***

The sound of my own screaming snapped me back into consciousness. Pain rippled across my scalp as I struggled to realize where I was or what was happening to me. My knees burned as they scraped across the barn floor. How was I moving this way? Why did everything hurt?

"Shut the fuck up you little pussy," Sir bellowed. "You wanna play tough? I'll show you tough."

Suddenly, I realized why my head was on fire. I could feel Sir's thick fingers wrapped around locks of my hair as he dragged me across the barn floor. The pain was unbearable, as though the skin might rip clean off my skull. My hands reached instinctively for his, desperate to release myself from his powerful grasp. But I couldn't get a good enough grip. It was as though my fingers were coated in syrup, a thick, slippery residue preventing me from prying myself free.

Why are my hands so wet? I wondered vaguely through the searing pain. Rather than bring them down to inspect what was the matter, I kept them planted as firmly as I could around Sir's wrists, frantic with the need for my agony to end.

But it was only the beginning.

Sir dragged me past the workbench through the back barn doors, across the lawn, and out to the slaughterhouse. My body trembled both from the unrelenting pain and the autumn chill working its way through my bones as I was pulled across the dew-covered grass. He pushed through the slaughterhouse doors, the stench of death assaulting my nostrils as I heaved in gasping breaths around each fresh scream that echoed from my lungs. The earth was stained a deep maroon color from all the cows that had been brought there to meet their end. As the scent of iron and copper clung to the back of my throat, I wondered if my blood would be next to blemish the soil.

Once through the door, Sir shoved my head away with his hand, the release of my follicles from his fingertips flooding me with relief in an instant, though not for long. As I lay on the ground, whimpering and running a shaky hand across the welt that was blooming across my scalp, I felt the edge of Sir's work boot connect with my ribs, sucking the air from my body. Vomit stung my esophagus as I writhed on the blood-drenched floor, struggling to breathe through the pain.

Before I could regain my composure, Sir was on me once more. He gathered my hands together above my head, looped a thick rope around my wrists, and bound them together. The twine dug into my skin as he pulled tighter and tighter, small fires igniting where the scratchy surface burrowed deep into my flesh. When he was finished, he threw me over his shoulder like a bag of feed, my ribs throbbing in agony as he carried me to one of the gambrel hooks that were used to hang the cows for processing after slaughter. As he slung my tethered hands over the metal hook, my shoulders stretched to the point of dislocation and I dangled like a dead thing from the rafters, feet too high above the earth to touch the ground and keep from swaying.

I wailed in anguish, still uncertain what I had done to deserve such a swift and terrible punishment. Sir had no tolerance for my screams. Holding true to his earlier promise, his fist connected with my teeth, dazing me into silence. I gagged as the blood gushed into my mouth, bubbling from my lips like a geyser. As I blinked through my tears, I saw a glint of metal flash from Sir's hand as he retrieved a knife from a nearby workbench. Urine flooded down my legs as he approached me, a sinister smile tugging at the corners of his mouth.

"You want to be an animal? I'll treat you like a fucking animal," he sneered.

I gasped as he placed the cool metal beneath my shirt and began to tear at the fabric, ripping the pajamas from my body as though he were skinning a freshly bled cow. When he finished peeling the shirt from my torso, he tore the boots off my feet, dragged my pants and boxer shorts off around my ankles, and tossed them onto the floor in a heap. I swung naked from the meat hook, body quaking equally from the cold as it was from sheer terror at what was still to come.

Sir exited the slaughterhouse without a word, leaving me exposed and afraid in the darkened kill room, moonlight spilling in through the open door through which he had departed. It seemed like hours passed before he returned, even if in truth, it had only been a few minutes; the fear and uncertainty of my predicament had skewed my perception of time. My vision was blurred from the deluge of saltwater leaking unimpeded from my eyes, but I could see that he was carrying something large in his arms when he finally materialized through the door. It took me a moment to realize what it was, but once I did, my heart grew numb with dread as the memory of what I had just done rushed into my mind.

The calf.

The shovel.

The screams.

The blood.

How could something so small have so much blood?

Sir placed the dead newborn down at my feet as though he were laying a child to rest. Again, I felt the fire rise within at the sight of his tenderness. So much care he had for this animal that he hadn't known for more than a few moments, giggling as it sneezed in his lap, wishing it a happy birthday while he had sent me to bed without so much as a bite of toast on the day that should have been a celebration of *my* life. It made me sick. It made me angry.

It made me hungry.

Giving the unmoving mass a gentle pat, Sir rose from the floor, seizing a fistful of my hair, the smell of nicotine on his breath fogging the inch of space that separated his face from mine as he peered inside my soul with cold, callous eyes.

"I always knew you were a waste," he hissed. "You will look at the mess you've made so you never forget why it was that I had to break you."

With that, he released his grip and proceeded to undo his belt buckle, sliding the thick leather strap out from the loops of his jeans in one fluid motion. He wrapped the belt around his right hand twice, giving him a firm handle on his makeshift weapon while leaving ample length with which to whip me. I had been on the receiving end of this particular brand of punishment before, but never unclothed.

Never buckle-side first.

I thrashed and shrieked, legs kicking out in all directions as I begged Sir for mercy. He said nothing as he disappeared from view, assuming his position behind me in the shadows. Through the sound of my desperate pleas, I heard him mumble something like a prayer. I didn't have time to register what he had said or if he had said anything at all. Before I knew what was happening, the buckle cracked into my back as thunderous as a bolt of lightning ripping through tree bark.

My neck muscles strained around a scream unlike anything I had produced before, stars blinking in my peripheral vision like a diamond-studded tunnel. One after another the blows rained down on me, the metal buckle tearing through my skin like tissue paper with each snap of Sir's improvised whip. He continued to hit me on my back until every inch of my skin was bloodied and bruised.

Then he started on my front.

I passed out the instant his belt connected with my stomach.

CHAPTER 4

September 8, 2004

School buses had a way of making me feel uneasy. Maybe it was the smell of unwashed leather or the thrust of inertia that pushed and pulled at my stomach contents each time the yellow monstrosity turned a corner. Or maybe it was the fact that the last time I had been on a school bus was during that long ride back from the apple orchard—the memories of that trip and all that had happened after it enough to make me nauseous. Come to think of it, I didn't have an appetite for apples after that day, either. The sweet acidic aroma of their juicy flesh was enough to make my mouth water with the urge to vomit.

But the queasy feeling in my stomach as I sat on the school bus that September morning had nothing to do with car sickness or poorly suppressed trauma. In fact, it was quite the opposite. I was buzzing with anticipation, insides twisting with possibilities that I hadn't allowed myself to entertain since the night Sir had beaten them out of me. Because I wasn't just returning to school. I was returning to Sudbury High School. The *only* high school in Sudbury.

The same school that Mia attended.

"Don't forget to pick your brother up at the bus stop after you get home," Mama had reminded me before I headed out the door that morning. The request normally would have irritated me, perhaps even been enough to awaken the voices from their slumber.

How dare she demand anything of you, I could almost hear them say. *After everything she's done? She should be grateful we don't take matters into our own hands.*

But I didn't need to silence the chatter that morning. I was in too good a mood to let Mama's petulance stand in the way of my happiness, no matter how laced her words had been with resentment. Besides, the passive-aggressive tone in her voice was a welcome reminder that her plan to use me as a cash cow had failed. After all, her decision to finally rescue me from Sir's ranch had nothing to do with the fact that she must have known about the torment he put me through. Nothing to do with the fact that I had been removed from the public school system immediately following my punishment in the slaughterhouse, homeschooled in an effort to keep prying eyes from inquiring about the source of the scars that decorated my body. Nothing to do with an innate desire to fulfill the maternal duties that she had willingly abandoned. Like every other choice that woman had made, her desire to take me back to her mobile home in Sudbury was driven only by her greed. Nothing more.

"You're sixteen now," she had beamed at me the day we left her father's ranch together, the decrepit cabin diminishing in the rearview mirror the further she drove. "You know what that means?"

I shrugged in response, eyes glued to the reflection of Sir's cattle fields. As though I were expecting his beat-up Silverado to come chasing us down the road so he could drag me kicking and screaming back to the ranch. Not that he actually *wanted* me there. But there was an air of reluctance I sensed in his demeanor as he watched us pull away from his house. Like he wasn't yet ready to part with his plaything. Like he had more lessons he wanted to teach me with the back of his hand.

Or his belt buckle.

"It means you're a man now," Mama answered her own question with an odd excitement in her voice. "Or at least, you could pass as one."

She gave me a wink and I tried to smile, letting her know I was in on whatever hidden meaning was woven through her words. But I didn't understand what she meant. Not until we made it back to Sudbury at least.

The place where she lived was different from what I remembered. Maybe my torment under Sir's care had led me to build up its grandeur in my mind, but the mobile home from my memories hadn't been nearly as bleak or dilapidated as the one that stood before me as we pulled into the trailer park. It was dingy and dirty, with chunks of powder blue paint missing from its vinyl siding and a tear through the mesh of the screen door. A worn leather armchair that should have been the centerpiece in a living room was perched on the front lawn beneath an awning that protruded from the roof of the tiny structure. Beside it was an overturned bucket that appeared to act as a makeshift side table, an ashtray resting on its surface that was blackened and crusty from years of abuse.

It's better than getting beat, I tried to remind myself as I followed my mother up the creaky wooden front steps and into the heart of the home. The inside was no more glamorous than its exterior, with drab, beige Berber carpet and wood-paneled walls that reminded me of Sir's farmhouse. Aside from a stray beer can or empty cigarette carton, however, the place was mostly tidy. Dismal and cramped, but tidy.

"Mama, Mama!" A whiny voice pierced through the air followed by a thunder of clumsy footsteps as a blonde-haired child wrapped his arms around my mother's knees.

"Hey, baby." She ruffled the little boy's hair with affection before bending down to plant a kiss on his cheek. I watched the exchange in silence, an alien observing the curiosity of familial adoration with equal parts fascination and fury. Mama unwrapped herself from the boy's embrace and cast a furtive glance in my direction, as though she could feel the revulsion of my stare embedding itself in her skin. She smoothed her sundress as she stood to face me, placing a protective hand on the child's shoulder.

"You remember Matt, don't you, honey?"

My gaze drifted down to the stupid little brat at her side. Of course, I remembered who he was. Though he hadn't come to the ranch often, on the rare occasion that he did accompany Mama during her visits, I had always been stricken with immeasurable jealousy by the way Sir had doted on him. I could recall only one time that my grandfather had reached across the dinner table to give my half-brother a little warning slap across the face for talking out of turn—a proverbial walk in the park compared to the daily beatings I had been forced to endure.

He blinked at me with uncertainty, his bony arms still latched around our mother's waist. At eight years old, he was half my age and half my height, with lanky limbs that would have made Sir laugh with ridicule if he hadn't somehow been so enamored with the boy. Aside from these obvious differences, however, looking at him was like staring into a mirror—albeit one that had reversed the passage of time by nearly a decade. We shared the same shaggy blonde hair, the same bronzed skin, the same icy blue eyes. Well, the eyes were almost the same. Unlike mine, his hadn't been robbed of their innocence. I wanted to hate him for it, but deep down I knew that it wasn't his fault. He was just a kid. I decided not to hold it against him—for the time being, at least.

"Yeah, I remember," I said, pushing my lips back into a tight smile. The effort to disguise my disgust seemed to do the trick. Matt broke out into a wide grin, unraveling himself from Mama as though the thin line of stifled loathing that my lips had become had broken some sort of spell. His arctic eyes twinkled with instant idolization as he peered up at me.

"Do you like trucks?" he asked, a hopeful tone in his voice. I thought about Sir's pickup, how he had forced me to sit in the truck bed "like the animal I was" whenever we had to make a run to town.

"No," I answered. His face fell with disappointment.

"Oh, I'm sure you two can find something else to play with together," Mama reassured him with a gentle nudge on his shoulder.

I cringed.

She loves him more than you, the voices observed. My fists clenched as my heart dropped into a pool of stomach acid. They were right. I knew they were right. It made me want to—

"Michael, why don't I show you to your room? I've got something special for you," Mama interrupted my train of thought, placing a thin hand on my back as she ushered me forward. I flinched away. It had been nearly a week since my last lashing and the wounds that Sir had inflicted in the slaughterhouse had long since healed, but my flesh still crawled whenever someone dared to place their hands on me. She didn't seem to notice my involuntary response to her touch, pushing me deeper into the home as we stepped down a narrow hallway and into the tiny room that was located through the last door on the left.

It wasn't much bigger than the room I slept in at Sir's ranch, with the same beige carpet that covered the floor throughout the rest of Mama's house and bare walls the color of eggshells. Somehow Mama had managed to squeeze in a full-sized mattress beside a rickety writing desk that looked as though it had been plucked from a dumpster. A metal folding chair was tucked beneath it like an afterthought. I stepped into the room and spun around to face Mama, who was leaning against the doorframe with her arms folded, beaming with pride.

"What do you think?" She raised a pair of expectant eyebrows in my direction. I shrugged and nodded.

"It's nice," I lied. "Thanks, Mama."

"Look on the desk," she jutted her chin at the piece of furniture against the wall, "There's something there for you."

I stepped over to the writing desk and found the prize in question. It was a driver's license with my name printed on the front. I plucked the piece of plastic from off the wooden surface for closer inspection, uncertain what to make of it. Though I was by no means an expert in driver's licenses—Sir had forbidden me from taking my exam at the DMV so I could obtain my learner's permit—I couldn't help but notice the obvious defects. There were air bubbles trapped inside the plastic and the edges felt sharp and jagged rather than smooth, the way I expected them to be. But there were other glaring abnormalities that I struggled to overlook as well. The person in the photograph beside my name looked at least a decade older than me, with blue eyes several shades darker than mine. As if that weren't enough, the listed birthdate showed October 21, 1984—two years earlier than when I had been born.

"I don't get it," I looked over my shoulder at Mama. "What is this?"

"Do you like it?" she grinned mischievously. "Steve had one of his buddies at work make it for you."

"Okay... but why?" I wasn't trying to sound ungrateful, but I could tell my reaction to the gift had not been the one Mama was hoping for. She stepped into the room and took a seat on the mattress, patting the empty space beside her as she gestured for me to join. I obliged, the mattress springs squealing beneath our shared weight.

"You know it's hard for us to make ends meet, don't you, Michael?" she began. "That's why I had to... why you had to... anyway, all that's behind us now. You're home, and we're so happy to have you here. Because now you're old enough."

She reached across to brush the shaggy hair away from my eyes.

"Old enough for what?" I pressed, still unsure what she was talking about.

"Old enough to help out," she answered. "You're all grown up now, and with you working at the gas station down the road—"

"Gas station?" I balked. "What about school?"

What about Mia?

"You've got your whole life to go to school, dumplin'," Mama assured me. "Right now, you need to help your family."

"But I—"

"We've got an interview lined up for you first thing in the morning," she interrupted before I could object any further. "It's more of a formality than anything else. The manager, Brian, is a good friend of Steve's. You'll be all set up for your first day by Monday, I'm sure of it. Between the three of us working, we'll be out of debt in no time. Then we can talk about school."

And there it was.

She didn't want me. She didn't care about me. She didn't love me. All she wanted was an extra source of income so she could get herself out of the mess she had made. My insides ached with anger, blood boiling through my veins as I struggled to slow my breathing and drown out the voices thundering in my ears.

She doesn't love you, they reiterated. *But we do. We'll make it better. We can—*

"Come help me in the kitchen," Mama got up from the bed, holding out her hand for me to take. "It's almost time for supper. Steve will be home any minute."

The following morning, I went in for the interview at the gas station just as I was told. As Mama had indicated, Brian didn't blink twice at the phony ID I presented to him when I arrived for my first shift the following Monday. There was a mechanic's garage on one side of the property where locals would come in for the odd repair. Attached to the garage was a small convenience store that sold snacks and toiletries and lottery tickets. It was here where I spent most of my days manning the cash register. Wishing I were doing anything that remotely resembled normal, teenage fun.

Compared to the grueling manual labor I was accustomed to on Sir's ranch, working at the gas station was a breeze. But the hours were long and the work was tedious, which would have been tolerable if I had at least gotten to keep some of the wages I earned. That, however, was entirely out of the question. I managed to squirrel away a few dollars here and there over the next year and a half, but the majority of my earnings went straight to Mama and Steve. Even that injustice would have been easier to swallow if I hadn't been so lonely.

There I was in the hometown I had been so desperate to return to, mere minutes away from the only friend I had ever known, yet I might as well have been alone, back on that ranch in isolation. I'd watch with envy from behind the glass storefront as my would-be peers rolled into the gas station, fueling up their cars before heading off on whatever wild adventures awaited them on the open road. Once or twice, I could have sworn that I had seen my suntanned goddess tucking strands of golden hair behind her ear as she reached for the gas nozzle. Even if it had been my Mia, what difference would it have made? I was a slave to my post at the station. There would be no road trips for me. No cars packed full of friends waiting to ride off into the sunset.

If it weren't for the babbling homeless man who loitered in the convenience store from time to time, I wouldn't have had any social life to speak of whatsoever. He'd come into the store with his filthy blonde hair matted to his forehead, shoulders hunched over beneath a tattered Tar Heels tee shirt as he ambled through the aisles, muttering under his breath. Maybe it was the combination of his sandy locks and the square-set jaw that I inherited from Sir mirrored in the homeless man's face that drew me to him. Or maybe I just needed a distraction from the emptiness that was threatening to devour me each time I clocked in for another miserable shift at the gas station. Whatever the reason, ours were the only interactions that I had to look forward to. Aside from the few conversations we shared, I had nothing and nobody. There was only work and sleep—if the voices allowed it.

I started to believe that my life might go on that way forever, caught in an endless cycle of mind-numbing monotony, but the summer before what should have been my senior year of high school, everything changed. Brian ended up selling the gas station, and when the new owners arrived, it didn't take them long to figure out that I had been lying about my age. One look at the photocopy of the fake ID in my employee file was all it took for them to terminate me. They had even threatened to call child protective services on Mama if she didn't get me enrolled in school. It didn't matter that I was old enough to "pass as a man" as Mama had suggested. I wasn't one. I was a minor. And the state had rules about minors—specifically, that they needed to be enrolled in an approved curriculum until the time they turned eighteen. Not skipping out on a formal education to play breadwinner for their families.

Initially, I was ecstatic that I had been laid off from the gas station—even more so when I realized that it meant I may finally get the chance to return to school. But part of me wondered whether Mama might seize the opportunity to take me back to the ranch. After all, she had taken me there out of desperation, too broke and sad and irresponsible to care for two children. Without her obedient workhorse there to provide an extra influx of cash, what good would it be to keep me there? How would she even afford it? Panic pinched like a vice grip around my nerves as she sat me down for a talk late one evening in June shortly following my termination.

"Steve and I have talked it over," she started, "and we've agreed that you can stay here. You're old enough now that you can take care of yourself, and if you're around, you can help out with Matt instead of us having to pay the neighbor to watch after him during our shifts. But, as soon as you graduate, you have to go back to work."

And so it was that two weeks later, I was taking a placement test to enroll for my senior year at Sudbury High School. I didn't even mind the fact that, once again, Mama was using my presence for her own benefit rather than keeping me around out of the goodness of her heart. My respect for her died the night she left me to be brutalized in her father's barn. The moment I received the notification that I would be permitted to go to school in September, I felt as though a weight had been lifted. I would finally know normalcy.

I would finally see Mia again.

These were the thoughts I carried with me on the school bus that September morning as I prepared for my first day of class. My palms were clammy with anticipation as the bus lurched to a stop outside of the high school. The driver hardly had time to fling open the doors before I made my descent down the grooved steps beside his captain's chair and onto the blacktop beyond.

The school was massive—much bigger than Red Rock Elementary had been—with a sandstone exterior that gave way to a series of expansive windows that formed a small atrium at the front lobby of the building. Through the glass entryway, the image of a roaring beast with bared teeth was painted along the linoleum with an inscription beneath that read, "Sudbury High: Home of the Lions."

I had gone to orientation the week before, so I was already vaguely familiar with the school's layout and where I needed to go to find my locker. The bell for first period wouldn't ring until seven-thirty, and the analog clock above the doors to the administrative office read seven-ten. If I moved quickly, I'd have enough time to drop my backpack off in my locker and roam the halls in search of my golden-haired angel.

Moving quickly through the hallways, however, proved to be more of a challenge than I thought. The building was teeming with students, each of them seemingly on a mission to keep me from reaching my destination with their incessant squeals and high-pitched laughter and long embraces. One chestnut-haired girl in a skimpy halter top and jean shorts that left nothing to the imagination sent one of her sneakers straight into my hip as she jumped into the arms of her long-lost bestie.

Slut, the voices hissed with repugnance. I didn't disagree with them, though I had no time to allow my anger to fester. This was supposed to be a happy day. I could forgive the unintentional shove from a stranger, so long as it meant that I would find the person I longed for more than anything.

My locker was located in the hallway by the science classrooms—a newly constructed wing, according to the student ambassador who had shown me the ropes during orientation. I rounded the corner, narrowly skirting past a gaggle of oversized meatheads consorting beside the water fountains. As I emerged from the thicket of jocks and lifted my gaze to the end of the hall, my breath caught in my throat. She was taller than I remembered, with gentle curves rolling along the length of her torso, transforming her from the stick-figured girl of my memories to a perfect hourglass. But everything else remained the same. That bronzed skin. Those blue eyes. That blonde hair. There was no doubt about it. I had finally found her.

My Mia Davis.

I floated down the hallway; the students parted a path for me as though I were Moses and they were waves undulating through the Red Sea. It felt like a dream—even the bright overhead lights seemed to soften to a rosy veil as I made my approach. The swelling in my heart propelled me forward, lifted me off my feet as I glided across the linoleum floors. It wasn't until I was practically on top of her that I realized the locker that she held open as she unpacked her bag was the one right next to mine. I couldn't believe my luck. It was almost too good to be true.

And it was.

I arrived at my locker, tongue-tied and befuddled by her beauty, but I couldn't think of a single word to say to her. Not that it would have mattered. When she finished unpacking her bag, she swung her locker door shut and turned her head in my direction. She looked straight at me—right into my face. Right into my very soul. But that was all she did. There was no smile in her eyes. No faint glimmer of recognition. Not even the natural realization that she had registered another human's existence. She simply looked past me, as though I were a ghost. As though I were nothing at all. Because I *was* nothing at all. I was no one.

In that instant, I felt as if my life had ended. All hope that I had allowed myself to feel vacated my body immediately. It was over.

She didn't remember me.

**

March 24, 2005

The sound of tires crunching along the gravel and dirt tied my stomach in knots as Mama and Steve returned home from work. It was almost midnight and I had to get up early for school the next day, but I couldn't sleep. Not after receiving that thick envelope in the mail from Green Valley University.

It wouldn't have occurred to me to apply to college at all—especially not after Mama had been so explicit in her instructions that I return to work after graduation so I could help support the family. But the moment I found out that Mia had her sights set on GVU, I knew I needed to follow in her footsteps.

"Coach says I'm a shoo-in for the soccer scholarship," I overheard her gloating one morning to the ever-present members of her posse as they loitered like starstruck paparazzi beside her locker. And who could blame them? With her bubbly personality, her effortless grace, her impossible good looks—Mia seemed to have a gravitational pull on everyone around her. Especially me. But with her devoted fans always circling her like a band of royal servants, I never had the opportunity to tell her how I felt, or to talk to her in any capacity at all for that matter. All I could do was eavesdrop on her conversations, a fly on the gilded walls of her castle lurking in the background in constant awe of her elegance.

"Any day now, I should be getting that acceptance letter from Green Valley University!"

"But what about Beau?" one of her doe-eyed companions chimed in. My heart hardened at the mention of *his* name. "Aren't you worried about long distance?"

I watched as Mia stroked the photograph that was hanging in her locker of the curly-haired brute she called her boyfriend. Somewhere inside, the demons stirred.

"We'll make it work," she shrugged.

Not if we have anything to say about it.

That same day, I spent my lunch period in the library's computer lab filling out my application for Green Valley University. I liked the library. I liked books in general. Aside from farm work, reading was the only activity that Sir permitted me to do on the ranch. Burying my nose in a book was one of the only ways I found that I could avoid suffering another one of his punishments. For this reason, I was an excellent student. Though I didn't have the extracurriculars that would have made me a stand-out applicant, I didn't think that I'd have any trouble getting into college. I felt confident that my grade point average alone was enough to secure me a spot for the fall semester.

As I prepared to hit send on the application, I realized there was another barrier that I had failed to consider: College applications cost money. Money that I didn't have—at least not with me in the school library. No matter; I knew I had enough cash tucked away beneath my mattress at home. I decided to print my completed application out and mail it to the university for consideration instead.

I knew that it would take several months to hear back regarding my candidacy, but when March arrived and Mia came barreling into school, bursting to tell her girlfriends about her acceptance into GVU, I began to lose hope. Since that first day of school when she had breezed right past me without a single ounce of recognition on her face, I had been plagued with the desire to speak with her. To make her remember the promise she made to me the last time we had been together.

It didn't matter to me that ten years had passed since then. I couldn't accept that she had somehow forgotten the day when we had ventured into the fields beside the blacktop that surrounded our elementary school during recess. How we had woven flower stems around each other's fingers between the sun-bleached stalks as we made a sacred vow to always belong to one another. Her promise was the only thing that had given me a modicum of hope during my time on Sir's ranch. I knew if we had a moment alone, I could remind her that we were meant to be. She would return to me. She would make me whole again.

But she was constantly surrounded by her adoring clique. At least if I followed her to college, I'd have a better chance at finding my opportunity to reignite our love. She'd be just as alone as I would, surrounded by strangers in a strange town, desperate for familiarity. A sense of kinship that only I could provide. But, the longer I had to wait for my acceptance letter, the more unrealistic the possibility became. I started to think I might have to develop a new plan to make my way to Green Valley until finally, the day came when that glorious packet arrived in my mailbox.

The jingle of keys twisting in the front door knob as Mama and Steve pushed their way inside the mobile home jolted me upright on my bed, tearing me away from my thoughts in an instant. I reached nervously for the oversized envelope resting on my desk, the sweat of my palms seeping into the stiff, fibrous surface, turning the edges flimsy as I stepped into the hallway and made my way to the living room.

"Sweet lord almighty!" Mama hollered when she saw me approach. She clutched her chest and steadied herself against the doorframe as Steve stepped into view on the front steps just behind her. "You scared the devil out of me! What are you still doing up?"

I cast a tentative glance past Mama's shoulder at her fiancé. He wasn't an intimidating man by any means, with a bony build and deep-set blue eyes that made him appear perpetually tired. Still, his presence made me apprehensive. Even before he knocked my mother up and forced me out of my home, he had always treated me with an air of indifference that bordered on outright dislike. It wasn't the same unwelcome feeling that I had on Sir's ranch, but it came close. The packet in my hand suddenly felt as though it were made of lead. I knew that if I tried to bring it up in Steve's presence, he'd convince Mama that it was a bad idea.

"Honey?" Mama inched closer to me, placing her hands on my shoulders. "Is everything alright?"

Steve locked the front door behind him as he entered the foyer and grunted an unintelligible greeting in my direction before ambling through the open archway into the kitchen where I could hear him rustling through the refrigerator for a beer. I turned my attention back to Mama, her piercing blue eyes beseeching me to speak.

"Yeah, yeah," I nodded. "Everything's okay. I just... wanted to talk to you—alone."

Steve reappeared in the living room, plopping down on the sofa as he took a long swig from his open beer can and began to flip through TV stations.

"Can it wait until the morning, honey? It's been such a long day and I—"

"No, it can't wait," I interrupted, the agitation obvious in my voice. Mama pulled her hands away and crossed her arms in disapproval of my tone. I sighed, "I'm sorry, it's just... it's important. Can we talk in my room? It'll only take a minute."

She considered me with a frown, her lipstick bleeding at the corners of her mouth, aching to be wiped away after a long day's work. Pinching the bridge of her nose in a brief moment of aggravation, she sagged her shoulders and released a frustrated breath before pasting a smile on her lips and turning to face me once more.

"Fine," she agreed. Together we walked single-file down the hallway to my bedroom. As I shut the door behind us, Mama took a seat on the edge of the mattress, crossing one leg over the other. "Well, what is it that's so important then?"

My hands trembled, the webbing of my fingers slick with sweat as I presented Mama with the parcel I had waited so long to receive. She accepted the offering, a dubious eyebrow raised as she proceeded to pry open the tear that I had made at the top of the envelope and extract the papers within. I watched her eyes flick back and forth as she skimmed the contents of the letter, her cheeks flushing a deep pink the longer she read. When she was finished, she tossed the papers onto the bed beside her as though they had scorched her fingers.

"Just what the hell is this about, Michael?" she demanded, the anger in her voice sinking like a stone in my stomach. "I told you that we need you *here*."

"I know, Mama," I answered. "But I've been doing really well in school, and I thought that I could—"

"Thought that you could what? Abandon your family?" she scoffed. "We need *money*, Michael—not a reason to assume more debt than we have already. I can't believe you would go behind my back like this. After everything we've done for you—"

"Everything *you've* done for *me*?" My throat was bitter, mouth full of cotton as I spoke the words. I peered through a blackened tunnel at the woman who had the audacity to call herself my mother, the voices in my head wrapping themselves around my tongue as I launched into a tirade that I'd been holding back for years. "You threw me away like garbage. Like I was nothing—all because you couldn't keep your fucking legs shut! Do you have any idea what that did to me? What *he* did to me? Of course, you don't. All you ever think about is yourself. The only reason you even came back for me is because you're desperate for money. And you sit here and talk to me about abandonment? You're no mother at all. You disgust me."

Mama rose from her seat in a flash, her eyes glistening with angry tears. A twisted expression morphed across her face and for a moment, she looked exactly like her father: cold and callous. Unfeeling. Before I could register what had happened, the imprint of her open palm was hot across my face.

"Don't you *ever* talk to me that way," she simmered. "You will stay here and you will work. I don't want to hear another word about it, understand me?"

Unshed tears burned in my retinas as my flesh puckered with unsuppressed rage. I narrowed my eyes and took a step forward, our noses mere inches apart as I peered into her face.

"I hate you," I told her. And I meant it. With every fiber of my being, I meant it.

A cross between a whimper and a scream escaped her lips as she pushed past me and exited through the doorway, leaving me quaking with anger in the center of the room. My fingernails dug into my palms until I was certain that I would draw blood, eyes lingering on the discarded papers still lying on my bed. In just a few short months, Mia would be three hours away in Green Valley University, and I'd be left behind longing for her once again. The thought turned my soul to fire, flames licking eagerly at my insides, begging to burn everything in sight.

You could do it, you know, the voices soothed me. I waited for them to explain but heard nothing except the sound of my ragged breath surging through flared nostrils.

"Do what?" I pressed them.

Burn it, Michael, they answered. *Burn it all to the ground.*

CHAPTER 5

August 13, 2005

Months passed after my confrontation with Mama, with the sting of her refusal eating at my gut like glowing embers coming to rest on a cotton shirtsleeve. True to her word (for once), she had forced me back to work at the gas station the moment I graduated from high school. Aside from a curt "hello" or "goodbye" to acknowledge the other's existence in passing, we didn't speak. There was no reason to. She had her mind made up that I would be the obedient slave child that her father had groomed me to be. But I had my mind made up, too. Very soon, it would all be over, and she'd realize what a mistake it was to hold me hostage. But, by that point, it would be too late. She'd be dead.

They all would be. Every single one. Including me.

The argument with Mama had emboldened my demons, amplified their voices until every thought was laced with darkness. They had become impossible to silence, even more impossible to ignore. And I didn't want to ignore them. Ever since the first day they called to me in the shadows of Sir's ranch, they had filled me with strength, made me believe that I was powerful. I was in control. Through every bully, every beating, every bitter betrayal, they had been the one constant in my life. The one thing I could trust to never abandon me. It was time to show them my gratitude, give them the sustenance they craved.

Burn it, they instructed me over and over again until I could practically taste the smoke on my tongue. *Burn it all to the ground.*

Admittedly, at first, I was hesitant to comply. Aside from the calf in the barn, I had never intentionally caused harm to another living creature. Okay, *maybe* I had conducted a few experiments on the rabbits prancing through Sir's cattle fields on occasion. Perhaps I had even gotten hold of a stray cat, submerged its helpless body in the creek beside the farmhouse just to see how long it would take to turn limp in my hands. But I had never harmed another human being, much less taken someone's life. I will admit, however, the thought had occurred to me before, planting itself deeper inside my brain with every brand of physical torment Sir saw fit to enact upon me. But people weren't like animals. I couldn't extinguish them on a whim without consequence. It required a level of meticulousness that I hadn't yet mastered.

But I was learning.

Though I had missed the deadline to enroll at Green Valley University, I was still determined to follow in Mia's footsteps. I decided that it wasn't necessary for me to be a student there; I simply needed to give off the illusion that I was just another college freshman among the crowd of newcomers. Of course, it wasn't possible for me to go so long as Mama and Steve were still around to hunt me down if I ran away from home. If I was going to succeed in winning Mia back, then I would need a more permanent solution. Under the voices' careful guidance, I had concocted a plan that would give us each the satisfaction we desired.

The idea was simple really: Wait until the family was asleep, douse the entire home with gasoline, light the place on fire, and escape to Green Valley before the authorities arrived. I had already secured several gallons of gas from the station where I worked, staggering my purchases over a period of several weeks so as not to attract attention. I'd sneak into the garage bay in the mechanic's shop attached to the convenience store, grab one of the endless plastic containers lined along the back wall, and fill it up to my heart's content.

"For the lawnmower," I would answer if anyone asked—but no one ever did. It appeared that the new owners' attention to detail was limited to ensuring that they were not actively breaking any child labor laws. They couldn't be bothered to inquire about my insatiable need for fuel in the same way they hadn't concerned themselves with implementing any meaningful security measures around the premises.

Rows of vehicles sat abandoned in a lot beside the repair shop from owners who had failed to pay for their services, not a single camera in sight keeping watch over any of them. That was fine by me. Their negligence made it all the easier for me to make off one evening with one of the unclaimed work vans parked at the back of the lot. The abandoned junker would be the perfect escape vehicle when the time came. It wasn't difficult to obtain; the keys to all the deserted vehicles were kept inside a desk drawer inside the lead mechanic's office. All I needed to do was wait for him to take one of his notoriously long bathroom breaks so I could obtain my prize.

I knew it would be weeks, possibly even months before anyone realized the thing was missing, and the last place they'd go searching for it would be in the thick woods located at the edge of the trailer park where I lived. Incidentally, the van also made a perfect storage space for all the red plastic containers I had filled up with gasoline, which meant I wouldn't have to worry about Mama or Steve discovering my stockpile.

But time was running out.

Move-in day at Green Valley University was in a week, and there was still one piece of the puzzle that I needed to fit into place before everything I had worked towards could be brought to fruition. Because it wasn't enough to burn the place down and leave the ashes behind. I needed to get away with it. And if I was going to get away with it, then I needed to be an equal victim in the destruction I planned to cause.

I needed to fake my death.

It needs to be convincing, the voices said. *You need another body. One that others wouldn't miss. One that could pass for your own.*

I was beginning to lose faith that I would find such a thing. After all, it wasn't as though I were drowning in social prospects. I had spent the majority of my senior year skulking in Mia's shadow, trying and failing to summon the courage to speak to her. And, ever since graduation, I had been so consumed by my careful plotting that I hadn't stopped to consider how I would achieve what was inarguably one of the most critical parts of my plan. It didn't just need to be convincing, as the voices had said. It needed to be someone who wouldn't be missed. Someone I could easily manipulate into entering my home in the dead of night. Someone I could subdue without issue. But where could I look?

As though answering an unspoken prayer, the bells above the convenience store door announced the arrival of a certain incoherent vagrant whose presence at the gas station had always been a source of comfort to me. A welcome distraction from the loneliness that made my long hours behind the cash register insufferable. As I watched his familiar form amble through the aisles, muttering to himself incessantly, I felt the corners of my mouth stitch themselves into my cheeks. Beneath all the dirt and grime and tattered clothing, I was reminded once more of all that we shared in common.

I sized him up from my post at the cash register as he shuffled along the tile floors. Like me, he was tall and muscular (though not so sinewy as to be a physical threat to me), with sandy hair and a rigid jaw that reminded me of Sir. His face wasn't the same as mine, wrinkled with age while my own was angry with acne. The eyes were a muddy brown color rather than the icy blue that swirled around in my irises. But these things would be unrecognizable in the aftermath of the fire. All I needed was a body that was convincing. A body that no one would miss. A body that could pass as mine once thoroughly blackened to a crisp.

He's perfect, the demons voiced their approval. With all of the pieces of the plan in place, it was time to set to work. The filthy hobo meandered over to the candy aisle, ogling the wall of sweets that stood before him with the same longing in his eyes as a toddler in a toy store. I knew that look, could feel the sharp pangs ripping through my abdomen as though the emptiness in his stomach had been transmitted into mine. He was hungry.

We both were.

"Hey," I heard myself say to him.

He didn't seem to realize that I had said a word, so I tried again. "Excuse me? Yeah, I'm talking to you. It's Jimmy, right?"

He hesitated a moment, peering at me with sheepish eyes as he extracted a candy bar from the shelf and approached the counter where I stood.

"I got money this time, Mike," he assured me, placing the Clark bar in his hands beside the register as he fished around in his saggy pockets for change.

"Don't worry about it, man." I waved my hand through the air as though erasing the need for payment. "It's on the house."

That's it, Michael. Put him at ease.

The hobo's dark eyes brightened at the gesture, yellowed teeth poking out from his cracked lips as he fixed me with a smile and thanked me for the kindness. Before he could remove the candy bar from the counter, I grabbed it away, dangling it in front of him as I pinched the edge of the wrapper between my thumb and index finger.

"You know, Jimmy, you come in here for candy a lot," I observed. His eyes followed the Clark bar as I waved it back and forth, a hypnotist with a pocket watch made of chocolate. "But this junk won't fill you up. What if I could give you a nice, hot, home-cooked meal instead?"

For the first time since arriving at the counter, his gaze locked with mine.

Sucker.

"I could give that to you," I promised him. "Would you like that?"

He gave a vigorous nod, the desperation in his stare as sickening to me as the reek of sweat and unwashed dirt wafting from his skin up my nostrils. But I didn't dare turn away. Instead, I leaned in closer, teeth gleaming beneath the fluorescent lights as I smiled wide around the cloud of noxious fumes that surrounded him.

"Come back here tonight around eleven when my shift ends," I told him. "You got a way to tell time, don't ya?"

"Yeah, yeah, yeah." He reached into his pocket and pulled out a cheap digital wristwatch with a silicon band, the face of it cracked and smeared with a greasy residue. I leaned back and tossed the Clark bar on the counter, satisfied that he had fallen into my trap.

"Great," I said. "I'll see you later tonight then, and we can get you properly fed."

***

Later that night, Jimmy returned to the gas station as I had requested. His punctuality was a pleasant surprise to me given his destitution; although, the promise of fresh food had likely given him more of an incentive to arrive on time. Had the circumstances been different, I probably would have felt sorry for him.

Together, we walked the short distance from the gas station to the trailer park where Mama and the family lived, the August heat still stifling despite the absence of sun in the sky. As we traversed the darkened streets, I contemplated how I might succeed in subduing him once we made it to our final destination. I had read in an online forum during my final weeks at school that soaking a rag in equal parts bleach and acetone could be a powerful sedative if held over one's face for long enough. Almost like chloroform, but far more accessible. I knew there was a bottle of bleach in the bathroom linen closet beside the bucket and mop that was stored within. And Mama had plenty of acetone tucked away beneath the bathroom sink for when she grew tired of whatever cheap polish happened to decorate her fingernails at any given moment.

Perhaps I would put the theory to the test, sneak up behind poor, unsuspecting Jimmy as he munched away on whatever leftovers I could find in the fridge, only to have a chemical-soaked cloth fixed to his face, panic increasing as his vision slowly faded to black. Of course, if that didn't work, I could always knock him on the back of the head with a frying pan before dragging him into my bedroom and drenching his motionless body in gasoline.

All the lights were out in the home by the time we made it to the front porch. It was a Wednesday, which meant that Mama and Steve were in bed, sleeping off the final remnants of exhaustion from their last overnight shift so they could repeat the process bright and early the following morning. I raised my index finger to my lips as I placed my key in the doorknob.

"Everyone's asleep," I whispered to Jimmy. "You have to be quiet."

He brought a dirty finger to his own lips, mirroring my actions to show me that he understood. Adrenaline surged through my veins as I twisted the key in the lock, opened the door, and stepped into the darkness. This was it.

There was no turning back.

We crept along the carpeted floor and into the kitchen through the open archway, the soft glow of the digital clock from the microwave providing enough visibility for me to find the light switch. There was a breakfast bar with a pair of wobbly stools tucked beneath the counter which I gestured for Jimmy to take while I rummaged through the refrigerator to fix him something to eat.

Though the food had been offered only as bait, I figured it was only right to offer him a final meal in exchange for his sacrifice.

I pulled out a few plastic containers from the fridge and removed a paper plate from the cupboard, scooping out mounds of mashed potatoes, meatloaf, and green beans before popping the smorgasbord into the microwave. Jimmy remained quiet the entire time, no doubt fearing that the slightest noise would get him thrown out of the house before ever getting to savor a bite of the meal he had been anticipating all day.

Before the final second ticked away, I removed the plate from the microwave, grabbed a fork from the drawer beneath it, and stepped over to the breakfast bar to place the meal in front of my disheveled guest. He wasted no time shoveling piles of food into his filthy mouth, a series of low grunts and snorts echoing from his throat that reminded me of the way the cattle swallowed greedy mouthfuls of feed at the trough. It was nauseating to watch, even more so to hear.

Do it now, the voices commanded.

Sensing their urgency, I excused myself from the kitchen and made my way to the bathroom down the hall, pausing at Mama's bedroom door to ensure she was still asleep. Gentle waves of soft snoring ebbed and flowed through the air, letting me know that neither she nor her fiancé were aware of the house guest sitting in their kitchen.

Satisfied that they were both asleep, I proceeded to the bathroom and extracted the mop bucket and bleach from the linen closet before removing the acetone from beneath the sink. I poured equal parts of each liquid into the plastic bucket. After giving the container a thorough swirl to mix the contents, I grabbed a washcloth from the linen closet and let it soak for a few minutes. Even without the rag placed over my face, I could tell my plan was going to work. The fumes were so powerful in the confined, poorly ventilated space that I began to feel dizzy just sitting there waiting for the cloth to soak through.

Once the washcloth was thoroughly drenched, I fished it out of the bucket and made my way back to the kitchen, careful not to make a sound as I stepped through the shadows. My pulse quickened as I inched closer to the transient licking his plate clean at my kitchen counter. The sound of his lips smacking together with pleasure provided the perfect cover for my approach. He was so intoxicated by the food in his mouth that he didn't even hear the droplets of homemade chloroform splashing against the kitchen tile as I stood behind him. Watching. Waiting for him to lift his head so I could wrap my hands around his face. It was sloppy and careless, I know, but I was too thrilled by the promise of what was to come to concern myself with discretion any longer. I needed release. I needed to feast.

Now!

He straightened up in his seat, the final mouthful from his meal sliding down his gullet as I seized my opportunity. I pulled him to my chest in a one-armed hold, covering his nose and mouth with the cloth in my right hand. He resisted for a moment, gripping at my arm with his grubby fingers as he sucked in panicked breaths through the wet rag held tight around his face. For a moment, I worried that he might overpower me or that the sound of the barstool rattling around on the kitchen floor from our struggle would be enough to wake Mama and Steve from their slumber. Or Matthew. But within a few moments, his thrashing ceased.

His limbs went weak as he succumbed to the poison and his head drooped to one side.

I continued to hold the cloth to his face for a few minutes longer, ensuring that he was indeed passed out before attempting to drag him to my bedroom. He was heavy in my arms, the full weight of his body slumped against my torso like an under-stuffed scarecrow. Once I was certain that he was unconscious, I placed the rag on the countertop next to the empty plate and slid the barstool out from beneath him. I hooked my arms under each of his armpits and began to walk backward through the archway, dragging him down the hall towards the last bedroom on the left, pausing every few steps to ensure the house was still asleep.

Move faster, the voices urged. *Hurry—he'll wake up soon.*

I knew my concoction had been a temporary solution. It wasn't likely that he'd be out for more than twenty minutes—a half hour, tops. I still needed to retrieve my van full of gasoline from its hiding place in the woods. There was no time to waste. I left the vagrant in a heap on my mattress and retraced my footsteps back through the sleeping house and out the front door.

The tree line wasn't far from Mama's trailer, and I sprinted most of the distance to the shadowy forest to cut my travel time in half. In under five minutes, I was sitting in the driver's seat of the work van, bringing the engine to life before rolling out from the woods and into the trailer park. I left the headlights off as I drove, not wanting to cast the eerie glow of suspicion through my neighbors' windows as I pulled up in front of the house. After parking the car, I went around the back of the van to open the double doors and began removing the gas cans within. There were ten total, which I felt would be more than enough accelerant to consume the nine-hundred-square-foot structure that contained my sleeping family.

Catlike and quiet, I crept through the house with a gas can in each hand, making my way back to the bedroom where I had left Jimmy. I was relieved to see that he hadn't moved a muscle when I reentered the room. He remained motionless as I poured the gasoline on top of his body, ensuring he was thoroughly drenched before dousing the rest of the room. When both cans were empty, I went back to the van to get two more.

And two more after that.

And two more after that.

I worked as fast as I could, coating every square inch of the mobile home until the floors were soggy with gasoline. Mama and Steve were surprisingly heavy sleepers, and the empty beer cans on each of their nightstands told me that it'd take much more than the sound of splashing liquid to wake them. Still, I was careful not to pour the gas directly on their fatigued figures as I doused the rest of the area. When I was satisfied that their room had been sufficiently drenched, I exited through the doorway, pausing to lock the door on my way out—just for good measure.

With two gas cans left, I made my final trip to the van and debated my next move. The idea of killing Mama and Steve excited me. I could think of no greater justice than to bring an end to the very people responsible for every ounce of suffering I had endured over the past ten years. While Jimmy had never done anything to cause me harm, I felt justified in taking his life, knowing his sacrifice was a necessary evil that would bring me closer to the life I was always meant to live. But then there was Matthew. Sweet, oblivious, innocent little Matthew.

Could I really go through with killing him? Though Mama's decision to ship me off to her father's ranch had been caused by my half-brother's birth, I never blamed him for the heartache she had caused me. He was just a child. And in the two years I had spent sharing a home with him, he had never shown me anything but kindness. Was it fair for him to share the same fate as his parents? I didn't think so, but the demons disagreed.

Finish this, they hissed as I hovered outside Matthew's bedroom door. *Time is running out!*

The immediacy of their demands sent an electric current through my spine, shocking me into overdrive. Rather than enter Matthew's room, I spread the remaining gasoline around the hallway and crept back towards the front door. As I exited the home for a final time, I propped the screen door open and left the front entrance ajar before stepping into the night beyond.

I shoved the empty gas cans into the back of the van alongside the rest that I had used up, diving into the duffel bag full of bare essentials that I had packed to grab the booklet of matches I had stashed away inside. My fingers trembled as I pried one of the matches free from the cardstock, pausing over the striker before dragging the head across its abrasive surface. The flame danced around the edge of the matchstick, its orange glow begging to be fed as urgently as the voices flicked inside my mind.

Do it, Michael, the demanded. *Burn them.*

With one final look at the mobile home, I stamped down any lingering doubts that might keep me from doing what I knew must be done. I placed one foot on the bottom step of the front porch, leaned forward, and tossed the lit match through the open door. A low rumble reverberated through my chest as the gasoline ignited, the force of combustion sending me stumbling backward from the sudden burst of flames. Hot air rolled over my cheeks as though the devil himself had turned his head in my direction and sighed out a laugh of approval at what I had done. For a moment, I laughed along with him, breathless as I basked in the warmth radiating from the burning building that stood before me. But as the initial delight worked its way through my bones, a cold trail of guilt was left in its wake.

Thoughts of Matthew's blackened body melting into his bedsheets turned my stomach to ice despite the oppressive heat gushing out from the open doorway. I recalled the way he had looked at me the first day I returned to Sudbury, how full of hope and adoration his eyes had been. Those eyes—an exact replica of my own, just as the rest of him had been. How it still could be if I had the courage to act quickly enough.

I scrambled to my feet and rushed to the driver's seat of the van, throwing the car into gear as I pulled up beside the home where Matthew's bedroom window was located. It was too high above ground for me to reach on my feet, but if I climbed onto the roof of the van, it would bring me level with his window, allowing me to break inside. I hoisted myself out of the driver's seat through the car window and made my way onto the roof, scurrying over to the windowpane. My fingers ached as I tried to lift it open to no avail—it was locked shut. If I was going to get inside, I would need to break the glass.

It's too risky, the demons warned. *Someone will hear.*

I didn't care; I couldn't leave him in there. Balling up my fists, I smashed through the glass with every ounce of strength I could muster, the shards raining down on my wrists, sinking deep into my skin. Blood oozed down my forearms, alerting me to the severity of my injuries, but there was no time to waste on dressing my wounds. Kicking the rest of the shattered glass from the windowsill with my boot, I slid into the smoke-filled room where my half-brother slept, completely unaware that his world was burning down around him.

The smoke was thick and blinding, billowing in through the closed door that hinted at horrors in the hallway. I surmised that the black plumes must have aided in lulling Matt into a slumber so deep that he couldn't be bothered to see what the raucous had been at his bedroom window. His breathing was heavy and labored. If I didn't get him out of there fast, he would die of smoke inhalation. I looked back at the window through which I had entered, the jagged edges of the remaining glass like the toothy maw of a ravenous beast. Pushing his fragile body through the opening without ripping him to shreds in the process would have been impossible—the blood dripping from my open wounds proved as much.

I coughed into my elbow crease as I turned to look at the ebony tendrils snaking in through the gaps in the doorframe, warning of the inferno beyond. I had saturated the hallway floors in gasoline, but I hadn't coated Matt's doorway or ensured an impossible escape in the same way that I had for Jimmy, Mama, and Steve. It would be risky, but maybe if I moved fast, I could make it out alive—we both could.

I wrapped Matt in a blanket, gathered him in my arms, and held him tight against my torso, winding the ends of his blanket around my hand to protect my palm from the burning heat as I reached for the doorknob and pushed open the door. A gust of hot air surged into the room, flames engulfing the doorframe in an instant as though I were standing before a portal to hell. It was now or never: Hugging Matt tighter to my body, I barreled through the fiery opening.

The roar of fire washed over us, crackling and popping as the flames engulfed everything in sight. As I squinted through the blinding light and smoke to find the front door, burning chunks of doorframe and ceiling came crashing onto my back, singeing the fabric of my shirt until I was sure it had fused with my already scarred and puckered skin. I ignored the pain, plunging deeper into my scorched surroundings. The front door was still open. I could see the promise of its blackness peering out into the night. A boiling sensation assaulted my chest and I realized that Matthew's blanket had caught fire, embers blooming between us until the smell of burning flesh swam hot and acrid through my nostrils. I fought the urge to drop him, pushing through the pain with all the strength I could manage. We were so close. I could taste the humidity of the outside air on my tongue. Just ten more steps.

Five more.

One more.

We tumbled down the front steps in a heap on the lawn, clothes melting to our torsos as the blanket continued to burn. I rolled us around in the grass, pre-dawn dew drops already forming along each blade, helping to smother the flames. Within a few moments, the fire was out but the flesh along my back and chest screamed in agony as though the embers were still eating away at my skin. The pain was disorienting, dizzying as I scrambled to Matthew's side and checked to see that he was still breathing. His breath was shallow, heartbeat weak as I pressed my fingers into his jugular, begging to feel his pulse.

He's alive, Michael, the demons assured me. *But you can't bring him. You have to leave him. You have to let him go.*

"But I can't leave him here," I responded. "He's going to die."

Somewhere in the distance, I could hear the steady crescendo of sirens as they neared the trailer park. Goosebumps prickled at the back of my neck as I realized what that meant. Someone must have reported the fire. If they did, did that also mean that they had seen me? Had they watched me do it? Were they watching me still?

Get up! The demons seized control, bringing me to my feet before I could protest. A familiar numbness surged through my body as I watched my feet pound against the grass, stumbling to the van that was still parked beside Matthew's broken window and throwing myself into the driver's seat. Without another moment's hesitation, I put the car into drive and sped away from the carnage. The image of the smoldering mobile home burned holes into my retinas as it fizzled from view in the side mirror. I watched until it was nothing more than a spark winking out at me from the shadows.

CHAPTER 6

November 1, 2005

The sound of knuckles beating against the car window jerked me out of a deep sleep. As I jolted into consciousness, the tattered blanket that I had obtained from a nearby dumpster slipped from my torso. I pulled it up to my chin, fastening it around my body like a cloak, not just to fight off the autumnal chill but to keep whatever intruder was knocking on the van window from seeing the monster I had become. The armchair groaned out in protest as I lifted myself from the singed leather cushion, hunching over as I hobbled from the back of the van to the front so I could greet my unexpected visitor.

As I lowered myself into the driver's seat, I caught a glimpse of my reflection in the rearview mirror. Even with the worst of my appearance disguised beneath the blanket, I looked horrible. Grease bled from my hair to my skin, which was black with sleeplessness beneath my eyes. My lips were cracked and flaky, jawline covered in patchy stubble that did nothing to mask the inflamed pustules screaming out from my pores. I looked every bit as homeless as Jimmy had in the moments before I took his life. Because I was homeless. Maybe that was all I deserved after everything I had done.

I tore my gaze away from the mirror and reached for the hand crank to roll down the window. A squat, chubby woman with emerald eyes and a bulbous nose stared back at me through the opening. She seemed irate, with her fists tucked into her paunch at her hips, foot tapping furiously so that the tremors of her impatience quaked all the way from her toes to the trembling flaps of her Rosacea-covered cheeks. I recognized her as the manager of the motel that stood at the far end of the parking lot where I had chosen to take up residence.

"Didn't I tell you to leave?" she demanded, her fleshy cheeks making a gradual transformation from red to purple. "This isn't a halfway house. If you're not a paying customer, you can't just post up in my parking lot."

Bitch, the voices spat. *Worthless fucking swine of a—*

"What did you just say?" Her voice rose up several octaves as the anger bubbled up inside.

Shit. I didn't think I had said that out loud, but it was first thing in the morning and the line between my conscious self and my demons had blurred since the night of the fire. It had become increasingly difficult to keep them contained. They hadn't been pleased with the way I disobeyed them in my rescue of Matthew, nor the things I had done since then. And I couldn't blame them. My recklessness had almost gotten us caught. Judging from the fury that danced in the eyes of the woman who stood outside the van, I was beginning to think that my capture was inevitable. As though confirming my worst fears, she gritted her teeth and issued a warning.

"If you're not out of here in the next ten minutes, I'm calling the cops."

With that, she turned on her heel and bounded back toward the front entrance of the motel. I rolled the window up before shuffling to the back of the van and flopping into the armchair, the worn leather creaking beneath the weight of the world I held on my shoulders. It wasn't supposed to be this way. I was supposed to be blending in on campus, getting a job to support myself, finding ways to wiggle back into Mia's life—not holed up in the back of a stolen van, filthy and penniless and fearing for my life. But perhaps the worst thing about my situation was that I had no one to blame for it but the person staring back at me in the mirror.

You had to save him, didn't you? the voices mocked as I sank my head into my hands. *We told you to leave him, but you wouldn't listen.*

"He was just a kid!" I protested. "He wasn't like the others. He didn't deserve to die."

You were a kid, too, once, they reminded me. *No one ever came to your rescue. No one except for us. And you betrayed us—for what? So you could pretend to be a hero? Look what your heroism has cost us, Michael.*

As though someone had grabbed my skull and forced my gaze downward, my head snapped to the floor, eyes landing on the discarded newspaper at my feet. I bent down and plucked it from the cold, metal surface, fanning it out to read the front-page headline as though I hadn't already committed every word of the article to memory:

Arsonist Strikes Sudbury Trailer Park, Police Seek Answers

Sudbury, NORTH CAROLINA—August 15, 2005—A mobile home in Whispering Oaks Trailer Park Community was consumed by fire in the middle of the night on Wednesday, August 13, killing two and leaving two injured. According to the Sudbury Police Department, the motive for the fire remains unclear, but arson is suspected.

"A preliminary investigation revealed high levels of accelerant used throughout the home," said Police Chief, Andrew Brady. No suspects have been named and the investigation remains ongoing.

The fire raged for ten hours before it was finally extinguished by the Sudbury Fire Department on Thursday morning. Among the victims were Michael Davies and Steven Hardie. Survivors Carolyn Davies and her youngest son were brought to Novant Regional Health Center where they are currently being treated in intensive care for their injuries. No other homes aside from the Davies family residence were impacted by the fire, further suggesting arson as the possible cause.

Police have established a hotline for any tips to be submitted regarding the case. If you have any information, don't hesitate to reach out to 704-555-TIPS.

I balled the newspaper up in frustration and tossed it to the floor, angry with myself all over again. After leaving the scene of the fire, I was too afraid to drive on open public roads all the way to Green Valley. The fire department had come much sooner than I had expected, which made me worry that I had been seen. If someone had spotted me, then surely the police would be on the lookout for a suspicious-looking work van in the area. I decided to lay low, parking the van in a copse of woods on the outskirts of town to wait and see what information would start circulating.

Those two days I spent in the woods were some of the most agonizing in my entire life. It wasn't just the uncertainty of my future that weighed heavy on my mind or the hunger pressing up against my empty insides. The damage my body sustained in the fire had been significant. Deep gashes dragged down the length of my forearms from when I had broken through Matthew's bedroom window, forcing me to use the spare shirt I had packed in my duffel bag as a dressing for my wounds to stop the bleeding. Though I couldn't assess the damage, the sharp burning sensation and deep ache that radiated through my body each time I moved told me that my back was in no better condition than my arms. I needed to see a doctor. At the very least, I needed to get to a pharmacy. But I couldn't. Not until I knew it was safe to do so.

I remained in the woods, flicking through local radio stations to see if any news stories mentioned the fire at the trailer park. Either the story wasn't big enough to make the airwaves or I had conveniently missed the segment by shutting off the car radio to conserve battery. By the time Sunday arrived, I was in too bad a shape to care about whether anyone was actively searching for me. I was starving, and the wounds on my wrists had become red and swollen around the edges. Pus oozed with the blood from my open lacerations, telling me that infection was inevitable if I didn't act fast.

When I couldn't take the pain any longer, I decided to make my way to a local pharmacy so I could get the supplies I'd need to fight off the impending infection coursing through my veins. As part of my plan, I had applied for a credit card in the months leading up to the fire so I'd have something to use to get a hotel room once I made my way to Green Valley. I was prepared to use the card to make my purchase at the pharmacy, but as I approached the cash register at the front of the store, the sight of the newspaper headline stopped me in my tracks.

Arsonist Strikes Sudbury Trailer Park.

A cold sweat collected on the nape of my neck, causing the burns along my back to shiver as I ripped the newspaper from the shelf and began to read the article. My name was listed there, right in the center of the page for all to see. But perhaps even more unsettling than seeing the news of my own death printed in black and white were the words that came before it.

No suspects have been named and the investigation is ongoing.

I swallowed my panic, the voices buzzing in the back of my mind as the gravity of what we had just read sank in. If the police were actively investigating arson and they were under the impression that I was dead, would they discover that a Michael Davies used a credit card at a nearby pharmacy as part of their investigation? I wasn't sure, but I didn't want to find out.

Fortunately, I had a small amount of cash that I had saved up for the occasion, so I decided to dip into that rather than risk using the card. I tugged my shirt collar higher up around my neck and avoided the cashier's eyes as I placed the peroxide, rubbing, alcohol, and newspaper on the counter and waited for him to ring me up.

"Hot one today," he commented. Panic thumped in my chest like a warrior beating against a drum. I could feel his eyes on me, probing into the fabric that scratched at the wounds I was hiding underneath. Suddenly I felt as if they weren't hidden at all. As if he could see straight through me, right into the rotten depths of my soul.

He knows, the voices whispered. *You need to get out of here.*

"That'll be five dollars and thirty cents, sir," the cashier announced. I slapped a ten-dollar bill on the countertop, grabbed the bag full of groceries, and ran out of the pharmacy, ignoring his calls of concern as I raced to the van and drove back to my hiding spot in the woods.

I remained hidden among the trees for two more days, munching on the crackers and peanut butter I had packed inside my bag to fend off the hunger pangs while I waited for my wounds to show signs of healing and contemplated my next move.

You can't stay in this town, my demons told me. *Someone will find you.*

"I don't have enough money," I argued with them.

We tried to warn you, they hissed. *You should have left him behind!*

"What am I supposed to do now?"

With the investigation ongoing, I didn't think I could get away with using my credit card to get a hotel room, even if I did make it all the way to Green Valley. I felt certain that the cops would find out. Though I had enough cash to get a room for a night, that was all the money I had to my name. I needed to be careful. Green

Valley was a three-hour drive away; the gas alone would cost me nearly half of what I had available to spend. But I couldn't keep sleeping in the driver's seat of that van. My body was aching all over from the burns, struggling to find an ounce of comfort in the stiff, unforgiving car seat. I was desperate for a bed—hell, even an armchair would have been preferable to spending another night fighting for sleep in that terrible van.

An armchair!

My mind jumped to the leather armchair resting on the front lawn beneath the awning of my mother's mobile home. I wondered if it was still there or if it had suffered the same fate as Jimmy and Steve, reduced to nothing more than ash in the wake of the fire. It would be a big risk to return to the trailer park, but with no money and a body exhausted by sleep deprivation, riddled with partially healed wounds, I was desperate for relief.

Do not go back there, the voices warned.

"I'll be careful," I promised. "Please... I need this."

If you do this, you must do it exactly the way we tell you, they insisted.

I promised them that I would obey. I would not deviate from their plan. I would never go against their orders again.

Under their guidance, I waited until it was well after midnight, nothing but the silver glow of moonlight hovering overhead as I drove into the sleeping trailer park. I left the headlights off and puttered up to the empty lot that once held Mama's mobile home. Even in the darkness, I was struck by the magnitude of what I had done. Aside from a few shards of glass and what remained of the attached awning, there was nothing left of the house except a pile of ash and rubble hidden behind strands of yellow police tape. Yet despite the obvious destruction, it appeared that all was not lost. At the edge of the lot closest to the road, that leather armchair was sitting beside the curb as though it were waiting to be hauled off with the trash. It was littered with burn marks along the back and reeked of smoke, but otherwise, it appeared to have been spared from the worst of the flames.

I listened carefully to the voices' directions, backing up as close as I could to the armchair before maneuvering it into the back of the van. At one point, they told me I was being too loud, so I stopped what I was doing, waited, and listened for their approval to continue. I didn't fight them as they took over my body; I let myself lapse into the numbness that always accompanied their control, welcoming it like an old friend as it snaked through my veins and dulled the fire in my back. Together, we were able to get the furniture into the van without so much as a porch light from one of the other homes in the trailer park intruding on our progress. Within fifteen minutes, we had made it out of there undetected and were finally on our way to Green Valley.

My original plan was to stay at a hotel for a few days, get settled, maybe find a job near campus before Mia rolled in with the rest of the freshmen for move-in day. But all of my rash decisions had delayed my arrival by several days, and I was in no shape to be considered a suitable candidate for employment. I couldn't use my credit card without running the risk of getting caught and I had very little cash on hand after the long drive, so I could hardly afford a bite to eat, let alone a hotel room. And, with my disheveled appearance and complete lack of personal hygiene, I'd be unable to blend in with the college crowd without attracting unwanted attention from nosy students with prying eyes. I couldn't even park on the streets closest to the university, each space marked by a greedy parking meter demanding coins that I didn't have to spare. Instead, I was forced to go deeper into the wrong side of the city, living out of my van in empty parking lots while the love of my life roamed just out of reach, completely unaware of all I had done to keep the promise we had made to one another.

When I stumbled across the motel parking lot, I thought that my luck had finally changed. It wasn't as far away from campus as the rest of the lots where I had been forced to park my van. From my place at the far end of the blacktop, I had a perfect view of Fifth Street—a popular destination for my would-be peers from what I could ascertain from the buzzing crowds who flocked there. It didn't take more than a day for the motel manager to make her feelings known about my presence there. *Trespassing*, she had called it, as though the word alone held enough power to get me to leave. But I was determined. Maybe if I stayed there long enough, I would catch Mia traipsing down the street, those big, blue eyes of hers searching through the sea of strangers for a friendly face she could trust. I would finally have my opportunity. I would—

You would only scare her away, the voices invaded my thoughts. *Look at yourself. You're dirty and deranged. Even if you found her, you could never let her see you like this.*

Though I didn't want to hear their logic, I knew they were right. Even though my wounds had healed the best they could without medical attention, they were still jarring to behold. And I didn't have any clothing clean or professional-looking enough to be considered anything other than an unskilled vagrant in the eyes of any potential employers. It was an infuriating Catch-22: The only way to get clean clothes was if I had a job, but I needed to appear respectable to secure employment in the first place. My only respite from the impossibility of my predicament had been in the vantage point that the motel parking lot I'd been sleeping in afforded me. But with that fat slob of a motel manager breathing down my neck, even that had been ripped away.

I sank deeper into the armchair, bringing the blanket up over my head as I disappeared into a cocoon of worn cotton and burnt leather. Mia was out there—I could feel the purity of her heart calling out to me somewhere between the city streets, beckoning me to find her, to make her mine once again. But no matter how close our paths came to overlapping, it seemed she was destined to remain out of my grasp. I wanted her. I needed her. I craved her, the hunger for her touch so all-consuming, I could feel it pressing up against my ribcage. Could hear the desire hammering through my veins with each rush of blood that surged through my aching heart.

Wait a minute...

That wasn't the sound of longing bursting through my body. It was the same incessant knocking that had jerked me awake moments before. My stomach lurched. Was that awful woman back to harass me again? Or worse—had she already called the cops? Would they haul me away in cuffs for trespassing only to uncover the truth of who I was? Of what I had done?

The thumping moved from the window to the side of the van, persistent as it beat against the metal and reverberated in my chest. I flung the blanket off of my body, nearly sending my skull into the ceiling as I lifted myself off the armchair in a rage and ripped open the back doors of the van. As I rounded the corner of the vehicle,

I was prepared to see the same chubby intruder who had pestered me earlier. Instead, I was met with an unexpected face.

He was a gaunt, gangly man with wiry limbs and thin skin that sank into his face, accentuating the angles of his cheekbones. Wisps of dark hair poked out from beneath the rim of a black knit beanie, his brown eyes bulging out from deep-set sockets as they combed over my body in abject horror.

"Jesus, man, what the fuck happened to you?" He took a step back as though whatever had transformed my body into a canvas of scars was contagious. I folded my arms across my chest, the action offering little protection neither from the November cold nor the stranger's probing stare as I faced him in nothing more than a white undershirt and a pair of loose-fitting sweatpants.

"That's none of your business." I hissed between chattering teeth. "What the hell do you want?"

"Hey, calm down, bud," he put his hands up in defense, "I don't want any trouble. I just... I overheard what was going on and I... fuck, are you sure you're okay, dude? That looks like it hurts."

He grimaced and I turned away, ducking back inside of the van to grab my flannel jacket.

"I said I'm fine," I snapped back at him.

"Alright, alright, don't bite my head off." He flashed a set of crooked teeth as he tried a half-smile to ease the tension. "Look, we got off on the wrong foot, okay? Let me start over. My name's Kyle."

He took a step forward, extending his bony hand in greeting. I let it hang in the air as a cool breeze blew in the space between us. A moment passed in awkward silence before he brought his neglected palm to the back of his neck, attempting to rub away his discomfort.

"What do you want from me, Kyle?" I prompted him again. He dropped his hand to his side with a heavy thud against his hip.

"Well, listen, I... I'm not trying to be nosy or anything, but I overheard what that bitch was saying to you before while I was at the vending machine and it just pissed me off, you know what I mean?" His eyes darted around when he spoke, tongue flying over his words as though he couldn't form them fast enough. It was obvious to me that he was high, though on what I couldn't be certain. "I've been where you're at, man," he continued his yammering. "I know how it is when you just need a place to crash and everyone's trying to get rid of you like you're garbage. Shit makes me so mad, you know? And threatening you with the cops like that? Fuckin' ridiculous. Bitch acts like she's runnin' the goddamn Taj Mahal out here. Like, hello! You're motel's a dump, lady!"

He spun around to face the motel, raising two middle fingers in the air as if the woman were still in the parking lot to see his obscene display of solidarity. Stuffing his hands in his pockets, he turned back to face me, the grin fading from his lips as he realized that mine hadn't moved an inch in response to his antics.

"Anyway," he cleared his throat, "I just figured I'd come by and let you know that I got a place to stay if you need one. It ain't easy on the streets. Trust me... I know."

His eyes drifted past me, as though he were peering into a distant memory, haunted by some awful ghost that only he could see. My shoulders relaxed as I let my guard down. He wasn't a threat. A drug addict, sure, maybe even a bit of a busybody—but not a threat. Plus, he had offered me a place to stay, and though the armchair had been a dramatic improvement over the driver's seat in the van, I was desperate to sleep on a mattress.

"Hey, I'm sorry about before," I offered, pulling Kyle out of his trance. "You just caught me at the wrong time."

"No worries, man, I get it." He smiled, the focus slowly returning to his eyes. "I'd be pissed off, too, if some piece of shit tried to threaten me with the cops. No hard feelings."

We stood together in silence for a moment, glancing up into the overcast sky, the initial steeliness of our conversation dissipating into the autumn air. I pulled my jacket collar higher up around my neck, fending off the chill that snaked its way around my tender scars.

"So," I ventured, "you said you have a place for me to stay?"

What are you doing, Michael? I pushed the voices from my mind. If Kyle had a place to stay, I needed to take him up on that offer. I needed a bed. Just one night of sleep.

"Oh! Right, yeah," Kyle clapped an open palm on his forehead as though he couldn't believe that he'd already forgotten. "I'm in Room 12 just over there."

He pointed back toward the motel at the room beside the vending machines where he had allegedly overheard my conversation with the manager. I raised a skeptical eyebrow in response.

"Oh, hey, don't worry, man," he laughed when he saw my expression. "It's not like that. There's two beds, okay? I don't swing that way."

"Oh, I wasn't... I'm not—"

"Shit, I didn't mean it like that. It's okay with me if you do. I just was saying I'm not—"

"I don't—I'm not," I stammered, fighting to regain control of the conversation. "I wasn't thinking about *that*," I explained. "I was thinking about *her*."

I jutted my chin in the direction of the main office where the manager had disappeared earlier. Kyle nodded his head in understanding.

"Right," he sighed. "Didn't think of that."

"She probably won't like me staying parked here, even if you are a *paying customer*," I reminded him. "I'd better just go. Thanks anyway for the offer."

"No wait!" Kyle grabbed my arm as I began to turn away. "There's a side street just around the corner where you don't have to pay for parking. Just leave your van there and walk your way back over—easy peasy."

This is a bad idea, the demons warned. But I ignored them.

I should have listened.

Instead, I thanked my drug-addled friend for the tip and followed his directions to the street where he had indicated I could park my van without fear of getting it towed. It was a short walk back to the motel, but the weather had taken a turn for the worse, the pale gray coverage overhead giving way to a downpour as I squelched along the sidewalk. By the time I made it to Room 12, the rain had soaked straight through my flannel jacket, racking my body with violent spasms as rivers of ice water trickled down my spine. My teeth clattered against each other, drowning out the sound of my fist as it collided with Kyle's door. After a moment of standing beneath the sheets of rain, he opened the door a crack, seeming unsure of who would be waiting on the other side.

"Oh, shit!" He slammed the door. I waited while he fumbled to unlatch the security chain before swinging the door open and ushering me inside. "Come in, come in!"

I stepped into the room, water pooling off me in a soggy puddle along the maroon-colored carpet at my feet. The ruddy color reminded me of that night in the slaughterhouse, how the blood-drenched soil on the barn floor warned of my impending fate. If I closed my eyes, I could almost smell the iron and death curling up in my nostrils, stinging the back of my throat.

Kyle followed my gaze to the floor and placed a hand on my shoulder. I flinched in response, flashes of Sir's beatings still as fresh in my mind as if he had just cracked the belt buckle into my back. My hands began to shake.

"Oh man, you must be freezing," Kyle said, uncomprehending, clearly oblivious to the real reason for my trembling. "Here, why don't you get to the bathroom and dry yourself off? I've got a change of clothes around here somewhere you can borrow..."

Kyle pointed to the door at the far end of the room and busied himself searching the piles of lazily discarded clothing on the floor while I navigated my way to the bathroom. Inside, the space was dimly lit, only a flickering fluorescent bulb hanging exposed at the ceiling and yellowing tiles covering the walls and floors. To the right of the doorway was a shower-tub combo, a metal rack bolted to the wall beside it with a towel dangling from the bar. I grabbed it from the wall and placed it on the cracked, laminated countertop before peeling the wet clothes from my body and patting myself dry.

As I disrobed, I caught a glimpse of myself in the mirror. It was the first time I had seen the full extent of the damage that the fire had caused. I gazed into my reflection in horror, twisting my torso around to get a better view of the scars that tattooed my flesh. Pink and puckered skin covered my shoulder blades like a series of unnatural bubbles dying to burst. Though my chest had suffered the least of the damage, it was still raw and red like a wrinkled newborn under harsh hospital lighting. No wonder Kyle had been so taken aback by my appearance.

I was hideous.

A knock at the door forced my attention away from the glass. I fastened the towel around my waist and opened the door an inch, hiding my body behind the wooden surface so Kyle couldn't see what I had seen.

"Found that change of clothes for ya," he announced. I widened the door enough so that he could stick his hand through with the tee shirt and sweatpants he had gathered together for me, consciously keeping my body out of view through the exchange. After a quick shower, I changed into the outfit that Kyle provided and scooped up the soaked clothing on the bathroom floor, joining my host in the motel room when I finished.

I took a moment to survey my surroundings. Just as he had indicated, the place was nothing special, though I had to admit that this had more to do with the assorted trash strewn around the room than any failures on the part of the motel staff. It was dated and drab, the walls partially paneled in dark wood while the remaining half was swathed in beige, peeling wallpaper patterned with tiny rosebuds that matched the maroon floors. Kyle was splayed out on one of the two lumpy mattresses, the bedsheets a tangled mess of faded polyester and curious stains. A boxy television set rested on top of a bureau across from the beds, the pulls on its drawers worn with age. Beside it was a desk that reminded me of the one in my room at Mama's place, its surface littered with thick sheets of paper surrounding a printer and what appeared to be folded pieces of plastic that looked like translucent wallets.

"For my business operation," Kyle blurted when he saw my gaze lingering on the desk. I raised a quizzical eyebrow in response, to which he clarified, "I sell fake IDs to the college kids around here. It's a good gig. Pays a lot. Probably would pay a lot more if I wasn't blowing all the cash on this shit."

He held up a glass pipe that looked as though it were filled with a white, powdery substance before grabbing a lighter off the nightstand and taking a hit. My nose wrinkled at the stench that followed, the harsh odor reminiscent of an unwashed restroom at an abandoned gas station. Kyle coughed out a cloud of smoke as his body relaxed into the mattress.

"You want a toke?" he offered. I shook my head, unable to shield my disgust. "Probably for the best," he assured me. "This stuff'll kill ya. But it sure helps take the edge off, know what I mean?"

I shook my head. No, I didn't know what he meant. Aside from the few moments when the demons had taken over my body, I was always on edge; I had never been able to find any peace. My mind was a maze of murderous rage, an unwatched pot frothing over with boiling water, longing to drown anyone who dared to get too close.

Kyle frowned.

"You mean you never just let loose?" I shrugged in response, taking a seat on the edge of the unoccupied bed beside his. He nodded as though my answer to his question had filled him with understanding. "That why you ah... you know? Tried to...?"

He made a gesture with his hand, dragging his index finger across his throat. I felt my eyebrows bunch together in confusion. Was he already high? How strong was that powder in his pipe? Sensing my bewilderment, he jutted his chin at my forearms.

"Your wrists, man," he said. "You suicidal or something?"

Warmth flooded my cheeks as I wrapped my arms around myself, attempting to hide the scars.

Don't say anything, the voices instructed. *Let him think whatever he wants.*

"Shit, man, I'm sorry." Kyle put his pipe on the nightstand as he sat up in the bed. "Sometimes I just say whatever pops into my head without thinking. You don't have to answer that. Forget I said anything."

"It's fine," I assured him, searching the room for something to save me from the unwanted probing into my personal life. My eyes fell back on the desk. "How long have you been doing all that?"

Kyle followed my gaze to the furniture filled with the tools of his trade, his dilated eyes struggling to find their focus through the fog of inebriation.

"Oh, the IDs? A couple of years or so," he answered. "You ever have one?"

"Once," I responded, my mind drifting back to the cheap fake ID that had both secured me my job and gotten me terminated from the gas station. Kyle grinned, his mossy teeth crowding one another, fighting for center stage through his cracked lips.

"Bet it wasn't as good as the ones I make." He waggled his eyebrows at me and I allowed one corner of my mouth to pull up in a half-smile. I thought about how terrible the ID had been, how its surface was laden with air bubbles, the plastic jagged and coarse along the edges, the lack of resemblance between the person depicted and the cardholder in question.

"No," I admitted. "I can guarantee you it wasn't as good."

"So stupid," Kyle laughed. "They're not even that hard to make well if you know what you're doing. Hey! Want me to show you how?"

"Oh, that's okay. I don't—"

"Oh, c'mon. It'll be fun!" He clapped me on the shoulder as he got up from the bed across from me. "It's not like we've got anything better to do. I'll make you a new one—on the house."

He reached under the bed where he had been sitting and pulled out a bulky laptop before moving over to the desk and clearing a space through the sheets of cardstock. I walked over to the desk, hovering in awkward silence behind him as he brought the laptop to life and opened up a design application.

"Almost forgot—we're gonna need a picture," he muttered more to himself than to me. Pulling open one of the desk drawers, he removed a digital camera and ushered me into the bathroom. "The lighting's better in here," he explained as he snapped my photo. "Plus the white background makes it easier to crop out your image later."

When he was satisfied that he had what he needed, I followed him back to the desk and waited for him to upload the picture to his computer.

"What'd you say your name was again?" he asked without facing me.

Don't answer that, the voices warned. I stayed quiet, not able to bring myself to disobey their commands. But the longer I stayed silent, the more uncomfortable I became. By not answering his question, I'd give Kyle more of a reason to be suspicious of me. I chose the first name that popped into my mind. The only one I felt certain that no one would know. No one would care about.

No one would miss.

"Jim," I mumbled while visions of the homeless man I had sacrificed flashed before my eyes, his mouth hanging open with hunger as I dangled a candy bar in front of his dirty face. "Jim Clark."

"Tim Clark, huh?" Kyle repeated in error. "Pleasure to meet ya, Tim."

"Actually, it's—"

"When's your birthday?" he interrupted. "It's always better if you use real details. Makes it easier to remember in case they quiz ya about it at the liquor store or whatever."

I gave him my birthdate and decided not to correct him on the false name I had provided. It didn't make a difference. I knew the real meaning behind it, and that was all that mattered.

Kyle guided me through the motions of creating the fake ID. He showed me where he kept his templates for every state in the nation; how to isolate an image and replace the background so that it matched what would have been used at the DMV; which color codes to use for the eyes and hair; how to get the signature just right so it passed "the sniff test."

"You gotta use a special kind of paper," he explained as he loaded the printer with a few of the sheets splayed around the desk. "It's called Teslin. It's not what the government uses, but it does the trick. Feels like the real thing, you know? And these?"

He grabbed one of the folded pieces of plastic and held it up for me to inspect.

"You only use these, okay? Don't use that laminate paper shit or you'll get real uneven edges when you cut it and blow the whole thing." He opened up the desk drawers and pulled out a small machine. "This is the laminator. After we print, you put the Teslin in the butterfly pouch, set the laminator to medium, and pop it in crease-first. Then you let it sit for about an hour, trim the edges and *bam!* You're done. Easy peasy."

I nodded to show him I understood. The printer sprang to life and, before long, the image Kyle created was etched across the surface of the Teslin paper he had shown me.

"How much do you sell these for?" I pressed.

"Depends," he shrugged. "Out-of-state IDs are easier to fudge, so those'll go for one-fifty. If they want a North Carolina license, though, I'll usually charge three hundred for that. Trickier to nail down, but you gotta give the customer what they want."

"Wow," I commented. "That's a lot of money."

"Yeah, well, like I said, it'd be a lot more if I didn't smoke so much crack," he said. "Probably would make a shit ton more if I had any help... hang on! Why didn't I think of this earlier? Oh, man. I'm such an idiot."

His dark eyes twinkled with excitement when he twisted around in the desk chair to face me. Something about his expression made my insides burn. It was the same hopeful look that Mama wore when she drove me away from Sir's ranch weeks after my sixteenth birthday. Greedy. Desperate.

"How would you like to go into business together?" Kyle suggested. "Between the two of us, we'll be rollin' in dough!"

Don't listen to him, Michael, the voices whispered. *He's nothing but a drug addict. Do not trust him.*

"I don't know," I said. "Sounds risky..."

"Ah, don't worry about it." Kyle wasn't going to take no for an answer. "I'll look out for you. What're partners for, right?"

"Look, I said I—"

"Oh, man, I'm so glad I ran into you!" he interrupted me again. Why did everyone feel the need to interrupt me? Was it so much to ask for others to hold their tongues while I spoke? I seethed in silence while he continued with his chatter, "We're gonna be rich, dude. You and me doing this together? Fuckin' dream team! This calls for a celebration. Hold up, I think I got something you might like."

He shot up from the desk in a rush and made a beeline for the bureau beneath the ancient TV, digging around in the top drawer until he found what he was looking for. When he turned around to face me, he held an orange prescription bottle in his hand.

"I know you said you don't do the hard shit, but this is different," he explained, shoving the bottle into my hands. "It's legal. Well, it's legal with a prescription, I should say. Just a little Valium—nothin' crazy. It won't get you high or nothin'. I mean... not if you take a little bit. Who knows? Might help with whatever you got goin' on up there."

He tapped an index finger against his temple, alluding to the inner turmoil he thought had been responsible for creating the scars on my wrists. I pocketed the pills and gave him a tight smile.

"Thanks," I said, though I saw nothing to be grateful for. "Maybe a little later."

"Oh, c'mon," Kyle whined. "Don't be a party pooper! You gotta live a little, man."

I shifted in place, his expectant eyes boring into my skin, making my flesh crawl with discomfort. After several moments of uncertainty, I jammed my hand in my pocket and extracted the pill bottle.

"Fine," I relented. "Maybe just one."

Michael, do not take those pills, the voices warned.

It's just Valium, I argued. *What's the worst that could happen?*

***

November 2, 2005

I woke up the next day feeling like I hadn't slept at all, my eyelids heavy with a fatigue that seemed misplaced, as though someone else's exhaustion had stitched itself inside my bones. It took me a moment to realize where I was, the feeling of the motel mattress foreign against the skin that had become so accustomed to sleeping on a leather armchair in the back of a van. I rolled over in bed and blinked the sleepiness away, allowing my vision to focus on the horizontal silhouette in the bed across from me. As I adjusted to the morning light, I realized that Kyle was facing me, his eyes open in a manner that suggested he was also beginning to wake.

"Morning," I grumbled, the word muffled and clumsy on my tongue. Kyle said nothing as I raised into a seated position, his body unmoving on the mattress. I stretched and yawned, still wondering why I felt so tired. My mind was a black hole, like there was something important I had forgotten, but I couldn't remember what it was.

I looked back at Kyle—who still had yet to move—wondering why he was being so quiet when he had been so eager to chat with me yesterday. Did something happen between us? Why was he being so strange? Had I imagined that his eyes were open? I leaned forward towards his place on the mattress to confirm what I had seen. Sure enough, his eyes were open. But the longer I stared, the more I realized that he wasn't awake at all.

He wasn't blinking. He wasn't breathing.

"Oh shit," I whispered. "What did you make me do?"

Get up, Michael, the voices demanded. *It's time to go.*

CHAPTER 7

October 7, 2006

Fifteen months had passed since I arrived in Green Valley. So much had changed by then: I was no longer living out of my van; I had money; my appearance was improved, my face cleared of acne and stubble, hair cut close-cropped and shiny with shampoo rather than slick with grease. Yet, despite all these strides, despite all the effort I put into normalizing my image, despite finally being able to blend in with the crowd on campus, one thing had remained the same.

I still hadn't found Mia.

Green Valley University was much larger than I anticipated, its sprawling campus strategically tucked away behind a perimeter of modest skyscrapers that comprised the city's downtown atmosphere. From the Main Street entrance, it wouldn't have been apparent that a college existed there at all—just a maze of concrete and glass storefronts typical of any other bustling city street. But once one wandered past the grand opening into the heart of the university's central courtyard, it was like stepping into another world.

Historic brick buildings flanked by ivory columns were broken up by perfectly manicured lawns where students read textbooks beneath the shade of weeping willows or sunbathed on blankets in between classes. I wasted many afternoons there, watching the sun trace shadows along the pavement until the silhouettes of every building that surrounded the university swallowed me whole. For weeks, I'd sit there among the blades of grass, heart swelling at every suggestion of Mia's golden locks only to be crushed by the realization that it had not been her at all, just another ugly imposter.

While my search for Mia yielded nothing but disappointment, being close to campus did help me earn enough money to remain in Green Valley so I could continue looking for her. It turned out that Kyle's instincts were right when he had asked me to go into business with him: I had a natural talent for forgery and was able to earn a great deal of cash from my amateur operation. Too bad my mentor never got to share in any of the profits; although, judging from our brief encounter, I doubted whether he would have used the money for anything other than supporting his drug addiction. Maybe that's why it was so easy for me to stop feeling guilty about taking his life. If I hadn't helped him into his grave, he would have found his way there on his own sooner than later. I did him a favor—at least, that's what I had chosen to believe after realizing what I had done. What I couldn't remember having done, even after spending months wracking my brain for the memory.

It was the same way with that calf in the barn, fragments of what had transpired surging to the forefront of my mind like puzzle pieces tumbling out of a cardboard box. If I stepped back, squinted my eyes, I could almost see how they fit together, could almost remember the exact moment I slipped the lethal amount of crushed-up Valium into his drink when he wasn't looking, could almost feel the weight of the pen in my hand as I scribbled out his suicide note and left it on his nightstand. Deep down, I knew I was responsible. But the images in my mind didn't feel like they belonged to me. It was as though I had drifted off to sleep only to wake with the memory of someone else's dreams.

At first, I was disturbed by the sight of Kyle's lifeless body, the pool of vomit that trickled out the sides of his open mouth, staining his pillowcase orange with bile. Though he was nosy and somewhat annoying, I didn't think that these qualities were malicious enough to warrant taking his life. Guilt gathered in my gut, freezing me in place on the bed despite the voices' demands that I get up.

"Why did you make me kill him?" I wondered aloud, my voice on the verge of breaking.

He was dangerous, the demons responded.

"He was nice to me!" I argued. "He was trying to help. He was—"

He was trying to use you, they insisted. *You saw the way he looked at you. Just like your mother. You were nothing but a payday to him. Now you'll be the one to profit.*

"Profit? What do you mean by profit? Profit how?"

It's all yours now, they answered. Before I could ask what they meant, my head snapped in the direction of the desk beside the bureau, the fake ID that Kyle had made me sitting on top of the pile of cardstock and empty laminate pouches.

Take it, Michael. Take all of it.

And so I did. Using a duffel bag that I had found shoved beneath Kyle's bed, I gathered up his laptop, the printer, the Teslin paper, the butterfly pouches, the laminator—everything I could fit inside the bag, I took. But perhaps the most significant thing that I took was the bag itself. Tucked away inside its pockets was enough cash for me to get a room at a hotel for at least two weeks.

I used the money to get a room at a cheap place on the outskirts of town, much further away from campus than the motel parking lot where I had been living. But it would have to do for the time being, at least until I figured out what I was going to do with all the things I had stolen.

It's a good gig. Pays a lot, Kyle had said about his "business" dealings. But in order for it to pay, I needed clients who were willing to part with their money for the services I could provide. Kyle had mentioned that the majority of his earnings were from college kids looking to buy alcohol, but with the state of my appearance, I didn't think any students would feel comfortable approaching me to ask what time of day it was let alone give me hundreds of dollars to make them a fake ID. If this was going to work, I'd need to reinvent myself. I could no longer be Michael Davies—the timid, awkward loser skulking beneath a mop of tangled tresses and a face full of acne. It was time to become someone new. Someone charming and cunning and confident. Someone approachable and attractive. Someone Mia—or anyone for that matter—would never forget, no matter how much time had passed.

And so it was that I began my transformation from Michael Davies to Tim Clark. After getting settled in my new motel room across town, I used some of the money from Kyle's duffel bag to get a proper haircut, some face wash, a decent change of clothes. The latter proved to be my biggest challenge. The scars trailing along my back and down my forearms made anything other than a long-sleeved button-down impossible to wear without attracting unwanted attention. I stocked up on as many of these shirts as I could find at the local thrift shop. They weren't stylish by any stretch of the imagination, but they concealed the damage I wanted to keep hidden. To any onlooker, I was as warm and welcoming as a quirky car salesman with questionable fashion sense. No one would detect the monstrosity lurking beneath the layers of fabric that held the secrets of my true identity.

It didn't take long for me to find my first set of clients. Unlike Michael Davies, Tim Clark possessed a level of magnetism that seemed irresistible—particularly to members of the opposite sex. With my shaggy hair and downcast eyes, my complete lack of confidence, existing as Michael had never earned me more than a polite "hello" in passing from any girls who dared to glance in my direction. But life as Tim was altogether different. Maybe it was the haircut or the clear skin or the sense of freedom that came from living as someone else. Whatever it was about my new persona, women seemed to gravitate toward it like moths to an open flame.

By the end of my first day sitting in the university courtyard hoping to catch sight of Mia, I had gotten ten orders—all from women who seemed far more thrilled with the prospect of having their picture taken in my motel room than they were by the idea of getting a fake ID. Some of them had even offered to pay me in sexual favors, throwing themselves at me as though their bodies were currency that I could use to keep a roof over my head. For the most part, I denied these transactions. I was more interested in the money than in seeking out any sexual gratification. But every once in a while, I'd make an exception for a blonde-haired, blue-eyed customer, always careful to leave my shirt on and the lights off.

After all, I couldn't have them gossiping about the scars on my body to their friends across campus.

Despite the fact that I hadn't gotten any closer to finding Mia, my days at the university courtyard had been productive. With the business I had earned, I was able to save up enough money to stay in that motel room all through the summer—even without the usual crowd of college students strewn about the campus. But by the time the fall semester started back up, the atmosphere began to change. It seemed the university had expanded its security team, the newly hired thugs patrolling around the lawn like hawks circling a fresh carcass. I couldn't conduct my business there without running the risk of getting caught, so I was forced to seek out my clientele elsewhere.

At first, I was annoyed by the change. After all, I still hadn't found Mia, and being driven further away from campus was the last thing I needed. But I'd have even less of a chance of finding her if I got arrested for selling fake IDs or driven back to destitution for being unable to pay for my room at the motel. So, I decided to change tactics and scope out potential customers by standing watch outside of the local bars and liquor stores.

That's where I first ran into Stephanie, and my entire existence in Green Valley changed overnight.

I watched her spill out of the Jarvis Street liquor store, her cheeks flushed as scarlet as the strands of fiery hair she had pulled back into a long ponytail trailing down the nape of her neck. She cast a fierce glare back at the glass storefront through which she had just departed.

"Stupid *bitch!*" she hissed. With a frustrated grunt, she leaned against the brick wall to the left of the liquor store, sliding the large purse that was slung around her shoulder down the length of her slender arm as she rummaged around for her cellphone, muttering profanities under her breath. I didn't need to overhear the curt, clipped conversation that followed to understand what was happening. I had seen enough students come tumbling out of similar establishments bearing identical expressions of disappointment and exasperation for me to ascertain that she had just gotten carded and subsequently denied her purchase. That was my cue to swoop in as the savior.

"Hey." I made my approach from the alleyway where I had been standing, a lion emerging through the tall grass, ready to strike his prey. "Everything alright?"

"Get lost, creep," she answered without looking up from her phone, her thumbs furiously dancing over the keys on her Blackberry as she typed out a long, fuming message to one of her friends. I shrugged and leaned up against the wall next to her.

"Okay," I sighed. "Guess you don't want me to help."

She tilted her head back and rolled her eyes, throwing the phone into her purse before turning to face me.

"I said get—" before she could finish her sentence, she trailed off abruptly as she drank me in with thirsty eyes. In a matter of seconds, the irritation melted from her features, transforming her irate expression into a puddle of infatuation. She reached around the back of her neck and pulled the length of her ponytail to the front of her chest, twisting the ends of her hair around her finger with a coy smile tugging at her lips.

"Sorry," she said with a soft giggle. "You just caught me at the worst time."

"Let me guess," I smirked, nodding my head in the direction of the liquor store entrance. "You got carded?"

"*Yes!*" she gasped, impressed by my observation. "How'd you know?"

"I've got an eye for these sorts of things," I told her, the nonchalance effortlessly dripping from my tongue as I delivered the well-rehearsed line. "What were you looking to buy?"

"There's a party tomorrow night at the Sig Nu house—you know about it?" She drew her eyebrows together, as though she were studying my reaction to gauge my trustworthiness. I didn't skip a beat.

"Of course, I know about it," I lied. "Who on campus doesn't?"

She grinned, relief smoothing away the concern that was stitched across her forehead just moments before. "Right," she laughed, "well, I think I just screwed the whole thing up. I'm in the sister sorority for the frat and it was my job to grab the alcohol for the party, but that stupid *bitch* in there must be new or something. They never used to card people here!"

I let out an empathetic laugh at her remark.

"Well, lucky for you, I'm here," I assured her. She folded her arms and leaned back, sizing me up with unmasked skepticism dancing around in her amber eyes.

"What're you, like, eighteen or something?" she scoffed. "You'll just get turned away, too."

"Actually, I'm nineteen," I corrected her, "and I can guarantee you that won't happen."

"Oh yeah?" she challenged. "I'll take that bet."

"Watch me," I dared her, extending my hand to shake on our friendly wager. "What were you looking to get?"

She gave me some cash along with her order—three bottles of vodka—and I tossed her a confident wink before slipping inside the liquor store to make the purchase. Within five minutes, I was back out on the street with a brown paper bag full of liquor and a dumbfounded sorority sister gaping at me in disbelief.

"I can't believe she didn't card you!" she huffed, accepting the bottles of vodka into her eager, outstretched arms.

"She did card me," I countered. "But I've got this, and you don't."

I reached inside my back pocket and extracted my wallet, removing the fake ID that was tucked inside and holding it in front of her face. She snatched it out of my hand, bringing it in for closer examination.

"Tim Clark, huh?" she simpered before placing the plastic back in my grasp. "Where'd you get a fake that good?"

"I made it myself," I replied. Her mouth fell open, the pink gloss coating her lips like a shiny ring hugging the curve of her astonishment. I had her right where I wanted her.

"Shut *up!*" She gave my shoulder a playful nudge. "You've gotta make me one."

"That can be arranged," I told her. "Why don't you swing by my place later and we can—"

"Stephanie!" A loud, booming voice echoed from across the street, followed by thunderous footsteps. Before I could turn my head in the direction of the noise, a thick hand clamped down on my shoulder and shoved me against the brick wall.

"Who the fuck is this?" my assailant demanded. "You puttin' a move on my girl, bro? She's taken. Why don't you get the fuck out of here before I—"

"Mark, stop!" Stephanie whined. "Let him go! He wasn't doing anything, I swear."

"Oh yeah?" Mark shot back without looking in her direction. Rather than back away, he held me pinned against the wall, his forearm wedged between my chin and my chest. "Looked a little too buddy-buddy from where I was standing."

Enough of this, the voices sneered. *Kick him in the groin and be done with it.*

Just as I was about to obey my commands, Stephanie latched her free hand around her boyfriend's shoulder and yanked back, forcing him off of me. I coughed and straightened myself, relieved to have my airways unimpeded but still seething over the confrontation.

"What the fuck?" Mark huffed, throwing his hands in the air. "You got a crush on this loser or something?"

"You should be thanking him," Stephanie argued. "If it weren't for this *loser*, your party would be ruined."

One of Mark's dark eyebrows shot up just beneath the brim of his backward baseball cap as he fixed his girlfriend with a dubious look. "Yeah right," he dismissed her with a wave of his hand, but she held firm, shoving the paper bag full of liquor bottles into his chest.

"See for yourself," she insisted. "I got carded and turned away, but he stepped up and got what you needed."

Mark rifled through the bag, the anger reluctantly dissolving from his face as he realized that his girlfriend was telling him the truth. He turned to me with a frown, shame and humiliation swimming in the ocean of his irises.

"Sorry, man," he grumbled. "Didn't realize..."

I smoothed down the front of my shirt and nodded, ignoring the voices' demands that I sink my fist into his teeth.

"It's fine," I told him. "I get it. No hard feelings."

His shoulders relaxed, thin lips stretched around a set of straight, white teeth that seemed almost blue beneath the twilit sky. As quickly as the tension faded from his body, a new emotion danced across his face, contorting his features into a tight ball of confusion.

"Wait a minute," he backtracked, assessing me with the same incredulity that Stephanie had in her eyes. "*You're* twenty-one?"

"No," I answered.

"Then how'd you get the stuff? You didn't get carded?"

I grinned and whipped out the fake ID that I had just shown to his girlfriend. "Doesn't matter if you get carded if you have one of these," I told him. At the sight of the plastic in my hand, Mark pushed the paper bag back into Stephanie's arms with enough force to send her staggering backward a few steps as she fought to keep the bottles from tumbling onto the sidewalk.

"Damnit, Mark! What the—"

"Woah!" Mark ignored his girlfriend's indignation as he snatched the card from my fingertips so he could take a closer look. "I've been wanting one of these for a while. Man, it looks so real. Where'd you get it?"

Before I could answer, Stephanie spoke for me, "*He* makes them."

Mark looked from the redhead back to me, his eyebrows raised as if to ask, *That true?* I nodded my confirmation, his eyes lighting up at the admission.

"Get out of here, man!" He nudged me on the shoulder in the same way his girlfriend had moments before he assaulted me. "You're really good at this. You sell a lot of these?"

I shrugged in response.

"A good amount, I guess. Used to sell more before they tightened up security on campus."

"Tell me about it," Mark rolled his eyes as though he understood my plight. "Those morons have been sticking their noses so far up our asses over on Greek Row, I'm surprised their faces aren't covered in shit."

The three of us laughed at the comment. Whatever remaining distrust that had been lingering between us drifted into the hazy night air with the breath from our lungs. As the laughter died down, Mark's face turned serious again.

"What year are you anyway?" he asked. "I haven't seen you around campus before."

"Sophomore," I lied. "I don't hang around campus much. Kinda try to keep to myself."

"Right on," Mark nodded. "That's cool. I'm a junior. Still got a few months before I turn twenty-one, though. Wish it was sooner. Would make things a lot easier for us over at the house."

"Well, I could make that happen for you," I promised. A wide smile spread across Mark's face in response. It only survived for a fraction of a second before it was replaced by a graver expression.

"How much we talkin' here?" He folded his arms, resting his elbow on one forearm as he held his chin in contemplation. I gave him my rate and he let out a low whistle, sticker shock written all over his face. "Damn. That's steep."

"Yeah," I conceded, "but it's worth every penny."

"Hmm..." He unraveled his arms and brought his hand to his cap, lifting it up to smooth back the mess of dark hair that was tucked beneath. "Tell you what," he started once he repositioned the hat on his head, "why don't you drop by the house later tonight? I got a couple more errands to run for this party we're throwing tomorrow, but I should be back around nine."

"Okay," I nodded at him tentatively, "but all my stuff's back at my place. If you're gonna get an ID, then it'd probably just be easier if you—"

"Just come by the house later, alright, man?" Mark clapped a hand on my shoulder. "I've got an idea that I think could solve both of our problems... if you're up for it."

Don't trust him, the demons screamed out inside my mind. *It's a trick!*

As I willed the voices to quiet down, I peered into Mark's face, searching his features for signs of dishonesty. Ever since the incident with Kyle, the way I had overlooked the notes of greed in his eyes when he had asked me to partner with him, I had been grateful to my demons for taking matters into their own hands. For protecting me from being someone else's puppet as Mama had made me out to be. Looking into Mark's face, I saw the same glint of avarice twinkling in his stare, that ghost of hunger haunting his expression, betraying the good intentions that he wanted to portray. But, despite what I had seen, despite my demons' protestations, something deep in my gut told me that I should meet him at the frat house. Like a ribbon of intuition snaking around my intestines, pulling my insides tight with anticipation, though for what I didn't yet understand. All I knew for certain was that I needed to be at the fraternity—no matter how bad an idea it had seemed to the voices inside my head.

"Okay," I said after a long pause. "I'll see you then."

Before he and Stephanie departed, Mark gave me the address for the Sig Nu house on Fifth Street, reiterating his instructions to meet him there at nine o'clock. I watched them walk together down the street until their bodies became silhouettes, disappearing into the indigo evening shadows.

***

October 8, 2006

It's a mistake, the voices insisted. Even though they were speaking to me from inside my head, it was still difficult to hear them over the pounding music, the squeals of laughter screeching out like a siren from the lips of every hussy in a halter top that surrounded me. *You should go back to the motel. You don't need their help.*

But there was no going back to the motel. I had already checked out and moved all my things into the basement of the Sig Nu house. It was done.

I was one of them now.

Wasn't the whole point of coming here so we could blend in and find her? I argued internally as I snaked my way through the throngs of drunk and gyrating college students. *This is our chance to make that happen.*

They're just using you, Michael, the demons warned. *When will you learn? Everyone has a game to play. Don't be so naïve.*

As if on cue, Mark rounded the corner through the archway of the kitchen, pushing his way through a group of girls with red plastic cups clutched in their hands. His eyes swam around in their sockets like two blue ping-pong balls floating in a pitcher of beer. He staggered over to me once he realized I was there, a wide grin spread across his face. With the blacklights bouncing off his smile, his teeth looked even bluer than they had the first time I had seen them glowing from between his thin lips the previous night.

"There he is!" he announced, clapping a clumsy hand on my shoulder. "The man of the hour!"

I bristled at his touch, nose crinkling from the burn of alcohol that wafted from his mouth. He didn't seem to notice my revulsion.

"I'm so glad I met you, man," he slurred as he leaned in closer. "This is a good thing we've got going. I can feel it."

I nodded and smiled, straining to disguise my disgust. Straining even harder to drown out the mounting objections echoing around in my skull.

"It's gonna work out great," I agreed. *It has to.*

After he and Stephanie had left me at the liquor store the previous night to run the rest of their errands for the party, I waited until nine o'clock and met back up with them at the Sig Nu house as planned. The house stood tall and narrow in the center of the lot, its white exterior hovering like a phantom between the blackened blades of grass. It was much larger and nicer than any house I had ever been invited to before, even with its creaking wooden porch covered in cigarette butts. Mark welcomed me inside so we could talk, gesturing for me to take a seat on the sectional sofa in the living room beyond the foyer.

That was where it happened. The conversation that changed everything.

Mark explained his troubles about the frat house falling under scrutiny for underage drinking at their frequent parties. He figured the best way to avoid getting in trouble was if everyone had a way to prove that they were of legal drinking age. That's where I fit into the equation. I'd make the brothers the IDs they needed, and in exchange, Mark would make me an honorary member of sorts, allowing me to stay in the spare room in the basement. He argued that the waived membership and housing fees more than covered the cost of the fake IDs I'd be making. At first, I thought the arrangement could work in my favor. I'd get to live closer to campus, be at the top of the social hierarchy, increase my chances of running into Mia. But unfortunately for me, there was more to it than that.

"Of course," Mark casually added after finishing his proposition, "if you're gonna be making IDs for us, you'll have to make them for the partiers, too. Not for free or anything like that. I wouldn't expect you to do that. But, if you're gonna be staying here, then I'll need a cut of the profit."

We told you, the demons mocked. *Do not trust him. Do not—*

"How much?" The question left my lips a little too loudly as I cut through the chatter in my mind. After a brief negotiation, Mark and I settled on twenty percent. But the plotting was far from over. If I was going to be mass-producing fake IDs for the frat, then I would need a way to do it in secret.

"We're under enough suspicion as it is," Mark reasoned. "We can't have random people dropping by the house all the time. It'll look weird."

"So, how am I supposed to take orders and drop them off?" I argued. "I need to take their photos. I need their names and addresses. There's a whole process. I can't just—"

"Yeah, yeah, I thought about all that," Mark assured me with a grin. "I think I've got a way to make it work. Stephanie, wanna tell him what you told me?"

The redhead joined the conversation for the first time since I had arrived at the frat house. She explained how she had recently gotten a job as a receptionist at the university library.

"It's so boring," she lamented, rolling her eyes as she sank deeper into the couch cushions. "No one ever goes there. The place is basically a graveyard."

"No one cares about how much you hate your job," Mark interjected, annoyed with his girlfriend's rambling. "Tell him what you told me about the restricted section, dummy."

"Oh, right." She sat taller on the sofa as she launched into an explanation about how the eighth floor was a restricted section that was off-limits to students unless they had a special key and were accompanied by the librarian. At first, I didn't understand how this was beneficial to our predicament. If students weren't allowed without a key, how would they get up there without raising further suspicion by the library staff? Stephanie answered before I could voice my concerns aloud.

"I'm in charge of handing out the key and coordinating visitation with Mrs. Cutler, the librarian," she explained. "But she has a staff meeting every Wednesday afternoon. She'll never know the difference if you're up there or not."

"And what about the students placing orders?" I argued. "How am I gonna get what I need from them to make the IDs?"

"You have a scanner, don't you?" Mark pushed back. I nodded, thinking about the printer that I had stolen from Kyle. Though I hadn't used its built-in scanner before, I distinctly remembered there being a glass window hidden beneath the plastic flap on top of the device, hinting at its dual functionality. Mark leaned back on the sofa, snaking his arm around his girlfriend's shoulders as he spoke.

"So, if they leave you a photo, you can just scan it and use that to make the IDs," he suggested.

"The eighth floor is mostly archives and old yearbooks," Stephanie added. "Once students get up there with their chaperone, the librarian will direct them to whatever it is they're looking for, then she'll just sit at her desk up there pretending to supervise them until they're ready to go back downstairs. We can have people place their orders in an envelope in one of the old yearbooks. They'll write their names and addresses on the back of whatever photo they want to use, then drop that in the envelope along with their payment. You can come collect and drop off the orders on Wednesdays during the staff meeting so Mrs. Cutler doesn't get suspicious about you needing to go up there so often."

I reflected on this plan for a moment. Though it wasn't perfect, it was a lot less risky than looking for clients by loitering outside of the liquor stores and bars around town. Plus it would mean that I would no longer have to interface with any of my customers. No one could point the finger back at me if they got caught with their phony license. How would they be able to? They'd never know who made it for them in the first place.

"So, you in?" Mark pinned me with a hopeful stare. Despite the demons screaming out in protest, I felt myself nod in his direction.

"Yeah," I said. "Let's do this."

The following morning, I checked myself out of the motel room downtown. I had ditched the van in the back of an alleyway after initially getting settled in the motel the previous year, nervous that the gas station in Sudbury would have reported it missing from the lot by that point. But I still had that armchair, so I made plans with Mark to help me load it into the back of his pickup so I could take it with me to my new life in the Sigma Nu house. It was hard work maneuvering the chair around the tight corners of the basement stairwell, but even under the heaviness of the furniture as we carried it down the stairs, I felt as though a weight had been lifted as I moved into the house that day. While the voices weren't happy that I had gone against their wishes, I had a good feeling about the arrangement between me and Mark.

It wasn't just the reduced risk related to my questionable business dealings that had me floating on air. Being a part of the frat would put me at the top of the food chain among my peers—even if it was all a ruse. With the brothers sworn to secrecy for fear of getting caught themselves, no one would know that I wasn't a true member. To any outsider looking in, I'd be just another friendly face at the frat house, just another body at the endless parties surging through Greek Row. I'd blend in with the crowd like I never had before. I'd be the person everyone wanted to talk to. Everyone. Including Mia. This was the thought I kept at the forefront of my mind as the party raged around me later that night.

"C'mon, man," Mark draped a heavy arm around my shoulders as he ushered me over to the bar in between the kitchen and the staircase that led to the second story of the Sig Nu house. He grabbed a Solo cup off the counter and submerged it in a punch bowl that was filled to the brim with a pink liquid that gave off a strong chemical odor. Its scent reminded me of the mixture I had used to subdue Jimmy before I dragged him to my bedroom and lit him on fire. Mark placed the plastic cup in my hands and smiled.

"Enjoy yourself tonight," he said. "You deserve it."

I gave him a half-smile in response and raised the cup to my lips, grimacing as the beverage burned the back of my throat. Mark patted me on the back, letting out a holler of approval as I swallowed hard around the bitter liquid. I had never consumed alcohol before, but it appeared that if I was going to play the part of frat brother, drinking was a non-negotiable term of the role. An intense heat trailed from my lips, down my esophagus, pooling in the core of my stomach as I drank. With Mark hovering over me, I felt pressured to guzzle the remainder of my drink in his presence. Only after he was satisfied that I had drained the glass in its entirety did he decide it was safe to leave me to my own devices by the bar. Though I had no intention of getting drunk before having my first drink, I found myself dunking the plastic cup back into the punch bowl for a second round. And a third.

By the time I had moved onto my fourth drink of the night, my eyes had gone heavy, lips numb and tingly, limbs like wet towels hung out to dry. The room was a blur of blaring music and neon technicolor blending together beneath the glare of blacklights that made me dizzy to look at. I hated the feeling, the sting of nausea mounting in my stomach with every thump of the bass from the stereo speakers reverberating in my chest. But my dislike of being drunk paled in comparison to the way my demons felt about the sensation.

This isn't right, they warned. *You need to be in control. Don't be a fool.*

But it was too late. I was already inebriated. My gut pinched as acid churned inside my stomach, the urge to vomit growing more difficult to ignore with every sip from my cup. The house was thick with body heat, intensifying my discomfort in the mauve-colored button-down that covered my torso. I needed water. As I turned toward the bar to address my growing dehydration, my heart lodged itself in my throat.

"There she is," I whispered to myself as my gaze fixated on the woman standing across the room. She looked just like I remembered her from high school with her blonde hair tucked neatly under her chin, blue eyes sparkling like aquamarine gemstones embedded in a bronze statue. There was no doubt in my mind.

It was Mia Davis.

Excitement ballooned in my chest, pressing up against my ribcage as I contemplated how to make my approach. I couldn't let the opportunity to speak with her pass me by again. It was time to make my move. It was time to get her back in my life. It was time to make her mine.

"Wait a minute..."

The earth seemed to fall out from under me as the exhilaration sobered my senses and my vision cleared. I blinked several times in disbelief, trying to convince myself that what I had originally seen had been the truth. But it wasn't. As much as I wanted it to be, the girl across the room wasn't my Mia at all. Just another in a long list of substandard doppelgangers who had tried to fool me ever since I arrived in Green Valley. I watched as the imposter played a game of

Rock, Paper, Scissors with her frizzy-haired companion, the sight of their game causing embers of anguish to erupt all over my skin.

It's not her, Michael, the voices confirmed what I still wasn't ready to believe. *Maybe if your mind was clear, you wouldn't have gotten your hopes up. Maybe you should listen—*

"Shut up!" I hissed, not caring if anyone heard me talking to myself. Thankfully, the music was too loud for anyone to notice. I tore my gaze away from the wannabe Mia and her unremarkable friend, the disappointment planting a golf ball-sized lump in my throat. Rather than continue my hunt for water, I sank my plastic cup into the punch bowl for a fifth time, bringing the alcohol to my lips so I could burn away the anger building in my veins. Suddenly, I felt as foolish and deflated as I had on the bus ride back from Sudbury Cider Mill, Mrs. Donavan's words echoing around in my mind, mocking me with their emptiness.

It's possible.

As I scanned the room with drunken eyes, I started to feel as though everything I had worked for in the past fifteen months had been hopeless. I had stolen a van, burned down my house, murdered three people—all to find a girl who, for all I knew, might not have even ended up going to Green Valley University. If the results of my search were any indication, she had probably accepted an offer to attend some other school in some other city, far away from the one person she had promised to love forever. I wanted to drown myself in liquid fire, saturate my tongue in vodka until I could no longer taste the heartache that threatened to rip me apart from the inside out. I wanted to scream until my vocal cords were nothing more than shredded tissue dangling around in my throat. But most of all, I wanted to—

"Hey!"

A voice called to me through the crowd, pulling me away from the darkness that was slowly swallowing me. At first, I thought that I had imagined it. But the sound had been so clear, so real. It had to have come from somewhere in the room. I strained my eyes, focusing through the fog of liquor to find the source of the noise.

That's when I saw her. Not a lookalike. Not a mirage. Not a drunken vision born out of desperation. It was real. It was her. At long last, it was my Mia.

I watched for a moment as initial uncertainty blossomed into unadulterated joy. She looked exquisite with her tanned skin sparkling beneath a sheen of sweat, the ends of her blonde hair hovering just above the plump curve of her cleavage that turned my throat dry with desire. The longer I stared, the more confident I became that I had finally found her. But my confidence gave way to terror as I realized that she was headed for the front door. I couldn't let her escape. Not after everything I had done to find her.

Follow her, the voices commanded, urging me forward into the crowd. Without hesitation, I obeyed their wishes. Before long, I disappeared through the throng of drunken partygoers into the darkened city beyond. She was there. I had found her.

And I was never letting her out of my sight again.

CHAPTER 8

October 13, 2006

At first, I thought that spotting Mia at the Sig Nu house was the beginning of a new life for me. It had all been so seamless in my mind when I'd gone to chase after her, like a scene from a movie. I'd catch up with her, plot the precise moment when we'd casually bump into one another beneath the golden glow of a streetlight. We'd share a flirtatious conversation, she'd tilt her head up at me, moonlight catching in the cerulean depths of her irises, hinting at an undercurrent of vague recognition in the moment just before our lips collided. Before either of us knew what had happened, we'd be planning out the rest of our lives. Together. Just like it was meant to be.

But none of it ever came to pass.

Instead, I stalked her in silence all the way back to her dorm, too drunk and insecure to summon the courage to act out the fantasy in my mind. It didn't help matters that she had been walking alongside some ugly, gawky stranger on her way back to campus. There was no chance for me to have the romantic rendezvous I had envisioned as long as she remained in the presence of that dreadful-looking tomboy. I staggered back to the frat house, resolving to try again in the morning. Now that I knew where she lived, all I had to do was wait for the perfect moment to make my move. Preferably at a time when my insides weren't fending off the poisonous side effects of alcohol consumption.

We told you not to drink that stuff, the voices scolded me as I stumbled through the shadows back to the Sig Nu house, already dreaming of how I would make my approach once the sun rose the next day.

"I'm getting really tired of the I told you so's," I complained. "We found her. That's all that matters."

Contrary to what I believed, however, finding Mia didn't put an end to my problems. If anything, it only made my life more miserable. In a strange way, not knowing where she was had given me a sense of purpose. A reason to keep going. But, once I found her, I was forced to contend with the same shortcomings that had kept us apart in high school. I found myself lurking outside her dorm building, waiting there every day sometimes for hours until she finally emerged, only to chicken out at the last possible moment. It was as if the mere sight of her had the power to steal my ability to speak. To think. To breathe.

After nearly a week of trying and failing to seize the opportunity to speak to her, I started to worry that I would never have the strength I needed to make her mine. I was frustrated, angry with myself for being such an insufferable coward. And I wasn't alone in my misery.

You're being pathetic, my demons informed me.

"I know," I sighed wordlessly to myself. I was seated at a table in the university library that following Wednesday, pretending to read from a textbook as I waited for Mrs. Cutler to make her way to her weekly staff meeting as Stephanie had instructed. "I want to talk to her, but I don't know how."

You just need practice, the voices suggested. *You've never done this before. It's only natural to be intimidated.*

I thought about all the girls I had slept with in that lousy motel room during my first year in Green Valley, how thrilling it had been to pretend that the swoons that escaped their lips as I thrust into them belonged to Mia.

"I've had plenty of practice," I argued internally. "I want the real thing."

Oh, we don't mean sex, the demons clarified as I boarded the elevator in the library and scanned the access key that Stephanie had given me to reach the restricted section.

"Say what you mean, then," I demanded. I was getting frustrated with the way they spoke to me, feeding me bits and pieces to get me to draw my own conclusions. Just once, I wanted them to be direct with me. To say something that wasn't shrouded in twenty different layers of impossible mystery.

You need a girlfriend, they replied.

"A girlfriend?" I balked. "The only girlfriend I want is Mia."

Oh, Michael, their dissonant chuckle consumed my eardrum as I stepped onto the eighth-floor landing and made my way to the yearbook that contained the envelope with the fake ID orders tucked away in the back. *Don't you understand? It doesn't matter what you want. It only matters what women want. And all women want the same thing.*

"Oh?" My hand paused over the back cover of the yearbook as I waited for the voices to explain. "And what do all women want?"

What they can't have.

I scoffed at the remark, shaking my head as I extracted the envelope from the back of the yearbook and pocketed the photos and money that were stuffed inside. Whatever the demons thought they knew, I felt I knew better. Mia wasn't anything like other women. She was special. She was different. Because she was mine.

She just didn't know it yet.

"Mia's not like that," I said to myself, making my way back to the elevator.

They're all like that, Michael, the voices asserted. *The sooner you realize that, the sooner you'll have her where you want her.*

My finger hovered over the elevator button, the demons' words arresting me in place. Maybe they were right. They had never been wrong about anything in the past. Every bit of suffering I had endured since they entered my life had been caused by my own disobedience, my failure to listen to their careful commands. Saving Matt from the fire when I should have left him to die; trusting Kyle blindly when all he wanted was to use me; getting drunk at the frat party when I should have been clear-headed enough to find Mia sooner and make my move. Maybe if I had been a better listener from the start, I could have already had the girl of my dreams.

"So, you think if I get a girlfriend, it could make Mia jealous or something?" I waited for the demons to speak as the elevator doors sprang open, but a response never came. It appeared that the darkness inside of me had been stunned into silence at the sound of the piercing scream that came from inside the elevator cart as I entered it. An involuntary spasm coursed through my body as I jerked around to see who had caused the commotion. As my eyes darted around the elevator, they landed on a mess of wild, dark curls sprouting from the head of a pale and pouty student who looked oddly familiar to me.

"I'm sorry, I'm sorry," she stammered, grabbing at her chest as though I had startled the breasts right off her body. "You just... you're not supposed to be up here."

Shit. My pulse quickened at the statement, sensing that I had been caught in the act of wrongdoing. I couldn't let her know what I was doing up there or it would blow the entire arrangement that I had at the Sig Nu house.

Be confident, Michael, the voices calmed me, regaining their composure in the face of potential danger. *Act like you belong here.*

Without another moment's hesitation, I produced the key to the eighth floor and held it out for the girl to see. Her almond eyes squinted at the object in disbelief, plump lips opening and closing like a fish gasping for water in a world full of air.

"But how did you—?"

"Stephanie gave it to me? Downstairs?" I slipped the key back into my pocket beside the envelope that held the orders I had come to collect. The girl's cheeks glowed bright red as I watched her search for the right words to say.

"Well, she's not supposed to do that," she said finally. As the words left her lips, the color on her face transformed from a soft pink to a deep purple. She seemed inexplicably mortified, as though she were nervous. But why?

She likes you, the voices observed. *Use it.*

I did as I was told, sidling up beside her with an easiness in my demeanor that felt almost foreign to me. *You're not Michael anymore,* I reminded myself. *You're Tim. Women like Tim.*

"So, are you gonna tell on me then?" I teased her, hoping she could detect the notes of playful flirtation in my voice.

"That depends." She smirked as she pressed the button to the lobby and the elevator began its descent. "What were you doing up there?"

I fed her a line about needing to explore the yearbook archives to get inspiration for a retro-themed party at the Sig Nu house. As we talked, I realized where it was that I had seen her before. Though the memory was hazy no thanks to the alcohol I had consumed, I felt confident that she had been the same girl playing Rock, Paper, Scissors with Mia's lookalike at the frat party the week before. She was much prettier up close than she had been from afar, with warm, brown eyes and angular facial features that made her appear almost exotic in a way. Standing so close to her, I had to admit that she had a nice body—even if she was flat-chested.

As I finished providing her with the reason for my intrusion on the eighth floor, she grinned up at me, a curious cockiness consuming the creases of her smile.

"I call bullshit," she announced. "But that's okay. As long as you didn't do anything that's going to get me into trouble, I don't care."

Oh, she really *likes you*, the voices confirmed. *Keep it going. This is what you need.*

I obeyed my commands, summoning all the nonchalance I could muster as I continued to flirt with the frizzy-haired stranger.

"So, why'd you come chasing after me then if you don't care?" I purred. She bent her head down, tucking loose curls behind her ear as the redness in her cheeks deepened.

"I don't know," she answered. Before I could respond, the elevator came to an abrupt stop on the ground level, sending her body crashing into my chest. I held her there for a moment, a palpable electricity pulsing between us the longer she remained pressed against me.

She's the one, the demons professed. *This is your practice girl.*

As quickly as the lurch of the elevator had brought us together, sexual tension pulled us apart. But I wasn't ready to let her out of my clutches.

"Well, whatever the reason you followed me," I began, "I'm glad you did."

We both are.

Before she could respond, the elevator doors opened to the sight of Mrs. Cutler, her obvious anger making her already stout frame even more impossible to circumnavigate as I attempted to take my leave. I squeaked past the fat, fuming woman before she could find a reason to trap me in the lecture she launched at her subordinate. As I left the library, it dawned on me that I hadn't caught the name of the girl with whom I had been flirting. But it didn't matter. A week later, I was back in the library for my weekly trip to the eighth floor, ready to conduct my business in secret. More than that, I was determined to see if what the voices had suggested held any truth. Maybe if I made myself unattainable as they had said, Mia would finally give me an ounce of the attention I craved.

I sauntered over to the front desk the following week, the look of anticipation swimming out of the receptionist's eyes as she watched me approach her all that I needed to confirm she was already mine.

"I didn't get the chance to formally introduce myself last week." I extended a hand across the countertop in greeting. "I'm Tim."

She slipped her hand inside my own and beamed up at me. "Nice to meet you, Tim." She blushed. "I'm Cat."

***

January 4, 2008

The demons were right about Cat: She liked me. A lot. In fact, I was pretty sure she didn't just like me—she was in *love* with me. And even though I was using her to get to the girl I really wanted, the more time I spent pretending to be Cat's adoring boyfriend, the more I grew to like her, too. There was something alluring about her, as though she also had a darkness within that she struggled to keep hidden. Whatever haunted her, I didn't think it was of the same magnitude as the voices constantly hissing in my ear, but I noticed a profound sadness in her eyes. Like me, she had been broken. Maybe that's why I felt so guilt-ridden when I asked her to move into that off-campus apartment.

It had been six months since Cat and I officially started dating when I learned that Mia moved into a brick duplex just across the Greene Street Bridge. Flaunting my relationship had been difficult enough when Mia was living on campus. Aside from the occasional sighting in the library or at the frat house, we rarely ran into one another. With her living further away, I'd have an even harder time making her jealous. It was infuriating to me. There I was, dating someone else just to get her to notice me, and not once did she ever turn her head in my direction. It made me feel as worthless and invisible as I had the day that she walked straight past me in the halls of Sudbury High School. In her eyes, I would always be nothing. I would always be no one. But when I found out that there was an empty unit available for rent in the same building where she lived, I thought it was the perfect opportunity to force us together.

Of course, there were obstacles that I needed to overcome in order to get what I wanted. Cat didn't know the full truth about my secret dealings in the university library. Out of necessity, I had told her that I was selling homework answers to students so she'd turn a blind eye to my frequent visits to the library's restricted section. Though the lie had helped explain away my presence on the eighth floor, it forced me into a corner when it came to moving into the apartment. Selling the fake IDs had earned me more than enough money to afford the place on my own, but I couldn't alert Cat to this fact without raising her suspicion about where the funds had come from. Not only that, but I thought that by leaning into the lie of my impoverishment, she would feel more compelled to help me.

If there's one thing women want more than the thing they can't have, it's being someone's savior, the voices had advised. *Give her a reason to rescue you.*

With that in mind, I decided to raise the stakes on my need to live off-campus. I told Cat that the university caught wind of my homework hocking in the library and they'd be conducting a raid on the Sigma Nu house to confirm the rumors. If I didn't get out of the house by the end of the fall semester, I'd be expelled. That seemed to do the trick. By the end of the week, we were touring the two-bedroom unit on the second story of the very duplex where

Mia resided on the ground floor. I laid it on thick about how badly I wanted to live there, even going so far as to push Cat to try and get the extra money for the place from her parents just to complete the picture of my desperation.

It was amusing to watch her bend over backward to accommodate me. I could almost hear the gears grinding away in her head as she tried to work out how she'd be able to give me what I wanted. To be my savior. I thought for sure that she'd cave and go running to her parents for the money, but it surprised the hell out of me when she came up with a terrible solution of her own.

"What if we ask Elaine and Evan to move in with us?" she suggested. "With four people to split the rent, it would only cost each of us four hundred dollars."

I groaned inwardly at the idea of sharing a living space with Cat's best friend.

Elaine. Just the sound of her name was enough to make my stomach turn sour. She was without a doubt one of the most provocative tramps that had ever set foot in the frat house, capable of capturing the attention of whatever brother was unlucky enough to have fallen under her spell—myself included. I couldn't help it. With her slender, suntanned legs, her blonde bob tickling the space just beneath her chin, her blue eyes glimmering from her pixie-like face, she was every bit as beautiful to me as my Mia.

And I hated it.

Hated the way she had fooled me that first night that I had seen her beneath the blacklights at the Sig Nu house. But what I hated even more was the scrawny, sulky string bean whom Elaine called her boyfriend. Evan was standoffish and sullen, which wouldn't have bothered me in the least had it not been for the unfiltered cynicism that filled his eyes whenever he looked in my direction. I tried to tell myself that it was no different from the way he looked at any of the other frat brothers, but even the demons seemed to be on edge in his presence.

Rather than shoot down Cat's suggestion that the four of us move in together, I pasted a wide smile on my face, swung her around in my arms, and sang her praises for having thought up such a wonderful plan. If that's what it took to become Mia's neighbor, what choice did I have but to play along? The performance I put on with my mock enthusiasm could have won me an Oscar. Within a week, the four of us had signed our lease and made plans to move in by the new year.

I thought that signing the lease would have filled me with hope. After all the time I spent tracking Mia from a distance, I was finally going to be caught in her orbit. Unavoidable. Inescapable. Exactly how I wanted it to be. But a strange thing happened in the weeks leading up to move-in day. Rather than joyful anticipation, I started to feel... ashamed. At first, I thought that I was just nervous about being in such close proximity to the girl who had held my heart hostage since second grade. But as the new year approached, I realized that my anxiety had little to do with Mia. A serpent of guilt coiled itself around my intestines, and trapped in the center of its vice grip was the face of the woman whom I'd been deceiving for more than a year.

My relationship with Cat wasn't supposed to last as long as it did. At most, I thought that it would be a few months of meaningless hand-holding through campus until Mia inevitably glanced our way and realized what she was missing. But nothing had gone the way I envisioned. Though it was obvious that she was enamored with me from the start, it took months of careful courting just to get Cat to agree to go on a date with me.

"I've been hurt too many times," she confessed shortly after our first encounter in the library. "I'm trying to take things slow now."

I didn't mind the glacial pace of our budding romance; as long as Cat was in my presence when Mia was around, I could give off the illusion of being worthy of a relationship, and that was all that mattered. But, as the months went by and my role as boyfriend earned an official label, something shifted inside of me. Suddenly, I wasn't just pretending to enjoy Cat's company. I wasn't holding her hand or stroking her hair or diving in for a kiss because I thought Mia would see. I was doing it because I wanted to. Because I liked it.

Because I liked her.

Cat wasn't like the other girls I had encountered on campus. She didn't harbor that lustful, hungry expression in her eyes when she looked at me, as though I were nothing more than a handsome face she wanted to add to her laundry list of lovers. She didn't giggle idiotically at the things I said like some mindless moron trying to disguise the fact that she didn't understand what I had meant. She actually listened to me. Peered inside of me rather than resting her gaze at surface level. I liked these qualities. But, most of the time, they scared me. Because the more time I spent in Cat's company, the stronger our connection grew, the closer she became to uncovering the monster inside me, and the weaker my chances became of having the life I really wanted with Mia.

I did everything in my power to fight my feelings for Cat. Though I had been happy to engage in the occasional one-night stand in my motel room, I couldn't bring myself to sleep with my own girlfriend. Something about it felt too real. Too intimate. I knew that she wanted it, and deep down I did, too. Maybe that's what made it feel so wrong. By giving my body to her, I'd be betraying Mia. More than that, I'd be defeating the purpose of everything I had done to get to Green Valley. All the plotting, all the lies, all the death and destruction—everything that my demons had helped me achieve would be proven pointless the instant I succumbed to the building desire inside me that was getting more difficult to deny with each moment spent as Cat's boyfriend. And moving into that apartment together would only make it harder to stave off temptation.

Don't lose sight of why we're here, the voices tried to keep me focused. *You're so close to getting everything you've always wanted. It's only a matter of time.*

But when January arrived and it was time to move into the apartment, all I could think about was what living together would mean for me and Cat. It wasn't just the expectation of sex hovering over us like a cloud of gnats buzzing around the heads of grazing cattle. Even if we never ended up sleeping together, sharing a living space meant that there were certain things I could no longer hide from her—not without giving her a reason to be suspicious of me.

Though I had trained myself to withstand the discomfort of long-sleeved button-downs in the sweltering southern heat, there was only so much I could bear. I looked forward to the nights when I could shed my layers and seek relief in the cool comfort of an air-conditioned room, feel the icy air on my mangled skin after a long day spent suffocated by my own body heat. There was no way I'd be able to keep the secret of my scars while sharing an apartment with my girlfriend. Sooner or later, she'd see me for who I really was. The thought terrified me. Not because I wanted to keep hiding, but because on some level, I wanted her to see. I wanted her to know me. All of me.

Cat was gracious with me, putting her job at risk at the library while she feigned ignorance about what I was doing on the eighth floor. True, she didn't know the full extent of my illicit activities, but while it was obvious that she disapproved of the falsehood I had given her about selling homework answers, she never once judged me for it. Her acceptance and unconditional allegiance to me made me wonder if I could trust her with the truth. Maybe if I told her about everything that was going on inside of me—all the anger and hatred and insatiable hunger that pulled at my insides until the need to devour the world around me became impossible to ignore—she might understand.

She might forgive me.

These were the thoughts that invaded my mind as I drove up in the Penske to Cat's childhood home in Williamsburg that crisp morning in January. She and Elaine had been best friends since grade school and lived in adjacent neighborhoods in the town just forty minutes north of Green Valley. I had agreed to help them load up their belongings and make the drive down to our new apartment. Cat's excitement at my arrival was evident in the way her brown eyes glistened with relief as I pulled up to her parents' Victorian manor, as though part of her had been expecting me to forget about our plans to move in together. But her renewed faith in me only intensified the conflict brewing within my mind.

Silence consumed the cabin of the moving truck as we hauled our belongings down to Green Valley, Elaine following behind in her pristine, white Mustang. I could feel my girlfriend's eyes on me, probing me for an answer as to the reason behind my reticence. But I refused to face her. I just kept my gaze on the road ahead, trying to ignore the cacophony of chatter echoing around in my skull.

If you keep behaving like this, she's going to suspect something's wrong, the voices warned. *You can't scare her away. Think about Mia. Stick to the plan.*

I knew they were right, but the war that was raging inside my head made it impossible for me to focus on anything other than the guilt I felt at getting involved with Cat in the first place. My troubled mind kept me quiet for the entirety of the drive down from Williamsburg.

The parking lot was empty when we finally arrived at the apartment building, the duplex's rich, red brick exterior like a droplet of blood inked into the icy winter horizon. I helped the girls unload boxes from the back of the truck, the manual labor providing a welcome distraction from the chaotic chambers of my mind. It reminded me of being on Sir's ranch, how I grew to look forward to the heaviness of the hay bales or the bags of feed crippling my shoulders as I filled the troughs—each menial task diverting attention away from the torment I had endured, allowing me the space to escape. To exist.

In the fog of conflagrated emotions, I had almost forgotten that Evan had moved into the apartment ahead of schedule and was surprised to see him standing in the open-concept kitchen as I lugged the first set of cardboard boxes into the unit. He gave me a curt nod in greeting, which I did not return. Thankfully, Elaine was there to save us from the awkward silence that followed. She crashed into her boyfriend's arms, the pink glaze of her lip gloss transferring onto his mouth as she pulled away from a passionate kiss.

"Why don't you make yourself useful and help us?" she teased as Evan rolled his eyes.

"Yeah, yeah, I'll be down in a sec," he assured her. Together, Cat, Elaine, and I went back downstairs to collect another round of boxes. With all my conscious efforts focused on trying to appear normal for Cat's sake, I didn't hear the tires crunch along the gravel or the thud of the car door as it slammed shut, alerting me that others had arrived. So when I heard that familiar twang cut through the January cold, I had to fight to keep the box from slipping out of my hands.

"Hey, there! Y'all movin' in?" Mia skipped up to the back of the Penske as though greeting a group of long-lost friends. My chest nearly ripped open at the warmth of her smile as she extended a dainty hand in my direction, begging me to take it.

"I'm Mia," she said sweetly. "I live in the apartment downstairs."

With my hands full of moving boxes, I couldn't reach out to return the gesture. Even if I hadn't been laden with cardboard containers, it wouldn't have mattered. As with every other encounter we had shared since that first day at Sudbury High, the very sight of Mia rendered me speechless. And with Cat standing inches away from me, I was even more lost for words.

This isn't right, I kept repeating to myself. *I shouldn't be here. I can't do this.*

Yes, you can, Michael, the voices reassured me. *Don't be a coward.*

"Hi, Mia." Cat filled the silence, slipping her hand inside Mia's untouched palm. "I'm Catheryn, but everyone calls me Cat. This is my best friend, Elaine, and this is my boyfriend, Tim."

Mia shook Cat's hand, then Elaine's, and gave me a polite nod, acknowledging the heavy boxes in my arms with an apologetic grimace.

"Evan—that's my boyfriend—he's upstairs," Elaine explained. "He moved in a couple of weeks ago. Maybe you've already seen him?"

"Oh, probably not." Mia shook her head. "We've been in Sudbury for the break at my parents' house. This is the first we've been back since last semester ended."

My stomach somersaulted at the mention of our hometown. But there was something else about her statement that made me instantly uneasy. That word. *We.* What did she mean by "we?" Who was she with? Why were they still together? Somewhere in my mind, a movie played of Mia caressing a portrait of her brawny boyfriend taped to the inside of her locker.

We'll make it work, she had said. Was that what had happened? Was *he* the other half of "we?"

As though reading my mind, a frumpy, freckled girl with stringy, auburn hair meandered over to Mia's side. I recognized her as the same pitiful tomboy who I had seen walking back to the dorms with Mia after I followed her out of the frat party.

"Rachel." Mia slung an arm around her friend's shoulder. "This is Tim, Elaine, and Catheryn."

Rachel raised her hand in a half-wave, refusing to speak a word. Something about her silence set me on edge. There was a weight to it—a heaviness. Like the calm that sweeps over the fields, bringing cattle to their knees just before the first raindrop plummets to the earth.

"Don't mind her." Mia gave her mopey counterpart a gentle nudge. "She's just shy."

Cat, Elaine, and Mia continued chatting with one another, the three of them hitting it off while Rachel and I contributed nothing to the conversation. Each time I thought of something clever to say, the words got lodged inside my throat, trapped in my trachea until they dripped down to my gut, eroded by stomach acid. It wasn't just the typical anxiety that I experienced in Mia's presence. I was paralyzed by shame. This was the moment I had longed for, the plan I had carefully concocted for over a year, cultivating my relationship with Cat so Mia would finally see all that she had been missing. So why didn't I feel good about it? Why couldn't I do anything but shift uncomfortably in place while the two women I cared for more than anything bantered back and forth like it was easy? Like I wasn't even there.

"Well, it was really nice to meet you all," Rachel interrupted the conversation, jutting her elbow into Mia's ribs as though trying to shut her up. My eyes narrowed at the gesture, teeth grinding together as I attempted to swallow down my indignation. *How dare she silence her like that?* Before I could find my voice, the tomboy continued, "We'll get out of your hair so you can get back to it."

"Come by anytime!" Mia hollered over her shoulder as the two sauntered toward the front entrance of the duplex. "We're just a floor away!"

Just a floor away.

The words careened into my chest where they wedged themselves into my heart, thrumming through my veins until my pulse became the echo of her open invitation. As I watched her golden crown disappear through the front door, a new refrain took over my heartbeat, skipping alongside the words she had spoken.

It's possible. Just a floor away. It's possible. Just a floor away.

"They seemed nice." Elaine's observation pulled me out of my trance. "I think we've actually seen that Mia girl at Sig Nu before, come to think of it. We should invite them up sometime."

"Yes, we should!" I wanted to shout. But I never got the chance to speak. At that precise moment, Evan came barreling into the parking lot, his light green eyes black as coal, lips pinched into a tight frown as though he were trying to keep the fire from erupting out of his mouth.

"*Mia?*" The way he said her name made me want to squeeze his neck until his eyes leaked out of their sockets. "No fucking way are we hanging out with *that* bitch."

My hands became slick with sweat, quiet rage quaking through my body until I was sure the skin would slither right off my bones. A profound emptiness corroded my stomach, carving itself deeper into my core so that all I could feel was the persistent pang of inescapable hunger.

"Geez, what the hell did she do to you?" Elaine put her hands on her hips, sizing her boyfriend up with unfettered skepticism. Evan's pale face took on a crimson complexion as he cast his gaze to the ground, desperate to escape his girlfriend's scrutiny.

"She just... forget it. I just don't fucking like her, okay?"

I watched his expression carefully, saw the cracks in his façade expose the truth that he wanted to keep hidden. In that moment, I felt like I was staring into my own reflection. The slight hunch in his posture. That unanswered longing in his eyes. The droop at the corners of his lips, as though his face were trying to slide right off his skull, conscious of the fact that it would never be good enough. I knew that look better than anyone.

He wanted her. And he couldn't have her.

"Oh my *God!*" Elaine screeched. "You fucked her, didn't you?"

"No, I didn't!" Evan denied.

"Yes, you did. Why are you blushing so much if you didn't?"

"Just drop it, okay?"

As the two continued their bickering, I could feel the earth slip out from under my feet. My throat felt dry and tacky, stomach twisted in knots, legs numb and rubbery. It didn't matter how many times Evan professed his innocence. I recognized that look on his face, could trace the outline of his yearning with the same precision that I had memorized the jagged edges of the scars along my wrists. Whether he fucked her or not wasn't important. The only thing that mattered was that he wanted to. It made me hollow.

It made me hungry.

"Is anyone else hungry?" The sound of Cat's question made me wonder whether the voices in my head had found a way to escape. My heart stuttered in my chest, returning to its natural rhythm only after realizing the question was born out of pent-up frustration with Elaine and Evan's arguing. The two had filled most of the afternoon with their impassioned exchanges long after the last of the boxes had been unloaded from the back of the truck along with my armchair and Cat's mattress. She tapped her foot, surveying the room with aggravation as she pursed her lips.

"I think there's a deli across the street," she said. "Elaine, want to come with?"

"Gladly," Elaine rolled her eyes, shrugging her boyfriend's hand off her shoulder as she rifled through her belongings to locate her coat. Evan ran his hands through his shaggy mane before dragging them down his face, as though he were trying to peel the skin off his body.

"I'm not hungry," he mumbled, stepping over a set of boxes and retreating to the room that he had chosen for himself.

"Me either," I added. Though my insides were aching with starvation, it wasn't food that I craved. It would take much more than a sandwich to quell the ravenousness that was ripping me apart inside. "I'll just wait here and start unpacking if you don't mind."

Cat's face fell, a deep crease forming in her forehead as she knit her thin brows together in concern. She inched between the boxes that separated us, her brown eyes overflowing with compassion as she peered into my face, as though she were searching the squalls of snow in my irises for signs of distress.

"Okay, well, I'll be right back," she promised, standing up on her tiptoes as she left a tender kiss on my cheek. "I'll see you soon."

With that, she and Elaine exited the apartment, leaving me alone with the voices in my head. And Evan. Darkness invaded my every thought, the urge to rip the door to his bedroom off its hinges overwhelming me. My body was a rubber band stretched beyond the point of elasticity, one end tethered by my undying devotion to a girl I had wanted to be with since grade school, the other hinging on an emerging desire to live a happy, normal life. To be rescued from the sickness I had let fester inside me. To let Cat be the one to save me.

For the first time since arriving in Green Valley, I allowed myself to reflect on all the things I had done—all the things I was still doing—to be with a girl who didn't even remember the promise she had made to me. Didn't even acknowledge that she had been my one source of hope, my one glimmer of happiness in a life consumed by heartache and hurt. I had lied for her. I stole for her. I killed for her. But it wasn't until I saw that same look of desperation etched into Evan's face, that unrequited craving that clawed at the depths of my soul mirrored in his sullen features, that I stopped to ask myself—was it worth it? Even if by some miracle, Mia and I ended up together, would I find the peace I desired? Could being with her fill the emptiness that lived inside me?

Could anything?

I sank into the armchair in the living room, peering out through the floor-to-ceiling windows. Through the towering glass, I could see Cat and Elaine crossing the stone bridge that spanned across the Tar River, the need to be by their side, by Cat's side, overpowering me. *She deserves to know.*

Michael, you're not thinking clearly, my demons almost seemed panicked as they tried to soothe me. *We've come so far. Don't do something you're going to regret.*

I thought about the calf in the barn, Jimmy's sunken eyes lingering on a candy bar, Mama and Steve's melted flesh, Kyle's vomit-soaked pillowcase in that dirty motel room.

I already have, I answered. *And you made me do it.*

We never made you do anything you didn't already want to do, Michael, the voices said. *Don't you understand? We are the same. All we did was give you permission. Give you the power to take what's yours.*

My eyes lingered on Cat as I watched her and Elaine occupy a bench across the river from my place in the armchair.

If taking what's mine means hurting her, I don't want it. She's innocent. She... she loves me.

Haunted laughter ricocheted around in my skull, the sound of it sending an icy finger trailing from the nape of my neck down to my tailbone.

No one loves you like we do, the demons taunted. *When you were alone, who came to you? When you were powerless, who gave you power? When you needed help, who helped you? We are the only ones who love you, Michael. Don't you ever forget that.*

My fists clenched, fingers digging into my palms until I could feel my nailbeds bend back to the point of breaking.

You're wrong. She's different. I know she is. She'll forgive me. She can fix me.

If you truly believe that, then you're a fool, they jeered. But I didn't care what they thought. My mind was made up. I could no longer harbor this darkness, could no longer justify the things I had done. I needed to tell someone. And I could think of no better person to confide in than the one who had already shown me forgiveness—even if it was for all the wrong reasons.

***

By the time Cat and Elaine returned, dusk was falling. The living room was shrouded in shadows, nothing but the soft glow of streetlamps trickling in through the massive expanse of windows that hung before me as I gazed in empty reflection from my place in that armchair. When they entered and flicked on the light switch, I didn't turn to face them, too lost in thought about the confession that I had been preparing to make all afternoon. I heard the soft exchange of their gentle murmurs before the sound of a bedroom door closing told me that Elaine had exited the room to be with her still-sulking boyfriend. I could feel Cat's eyes on me, nervous excitement swelling in my chest as the moment I had been anticipating finally arrived.

"Come here." I patted the arm of the chair, inviting her to take a seat on the leather upholstery still burnt and battered from the housefire I had caused. "I need to talk to you about something."

She crossed the room noiselessly, taking a seat on the armrest.

"Hope you don't mind I unpacked your blanket," I told her, wrapping the fabric tighter around my body, not yet ready to expose what was hidden beneath. She said nothing in response, her expression unreadable as she watched me with hollow eyes. I swallowed hard. It was now or never.

"Look, I wanted to apologize to you. I know I haven't been acting myself lately. It's just..."

"You want to break up," Cat guessed. Ice formed in the pit of my stomach at the words. Is that what I had made her think?

"What?" I stammered, fumbling through the blanket to take her hand, careful not to let the fabric slip down around my otherwise uncovered arms. "No, that's not it," I promised. "That's not it at all. I love you, Cat. More than you probably know."

I kissed the top of her hand, resting my forehead on her knuckles, willing her to believe me. It was the first time that I had ever spoken the words aloud, acknowledging the significance of what existed between us. As I waited for her response, it dawned on me that she had never said the words either. A shiver of panic worked its way along my spine as her silence stretched out before me. Were the voices right about her? Did I imagine her feelings about me the same way that I had imagined I had a chance with Mia?

"I love you, too," she said finally, lifting my chin with her free hand as she stared into my eyes. "But I need you to let me in."

"I know, I know," I sighed, sinking back into the chair as I braced myself for what I wanted to tell her. What I *needed* her to understand. "I... I want to tell you something, but I don't know how."

I paused for a moment, wondering how to proceed. As I shut my eyes, struggling to find the words, Cat supplied them once again.

"There's someone else, isn't there?"

Before I could stop it from bubbling to the surface, a nervous laugh escaped my lips. Had she noticed the way I looked at Mia when we met her in the parking lot earlier? Was I as obvious as Evan? But the mixture of pain and uncertainty in her eyes told me that her comment was just another false assumption. I decided to play it off like it was nothing. Because it was nothing. I hadn't done anything with Mia.

"Oh my God, no, are you kidding me?" I snaked my arms around her waist and slid her off the armrest to hold her in my lap. "I'd have to be a complete idiot to cheat on *you*. I'm just... scared, I guess."

"Of what?" she whispered. I took a deep breath, ignoring the shouts of protest ringing in my ears as I prepared to deliver my response.

"Me," I said. She bunched her eyebrows together, befuddlement oozing from every pore as she twisted around to look at me. "Cat, I haven't been completely honest with you."

"What do you mean?" A nervous waver caught in her voice, like a child calling out to a bump in the night, not wanting to know the answer to what made the noise but unable to keep herself from asking the question. "Tell me what's going on."

"Okay, just... listen for a minute." I breathed in again, trying to summon the courage to push through what I had to say. "We're going to be living together now, which means you're going to find out things."

"What're you talking about? What kind of things?"

The panic in her voice spread to me. I couldn't look her in the eyes, unable to bear witness to the effect that my confession would have on her. If the voices were right, she would find me repulsive. She would leave me. She might even report me. And what would I be forced to do then? But she had told me she loved me. It wasn't just me imagining things. People who loved each other forgave each other—didn't they?

"I'm not the person you think I am." I let the words spill out, still unwilling to watch her reaction as I kept my gaze fixed on the river raging through the living room window. In the water's depths, I could see the faces of every person I had harmed, the ghosts of my past rippling in the glassy surface, daring me to speak their names.

"Tim, please look at me." Cat tried to pull my face towards hers, but I couldn't face her. The sound of my false name on her lips only made me feel dirtier. I bit down on the words that wanted to pour forth from my mouth. *My name is Michael. Tim isn't real. He's just the mistaken identity of the real man I murdered.* But I couldn't say any of that. I needed to play this right. I needed to make her understand.

"There's a lot you don't know about me," I whispered. "Everything I've told you about who I am and where I come from? It's not true."

I watched confusion and anguish wash over her face as she registered what I had said. Throughout our relationship, I had always told Cat that I was from out of state, not wanting her to know any part of who I really was. But, as I searched her eyes for understanding, all I wanted was to tell her everything. To show her everything I kept hidden.

"I don't understand." Her voice was quiet, crackling with emotion. "Why would you lie about something like that?"

"Because I didn't think I could tell you the truth," I answered, anxiety mounting as I selected my next words. "I had a really, really fucked up life," I began. "There's a lot going on up here that I don't like to talk about. And I'm afraid that if I tell you about it, you might not like what you hear."

I tapped an index finger on my temple, alluding to the demons that were trying to drown out the sound of my voice as I spoke. Compassion and concern swam in the depths of her chocolate eyes as she twisted her fingers between my own.

"You can tell me anything," she assured me.

And I believed her. With all my heart, I believed her.

"I... I'm from Red Rock, North Carolina, but I didn't always live here." The words tumbled out of my mouth faster than I could articulate them. "When I was eight, my mom got pregnant with my half-brother. She couldn't afford to feed two kids, so she sent me away to live with my grandparents on their cattle ranch. She told me it was just for a few months until she could get everything worked out, but I didn't see her again for nine years."

It wasn't the full truth. Even though I wanted to tell her everything, it was like the voices in my head had intentionally confused reality. I could feel them fighting for control, that familiar numbness tingling at the base of my neck, traveling down my arms, threatening to overpower me. But I kept pushing back. I needed release.

"Oh my God," Cat gasped. "Tim, I'm so sorry, I didn't—"

"She just left me there," I whispered. "She left me there like I was nothing, and she knew exactly what would happen to me. She had to have known... she had to have known..."

She did know, Michael, the demons reminded me. *She deserved what you did to her. We made that possible.*

I shuddered in response, drawing the blanket tighter around my torso as though the fabric could fend off the memories I wanted so desperately to escape.

"Tim?" Cat called me back to reality. "What... what happened to you there?"

My throat tightened, flashes of Sir's belt buckle catching on moonbeams in the shadows of the barn as he beat me to a bloody pulp playing through my mind on repeat until I wasn't just seeing it. I was feeling it. Right there in the armchair, I felt every lash on my back as though it had just happened. As though it were currently happening. As though I had never left the slaughterhouse at all that night.

"I tried to be good." My voice was inaudible over the sound of my distance screams. "I tried so hard to be good. But it didn't matter. I... I couldn't control it."

I was trembling, so lost in the memory of what I had tried to suppress for so long that I didn't even realize that Cat had slipped off my lap and onto the floor. She knelt down in front of me, taking my hands into hers, the blanket falling away from my skin, revealing myself to her for the first time.

"*What the fuck?*" she breathed, her eyes transfixed on my wrists with the same horror-struck expression that Kyle wore when he had first seen them. "What are these? Tim, what happened to you?"

"I did things," I told her. "I tried to... sometimes I still want to—"

"Don't." She crawled up to rejoin me on the armchair, placing a finger to my lips to keep me from speaking. "Don't say it," she whispered. "I can't hear you say it. Just promise me you'll never, ever act on it. I don't know what I would do if I lost you."

I thought about that day in the motel with Kyle, how he had assumed that the scars on my wrists had been self-inflicted. My heart sank as I realized that Cat had made the same assumption. She didn't understand what I was trying to tell her, but maybe that was a good thing. Maybe I didn't need her to. Maybe all I needed was confirmation that someone *could* love me, and that would be enough. I would be enough.

I leaned into her, hugging her against me as I slipped my tongue over her lips, tried to tell her with my body what I couldn't ever speak aloud. When she pulled away to catch her breath, she cupped my face in her hands.

"Don't ever leave me," she begged. I tucked a loose curl behind her ear, traced the line of her jawbone with my index finger until it came to rest beneath her chin. As I drowned in the chocolate depths of her gaze, I saw the promise of a life that held no darkness.

A life that was normal. A life that could be mine. And all I needed to do was promise to never leave.

"I won't," I assured her.

And, at the time, I meant it. I really did.

CHAPTER 9

May 18, 2008

Maybe in another life, things could have been different. I could have built a life with Cat. Could have had happiness. Had normalcy. All the things I had done could have been left in the past. Erased. Lost to the sands of time.

Demons aren't so easily dismissed. After years of sinking their claws into you, dominating every thought, you start to lose track of where the pieces of you end and they begin. Voices that you once had the clarity of mind to distinguish as separate from your own become impossible to differentiate. Impossible to ignore. Every thread that wove together the tapestry of your existence becomes frayed until you don't even recognize the fabric that once held you intact, defined your very core. Sooner or later, you're forced to admit that you are no longer in control.

And you don't even want to be.

A lot had changed in the months since Cat and I slept together that first night in the apartment—and not in the way I had been anticipating. Though our intimacy had given me hope that I could be healed of the sickness clouding my mind, the peace I felt was short-lived. Before I knew it, the voices had returned with a vengeance, and I could do nothing but succumb to their every whim, my resistance growing more futile as they molded me like clay. Coaxed me into compliance.

Under their renewed control, I began to see the world and everyone in it as nothing more than a massive expanse of farmland waiting to be worked. Manipulated. In many ways, the artful puppeteering that I was learning to master reminded me of the cows on Sir's ranch. Cattle were predictable animals, after all. Apply enough pressure in the right direction, and even the most stubborn bull will become putty in your hands, marching confidently to his own demise without so much as a sidelong glance back to pasture.

Humans were no different.

With enough practice, patience, and painstaking observation, you could learn which buttons to press to get them to do exactly what you wanted. Lucky for me and my demons, Evan's buttons were especially easy to find as we sat together in the apartment, passing the time until our girlfriends returned home, ready to go to a surprise party that he knew nothing about. A party that I had helped plan at the demons' request.

"Let me get you another," I insisted, leaning forward on the leather armchair to take Evan's empty glass from his hands before he could place it on the coffee table. Although judging from the dizzy look in his eyes, I doubted whether he possessed the coordination necessary to perform such physical feats as placing a tumbler on a stationary surface. It was only seven-thirty in the evening, an orange glow spilled across the hardwood through the floor-to-ceiling windows of our living room as the day prepared its descent into nightfall. But Evan was already wasted and had been for most of the afternoon.

I had made certain of it.

"My man!" He hiccupped as I grabbed the cup from his outstretched hand, a lazy smile splaying over his lips. With the sheen of saliva shining across his chin, the reek of whiskey fogging from his mouth, streaks of sweat sliding down his temples, the sight of him normally would have repulsed me. But as I peered down at the pathetic mass of human sludge that sat half-consumed by couch cushions, I couldn't help but feel a rush of excitement. Everything was going according to plan. In a few short hours, my life would be changed forever.

And so would Mia's.

Of course, if that was going to happen—and it was, it needed to, there was no other option—then I would need to do much more than get Evan drunk. He needed to be angry. More specifically, he needed to be angry with Elaine.

I knew this wouldn't be difficult to achieve. The bickering between the couple on move-in day had been a mere sampling of their explosive argumentation. It wasn't uncommon for them to spend hours in open hostility, the volume of their screaming matches often greeting me in the stairwell as their heated words rumbled through the paper-thin walls of the aging building that contained our apartment. But even if we hadn't been roommates, even if I hadn't been privy to every irritating argument, every loathsome lover's quarrel, my observations at the Sigma Nu house would have been enough to tell me exactly how to get inside my target's mind.

Though I had moved out of the frat house, my decision to relocate hadn't terminated the agreement that existed between me and Mark. I was still expected to maintain the appearance of being a brother, furnishing fake IDs for all the members while also ensuring the partygoers who were interested in obtaining one had gotten theirs as well. That meant I was forced to suffer through their bizarre social rituals, sandwiched between sweaty bodies undulating en masse to shitty pop music while a haze of cheap beer and body odor filled the air.

It wasn't all bad. In fact, it was my forced presence at these parties that shined a light on the ever-present undercurrent of jealousy that would allow me to pull the strings on Evan's back like the pathetic puppet he was. Though I shared his lack of enthusiasm in being at the frat house, I was much more practiced at masking my animus than he had been. He'd remain pinned against the wall with his hands stuffed into his pockets, glowering into the crowd with his features contorted into an expression that could only be described as menacing. At first, I thought the source of his contempt had been the brothers themselves. It didn't take long for me to realize what was truly fueling the fire behind his eyes.

Elaine's uncanny ability to ensnare the hearts of every man who had the extreme misfortune of being caught under her spell was a constant source of contention between her and Evan. It wasn't just that the brothers had found her attractive. It was the way she encouraged their advances. She was distracting and beguiling—and she knew it. There was an air of confidence, of *expectation* in the way she traipsed around the frat house that proved to me she was well aware of the effect she had on men. She was nothing more than a tease, grinding her backside up against her eager audience while her boyfriend stewed in bitter silence, too weak and scrawny to do anything but watch from a distance. While it was irritating to endure the incessant bickering that came a result of Elaine's debased demeanor, the couple's argumentation had given me plenty of ammunition to work with that would help me set my plan in motion.

I made my way to the kitchen counter with Evan's empty glass and reached for the bottle of Jack Daniels. It was vaguely impressive to me that he was still conscious given the fact that he had drunk three-quarters of the bottle all on his own. Of course, he didn't *know* that he had been drinking by himself. The sweet tea I sipped from my own glass had been the perfect disguise—a trick I had learned to keep from suffering the scrutiny of suspicious Sig Nu brothers who had a zero-tolerance policy for sobriety. I had learned my lesson about alcohol since that first party, no longer willing to risk my ability to concentrate, to plan, to hunt in the name of fitting in. While I had no desire to partake, I did like the way liquor made others more pliable, and my serendipitous ability to imbibe without becoming intoxicated seemed to encourage those around me to drink more heavily—as though we were engaged in some unspoken competition.

"Cheers!" I clinked my glass against Evan's after handing him the tumbler full of freshly poured whiskey, iced tea sloshing up the sides of my own container as we completed our toast. The corners of my mouth pulled up in a satisfied smirk as I reclaimed my seat in the armchair and watched him bring the liquor to his lips.

Drink up, little pawn, the voices egged him on from the darkened corners of my mind. *Good, good. Now, poke the bear.*

I straightened my back against the leather upholstery and waited for Evan to finish taking a long swig from his glass before making my move. His pupils were like two pinpricks drowning in a pool of absinthe as his gaze found mine. *Pathetic.*

"I'm really glad we could get the chance to do this," I lied through bared teeth. "It's funny, we live together and we party together, but we don't really *know* each other, you know what I mean?"

Evan grimaced as he gulped down another mouthful of whiskey, nodding his head in agreement. He set his glass down on the coffee table, resting his heels on the surface beside it as he sank back on the sofa and focused his attention on the television show that was playing in the background.

Push harder, the voices commanded. *Time is running out.*

I glanced at my watch for confirmation. Once again, the demons were correct: It was seven forty-five, which meant Cat and Elaine would be back from the library soon. I needed to act fast if my plan was going to work.

"We should hang out more often," I continued. "Hey! You know what? You should join Sig Nu."

Evan snapped his head in my direction at the comment, eyes seasick with anger.

Gotcha.

"I'd *never* join Sig Nu," he grumbled incoherently, folding his skinny arms across his chest. I struggled to suppress a smile at my marionette's defiant little display. It was almost too easy to pull the strings.

"Right." I nodded. "I guess I can't blame you for that. I'd probably feel the same way if all the guys there treated Cat the way they treat Elaine."

Evan ripped his legs off the coffee table, nearly knocking his drink over in the process. His brows pulled together, casting garish shadows over the acidic stare emanating from his eyes.

"What the fuck is that supposed to mean?" The question blended together into one long word as his tongue struggled to enunciate around the alcohol. I threw up my hands in defense.

"I'm just saying, I get it, is all." I gave a casual shrug as I leaned back in the armchair. "Honestly, I don't know how you deal with that. Doesn't it bother you that she's always wanting to go over there? Always the center of attention? I mean... what's that all about?"

Oh, that's good, Michael. Very good.

"Hey, fuck you," Evan sneered as he reached for the glass on the coffee table.

"Ah, shit, I'm sorry, man." I waved my hand through the air as if erasing the words I had spoken. "It's just the whiskey talking. Forget I said anything. I'm just glad we get to hang out, is all."

Evan tilted his head back, draining the last of the whiskey from his tumbler. He swayed in place as he rose from the couch, his frail body appearing even weaker than usual as it battled the liquor's effects.

"I gotta use the bathroom," he mumbled, stumbling past me as he meandered over to his bedroom door. Each of the two bedrooms in the apartment had an en suite bathroom, which I knew had been a major attraction for Cat when we had gone to look at the place at the end of the previous semester. But I didn't care about double master suites or stainless-steel kitchen appliances or hardwood floors. The only luxury in our second-story apartment that I cared about were those floor-to-ceiling windows and the unobstructed view they provided of everybody's comings and goings. Cat's. Elaine's. Evan's.

And Mia's.

Over the past few weeks, I had spent hours in front of those windows watching. Waiting. Committing every move to memory, all from the comfort of that worn, leather armchair. My constant reminder of what I was capable of doing. Who I really was.

Who we molded you to be.

While I waited for Evan to make his return, I peered beyond the glass into the street below, surveying my surroundings with pride. A twinge of excitement fluttered in my chest as my gaze landed on the stone bridge that was situated across from the brick duplex. It wouldn't be long until I would meet Mia there, intercepting her on the way back from her student government meeting.

Very soon, it'll all be over, the voices whispered. *We'll finally have her—one way or another.*

I reached into my pocket, fingering the edges of the note secured within. As I fantasized about how the rest of the night would unfold, a thrill rushed through me at the sight of two bodies making their way across the bridge. It was Cat and Elaine.

Right on time, my demons commented with delight. I raced to the front door of the apartment, pressing my ear against the surface so I could hear them enter the building. Moments later, the sound of footsteps echoed through the stairwell, signaling the girls' arrival. I braced myself, screwing my face up in a manner that I hoped would convey concern before I pressed through to the landing, ready to lay the groundwork for the next part of my plan.

***

April 27, 2008

That night with Cat back in January changed me—just as I had feared it would. For the first time since they had called to me in the shadows of my bedroom on Sir's ranch, the voices in my head went quiet after I finally gave in to temptation and allowed myself to explore my girlfriend's body. Allowed myself to feel something other than emptiness. Afterward, the constant chorus of whispers that ate away at my ear had gone, replaced with a nothingness, a normalcy that I never thought I could achieve. Not without Mia by my side.

But Cat changed that. It didn't matter that I hadn't told her the full truth. The mere fact that she had opened herself to me, forgiven my dishonesty, allowed me to burrow the darkest parts of myself inside her when she had every right to be repulsed by my very existence—it was proof that I could be something more than a broken shell haunted by the ghosts living inside my mind. Weeks would go by and I didn't even think about Mia Davis. Didn't even entertain the longing that had torn apart my soul for so long. But then February came, and everything went back to the way it was—only worse.

Memories of the Valentine's Day party were still swimming in my mind when I showed up at the Sig Nu house months later on that bitter day in April, the unseasonable chill that swept through campus sharpening the visions in my head that had dominated my every thought since the night it happened. The night that Mia recognized me.

It had happened so fast that part of me wondered if the whole thing might have been a dream, but the ongoing unrest between Elaine and Evan that followed told me that it was real. The four of us had gone to the Sig Nu house for our usual Friday night festivities, the holiday providing even more of an excuse for the fraternity to celebrate well into the early morning hours. Elaine had put on her typical display of debauchery, dressed in nothing more than what equated to a red, sequined bikini as she pressed herself against one of the frat brothers who was in a similar state of undress. Of course, Evan leered at her from his place beside the bar beneath the staircase, too chicken shit to do anything to fight off the gyrating gym rat lusting after his girlfriend. Part of me felt a bit sorry for him. But any pity I felt melted away the moment I watched him peel himself from the wall and head straight toward the pretty blonde in line at the bar.

"Oh no," I heard myself say above the thrum of music as I watched the scene unfold. It appeared that Evan was determined to give his girlfriend a taste of her own medicine. He stumbled over to the back of the line, his legs weak and wobbly beneath the volume of whiskey that had been coursing through his veins all day well in advance of our evening excursion. As he approached the line of partygoers waiting to retrieve their drinks at the bar, he latched one of his bony hands onto Mia's shoulder, twisted her around, and proceeded to stick his tongue down her throat.

My vision blurred, blood rushed past my eardrums, drowning out the sound of music thumping somewhere in the distance. A slow, steady burn clawed at my throat from the depths of my stomach, urging me to scream, but the sound never came. All I could do was stand and watch as Evan acted out the fantasies that had consumed my every thought for almost twenty years. I wanted to cry. I wanted to vomit. I wanted to—

Kill him.

A familiar numbness crept over my skin as the voices caressed my ear like shadows inching across darkened floorboards, reaching out with their spectral fingers until I was firmly in their grasp. All at once, they flooded my body, their hungry whispers humming through my brain until my veins vibrated with the need to eat.

Kill, kill, kill, kill, kill.

"What the fuck do you think you're doing?"

A deep, booming voice consumed the room before its owner stepped into view. He was a hulking beast of a man, rage rippling through the puddles of blue that bled from his eyes through his mop of thick, messy curls. Though I had never seen him in person, I recognized his face, had it tattooed in my brain since the moment I first saw his photograph taped inside Mia's high school locker—*her boyfriend.*

"Beau, don't!" Mia screamed as he slammed Evan's drunken body to the floor. The terror in her voice sparked something inside me.

Protect her, the voices commanded. I needed no encouragement. Within a moment, I sprang into action, leaping across the room to place myself between Evan and Beau. This was it. The moment that would bring us together. If I played my cards right, acted like a peacekeeper, Mia would have to take notice of me.

"Let's just calm down a minute," I said to Beau, putting my hands up as though attempting to coax an uncaged beast back into his den. "My friend here is just a little too drunk, okay? He didn't mean anything by it."

"Yeah, Beau," Mia chimed in, "this is Mike—"

I didn't hear anything else after that. Didn't listen to the rest of the argument as it erupted around me. Barely registered the feel of Beau's hands on my shoulders as he pushed me to the side and proceeded to pummel Evan into the ground.

"This is Mike."

The sound of my name—my *real* name—slipping off Mia's tongue made the entire world fall away. She said it with such confidence, such knowing, as though she had always known it to be true. In that moment, all the fear and the doubt and the uncertainty that she would ever be mine melted away. Somewhere deep down, I knew it wasn't a coincidence.

She recognized me. On some level, she knew who I was.

Mia's brief moment of clarity gave me renewed hope. I played the sound of my name rolling around in her mouth on repeat, addicted to the song it created in my mind. The faint glimmer of recognition in her voice was like sucking in a lungful of fresh air after drowning in a sea of uncertainty. I was so elated by the notion that she remembered me in any capacity that it inspired me to dig up that credit card in my old name. I used it to book a room at the Holiday Inn for the weekend with Cat so we could escape the sound of Elaine and Evan's makeup sex following the fallout from the fistfight at the Valentine's Day party. Everything inside me wanted to abandon my existence as Tim Clark. I had never wanted to be Michael Davies more than when I had heard the name spoken aloud by the one who I thought had forgotten me. As Cat and I tumbled together between the bedsheets in our hotel room that weekend, my only thoughts were of Mia and how good it would be when it was her body writhing in pleasure beneath mine.

An incoming text message from none other than Mia's doppelganger ripped me away from the memory of that weekend as I stepped onto the front porch of the frat house on Fifth Street:

> **Wednesday, April 27, 2008, 12:02 p.m.:**
> Meet me at Sig Nu. Alone.

What the hell does she want?

The thought of meeting one-on-one with Elaine was as appealing to me as launching myself over the edge of the Greene Street Bridge. Even after spending months together in cohabitation, I hadn't softened towards her. I found her obnoxious and controlling, somehow repulsive despite her close resemblance to Mia. Part of me thought about ignoring the message altogether, dropping off the fake IDs for the brothers like I had planned following my weekly Wednesday visit to the library and heading straight back to the apartment. But I knew it wouldn't fly.

Keeping up appearances as Cat's boyfriend meant that there were certain things I couldn't refuse, certain requests that couldn't be ignored lest I be discovered as a wolf roaming the fields of grazing, braindead cattle that surrounded me. The world was full of spineless yes-men, the word "no" so far removed from their vocabulary that to even think it too loudly was a transgression so egregious that it had the potential to destroy a person's reputation. So, when Elaine texted me asking to meet her at the Sig Nu house, I knew I couldn't say no—even though I had zero desire to be in her presence.

Within an hour, she was bounding up the sidewalk toward the frat house, gripping her torso as she attempted to fend off the bitter cold that billowed through the blades of grass.

"Hey," I called to her from the porch, "is everything okay?"

"Yeah, sorry." She smiled. "Didn't mean to scare you. Just had something I wanted to talk to you about—in private."

No shit. I fought the urge to roll my eyes. To let the voices in my head do all the talking.

"Um... okay?" I landed on polite confusion instead. "What's it about?"

Just as she was about to answer, a fresh gust of wind blasted across the yard, sending a shiver down both our spines. She hollered out in protest of the cold. Despite my usual attire, the long sleeves of my button-down did little to keep the frosty air from raising a trail of goosebumps along my arms. Given the icy climate, we decided to take shelter inside the frat house before continuing our conversation. As I turned to open the door, I felt an unexpected body crash into mine, sending the yearbook full of fake IDs that I held in my arms tumbling to the floor. My first instinct was to drop to the ground and gather up the evidence of my side hustle before anyone could see. But as I realized who it was that had bumped into me, I couldn't move. I couldn't speak. I couldn't breathe.

It was her. Of course it was her. It was always going to be her.

"Oh my goodness, I am so sorry!" Mia's eyes widened at her blunder. "Here, let me help you with those."

"I've got it," Elaine barked, "you've done enough."

Bitch, I wanted to say. *Stay on the ground where you belong, you filthy whore.*

The arrival of a second girl in the doorway of the frat house kept those demonic words trapped inside my throat. It was one of the brother's girlfriends, Lisa. With her face caked in makeup, she reminded me a bit of Mrs. Donavan. The only difference was her hair color—a deep brown where there should have been a shock of scarlet.

"Geez, Mia, what the hell happened here?" She giggled at the mess on the ground that Elaine was still busy cleaning up. As Lisa waited for a response, her boyfriend, Sean, appeared behind her, strands of ginger hair poking out from his baseball cap. He tapped a pack of cigarettes against his palm as he took in the scene, waiting with his girlfriend to hear Mia's explanation.

"I was just coming through the door when I knocked straight into Mike here and—"

"It's Tim," Elaine interrupted haughtily. But I couldn't hear anything over the sound of blood hammering through my veins, bursting to escape my body as elation overtook my senses.

Mike.

Again, she had said the name—*my* name—as though she had kept it held inside her heart, waiting for the perfect moment to release it. In the months that had passed since the Valentine's Day party, I started to have doubts that I had heard her correctly. Every time that we had bumped into one another in passing at the duplex since then, she had given no indication of having recognized me the way that she had at the party. But as I stood before her, listening to the sound of my name spill out of her mouth, there was no denying what I had heard. It wasn't just possible. It was real.

She remembered me.

"Shoot, I'm so sorry, sugar." Mia placed a hand on my shoulder in apology, sending a jolt of electricity through my body in response. "I don't know why I thought your name was Mike. Sometimes I can be so forgetful."

Before I could respond, Lisa wrapped her arms around Mia from behind, resting her hands on Mia's abdomen with a roguish grin tugging at her glossy lips.

"Don't mind Mia and her baby brain, you guys," she snickered. "Somebody's thinking for two these days."

As quickly as my world had been rebuilt, everything came crashing down around me. I stood as if on the edge of a cliff, the craggy precipice eroding beneath my feet, coaxing me further into oblivion. The taste of metal flooded over my tongue, hot and thick. A powerful ringing sounded in my ears, deafening the conversation that surrounded me until the only confirmation of speech came from the movement of lips. And, above the piercing drone of tinnitus, for the first time, I heard not a chorus, but one single voice calling out to me from beyond the ether:

She said forever.

She broke her promise.

She will pay for this.

"Tim, you and I have to talk later, man." Sean's voice sounded like it was underwater as he spoke. "Lost my ticket to that bitchy bartender at Lucky's, so I'm gonna need a replacement, you feel me?"

I couldn't find the words to respond to him. Couldn't do anything but stand stupefied and shattered. Visions of Mia's unborn child billowed through my mind like a heavy fog. Suffocating. Toxic.

She will pay for this.

"C'mon." Elaine elbowed me in the arm and jutted her chin towards the front door, pulling me out of my trance, away from the terrible refrain still echoing through my skull.

She will pay for this.

She will pay for this.

"You good?" Elaine scrunched her eyebrows together, tilting her head up at me with concern etched into her features.

"Yeah, yeah," I lied, shaking the thoughts of Mia's gestating fetus out of my brain. *She will pay for this.* "Just thinking..."

I didn't complete the thought, didn't have the words to express the poison coursing through my brain, wrapping its inky tendrils around my every thought, beckoning me into darkness.

She will pay for this.

"Thinking, huh?" The corners of Elaine's mouth quirked up in an evil half-grin that I wanted to reach out and rip right off her face. She held out the yearbook that she still had in her arms from when she gathered up the fake IDs that spilled across the porch moments before. "Thinking about what's inside that library book? I'm surprised at you, Tim. I didn't peg you for much of a rule breaker, let alone a criminal."

Heat rose from the depths of my gut, crawling up my neck where the fear blurred the edges of my vision. The meaning of Sean's earlier words slowly sank in. I snatched the yearbook out of Elaine's hands and clutched it to my chest.

"You're not supposed to know about that," I sputtered. "Not even the guys are supposed to know about that. Goddamn Sean and his loud ass—"

"*Relax*," Elaine smirked. "I knew before Sean said anything. All your shit spilled out on the floor, but don't worry. I'm not going to tell anybody. I'm a customer, after all."

At first, I didn't understand what she meant. I had made hundreds of fake IDs for students over the years, but I didn't recall ever making one for Elaine. Then it hit me: I hadn't made one for her.

But I had for Evan.

I remember when the order was put in at the end of our sophomore year. It was right around the time that Cat and I officially started dating, and I recognized the photo of Elaine's boyfriend when I found it tucked away in the back of the yearbook on the eighth floor along with the other orders hidden in the envelope. There had been a special request written on the back of his image—one that stood out to me:

Choose a name and address.

It struck me as odd that Evan would want a fake ID that had a separate name and address from his own. I remembered what Kyle had told me when he first showed me how to create them in that dingy motel room.

"It's always better if you use real details."

Maybe it was the sound of Kyle's words haunting me from the grave I had put him in, or maybe I just wanted someone else to share my burden. Whatever the reason, I did end up giving Evan a real name and address on his fake ID. A name that I was determined to distance myself from—at least until I had heard Mia speak it aloud at that Valentine's Day party.

Michael Davies.

I felt confident passing my identity onto someone else, sure that no one would connect the dots that I had been the one responsible for saddling Evan with it. But as Elaine stood across from me in the frat house, winking at me with a knowing smile on her face, I felt paralyzed.

She knows.

Panic gripped at my intestines as the illusion I had worked so hard to create began to chip away. If Elaine knew my secret, how soon would it be before other people found out about it?

"Please don't say anything to Cat," I begged. "She doesn't know about this. She thinks I'm selling homework, which is already bad enough. I don't want her to think… she can't know that I'm… what I really am."

"Like I said, your secret's safe with me," Elaine said. "But since we're on the topic of secrets, I need you to help me with one of my own."

"Oh?" I cocked my head. "What did you need help with?"

A smile spread over Elaine's lips as she launched into an explanation about how she wanted to use the frat house to plan a surprise party for her boyfriend. I tried to focus on what she was saying, but my mind kept bouncing back and forth between Mia's pregnancy and the fake IDs. My lungs shriveled inside of my chest, like two raisins starved of oxygen.

I had to admit to myself that it was over. Any delusions I had at sweeping Mia off her feet in a daze of nostalgia had been effectively erased the instant I learned that someone else had gotten her pregnant. She had betrayed me. She had broken me. And I wanted to break her, too. Needed her to feel the hurt and the emptiness she had planted inside me all those years ago. But how? When?

"Of course, if you don't help me," Elaine's voice crashed in on my thoughts, "I might accidentally tell Cat what you've been up to in the restricted section. Your call."

She's trying to blackmail you, the demons growled.

My grip tightened around the yearbook, jaw clenching as I ground my teeth together in disgust. On top of everything, now I had to worry about getting outed as a criminal by some bitch who had the audacity to blackmail me all so she could throw a birthday party for a boyfriend who didn't even enjoy going to the frat house. It made me want to wring her neck right there in the foyer. Seeing no way to actually get away with that, I relented.

"Fine," I growled at her through gritted teeth. But as I allowed my ire to settle, a wave of terrible genius washed over me. Pieces of a puzzle I didn't even know that I had been fitting together seemed to connect before me. A sinister smile worked its way across my lips as I allowed my demons to consume me, all the while that phrase was pulsing through my brain, beating against my temples with such ferocity, I felt certain that Elaine could hear it, too. I felt like a soothsayer, peering into a future that was mine alone to manifest.

She will pay for this.

***

May 18, 2008

Adrenaline surged as my feet pounded against the pavement, racing to catch up with Evan after his brilliant performance. Granted, he couldn't take all the credit for the way the night had unfolded. I had done more than my fair share of directing to help my little actor step into his role.

After the girls returned from the library, we attempted to sober him up with a cup of coffee before dragging him out to the Sig Nu house for the surprise party. I was getting antsy about the timeline; I wanted to make sure we were well on our way to the frat house before Mia was due back from her student council meeting. If everything went as planned, I could get Evan to have a meltdown the magnitude of which Elaine had never seen. She'd crumble, Cat would spend the night consoling her, and I'd pretend to be the hero as I tried to smooth things over.

At least, that's what they'd think.

The plan worked—even better than I had expected it to. I waited until we were half a block from Fifth Street before I let it slip that we were headed to Sig Nu. With the conversation that we had shared regarding Elaine's promiscuity with the brothers fresh in his mind, the mention of the frat house was all it took to set Evan off. He screamed at her in the street, leaving his girlfriend a broken, sobbing mess in Cat's arms before he sped away from the aftermath of his drunken rage, promises of going to the liquor store on his lips.

"I'll go see if I can talk some sense into him," I excused myself from the scene, hustling down the sidewalk to catch up with the fuming drunkard who had dissolved Elaine into a puddle of tears. It didn't take long to close the distance between us, his limbs still weak and wobbly from the day drinking I had forced upon him.

"Hey, Evan!" I hollered after him. "Wait up!"

"Fuck you," he slurred. "Just leave me alone."

I slowed down, falling in step beside him as we walked in the opposite direction of the frat house back towards the Greene Street Bridge. If the careful watching I had done from the armchair in our living room was correct, then Mia would be making her way back from her meeting any minute. I needed to steer Evan away, make sure he kept his promise to head to the liquor store on Jarvis Street so I could be left alone to do what needed to be done.

"Look, man, I'm sorry about all that back there." I tugged at the strings on my little marionette as much as I could without snapping them. "Elaine asked me to plan the party, and I just wasn't thinking. We cool?"

Evan puffed out a sigh, staining the air around him with the stench of whiskey.

"Whatever," he muttered.

"You heading to the liquor store still?"

Say yes.

"No," he grumbled. "I don't have any money."

I placed a hand on his shoulder and stopped him in his tracks at the intersection of Greene Street and Jarvis, reaching into my back pocket to grab my wallet.

"Well, hey, let me make it up to you," I offered as I placed a wad of cash in his hands. "Go grab whatever you want to drink and I'll meet you back at the house. The night is young. No need to ruin the rest of your birthday over this bullshit."

He squinted at me through the waves of alcohol swimming in his eyes. After a moment of private debate, he snatched the bills from my outstretched hand unceremoniously. He stuffed the money in his pocket and turned down Jarvis Street without another word. The liquor store was at least a ten-minute walk from where we stood—longer in Evan's inebriated condition. That gave me at least a half hour to meet Mia at the bridge. To make her mine. Forever.

The night air was cool and still, chilling the sheen of sweat that ran slick over my skin in anticipation of what I knew was coming. Very soon, it would all be over. I'd finally have her. Even if it meant keeping her with the rest of the ghosts I had created. She deserved it after everything she had done. I'd make sure she'd never break a promise again.

I kept my head on a swivel as I approached the bridge, looking out for any passersby who might interrupt my plan. It was the last week of the semester, and most students had already left campus for summer break. Green Valley wasn't a bustling metroplex by any stretch of the imagination. Once school let out, the place became a ghost town, haunted only by bored housewives desperate to escape their miserable existence on the rural outskirts, searching for a bargain or a bite to eat that hadn't been prepared by themselves. As I scanned my surroundings, my eyes confirmed what I already suspected would be the case.

The streets were empty; I'd have her all to myself.

I made it across the bridge in a hurry, eager to conceal myself in the shadows behind the scattered trees that bordered the edge of the stonework and led down to the bank of the Tar River. Blood hummed in my ears as excitement swelled in my veins, thoughts of Mia's body going limp in my arms making me dizzy with impatience. I glanced down at my watch, wondering what the fuck was taking so long. It was almost nine o'clock. She should have been well on her way back from the meeting by this point. I was sure of it. I had watched her countless times over the past few weeks.

Even followed her to a few meetings just to be certain of where she was going—and how long it would take for her to return. For her to fall into my trap. So why wasn't she here by now? Why wasn't she—

Listen.

Mingling with the sound of the river as it lapped up against the rocky shore was a distinct whimpering noise swimming through the shadows. It was the sound of a woman crying. My stomach gave an unpleasant lurch at the realization. Was it Elaine? Had Cat chosen to bring her to the riverside to console her just as she had done after the argument on move-in day? No. That couldn't be. I would've seen them walk past me and Evan if that had been the case. So who was sobbing in the darkness? As though the sound itself were a rope lassoing me around the waist, I inched toward it, unsure of what I might find.

I placed careful steps along the rocks at my feet, not wanting to alert the crying stranger to my presence. As the gentle decline of loose rocks and gravel tapered off to the shore, I saw her perched on the water's edge, knees hugged to her chest as her body quaked between heaving, rasping sobs. Moonlight poured over her, highlighting her blonde crown like a halo, as though even the heavens knew what her fate would be. The sight of her caught me by surprise, causing me to lose my footing on the rocks. She gasped, twisting around to face the noise, her gaze landing on mine.

"H–hello?" she choked. "Who's there?"

I stepped out from the shadows, allowing the moon to illuminate me. Her shoulders relaxed as she breathed a sigh of relief.

"Oh, it's you," she sniffled, dragging a sleeve across her tear-stained cheeks.

Do it, Michael, the voices urged. *Take her now. Make her yours.*

I took a step forward, preparing to make my move. But something held me in place. She seemed so vulnerable. Shattered. Had something happened with her boyfriend? Had something happened to the baby? I needed to know.

Moving along the rocks, I joined her at the river's edge and took a seat beside her.

"Hey," I spoke softly, the first word I had said to her since being forced away to Red Rock in second grade. "Is everything alright?"

The question seemed to crush her, tears flooding to the surface so fast, it appeared as though she were channeling the river. She bent her head into my chest, the warmth from her tears saturating the space surrounding my heart where she had lived for so long. My breath caught in my throat. Was this finally going to happen?

"No," she sobbed. "Everything is terrible. Everything is terrible, and I don't know how to make it right. I don't know what to do. Oh God, I can't do this. I can't—"

"Shh, shh," I stroked her hair with one hand, hugging her closer with the other. "It's okay. I'm here. I'm right here."

She continued to cry incoherently, trembling in my arms as the water lapped at our feet. For a moment, I thought that everything might resolve on its own. I wouldn't have to go through with it. I wouldn't have to steal her to make her mine.

Suddenly, she pulled away from me, the embarrassment evident on her face.

"I'm sorry," she stammered. "I shouldn't have done that. You probably think I'm such a mess."

I put my hand under her chin, forcing her to look into my eyes, willing her to see who I was. To recognize me. To feel what I felt.

"I could never think that about you," I told her, brushing away the stray tears on her face with my thumb. Before I could stop myself, I leaned into her, hungry for the taste of her lips on my tongue. The moment our mouths collided, I felt her entire body grow tense in my arms. She placed her palms on my chest and shoved with all her might.

"What the hell are you doing?" she demanded. "What is the matter with you? I don't even know you!"

She wiped her mouth with the back of her hand as though my kiss had poisoned her. Before she could stand up to leave, I gripped her by the wrist.

"Mia, wait," I begged. "You *do* know me. I know you know me. You've said it before. I'm Mike—remember? From second grade? I know you remember me. Please just—"

Thwack!

Her open palm scorched across my cheek and sent my mind stumbling back. It wasn't just Mia's hand slapping me across the face. It was Sir's. It was Mama's. And I would only ever be that small, scared, lonely boy stuck on a promise that never existed in the first place. Nothing and no one to care about me except the darkness that swirled inside my mind.

"Stay the hell away from me!" Mia hollered as she stood up to go. But the rage inside me was too quick. It was time.

She wasn't going anywhere.

Before she could grab her purse from the ground where she had abandoned it at her side, I wrapped my hand around the biggest rock I could find and drove it into the back of her skull. The sound of her bones splintering sent a terrible crack through the night air, but she didn't scream. She simply raised a hand to her hair, as though trying to locate the source of the searing pain that ballooned inside her head. Just as her fingers grazed the ends of her hair, she collapsed to the ground.

Finish her, Michael, the voices commanded.

But I couldn't move. I couldn't breathe.

The last thing I remember before the darkness took me was the sound of the river splashing against Mia's skin.

CHAPTER 10

May 19, 2008

I woke the next morning to the sound of knocking at the front door. When I answered, a pair of police officers were staring back at me. The white officer with the hook nose and dark hair spoke first.

"I'm Officer Gildan and this is Officer Michaels," he stated, gesturing to his dark-skinned companion. "Your neighbor downstairs, Ms. Davis, was found dead this morning in an apparent suicide, and we'd like to ask you all a few questions."

I knew I should have felt panicked by their presence, but I didn't. Instead of anxiety, I felt a wave of calm wash over me, visions of the previous night printed on the back of my eyelids like a private screening of some indie horror flick. Hitting Mia over the head. The demons taking over, dragging her limp body into the river, holding her underwater until the final bubble floated to the surface, confirming she was gone.

She was mine.

They made me go through her purse next so I could find her car keys and plant the suicide note I still had tucked away in my pocket on her driver's seat. Part of me wasn't sure if it had been convincing enough. I had planned to make it look like a suicide, just like I had done with Kyle. It was supposed to be quick, easy—a simple push over the edge of the bridge on her way back from her meeting. I wasn't supposed to hit her. Wasn't supposed to give a reason to doubt the story of her suicide. But as the officer delivered the news at our doorstep, I breathed a sigh of relief. He believed the version of events that I had hoped he would.

It was over. I finally had her all to myself. My Mia Davis.

"I don't get it." Cat came up behind me to greet the pair of policemen at our door. "If it's a suicide, why do we have to be questioned?"

She has a point, the voices interjected. *Something's not right.*

"It's just standard procedure," the African officer standing beside Gildan chimed in. "We're just trying to establish a potential timeline for when she may have passed. See if anyone might have seen her beforehand."

His chocolate eyes seemed to bore into mine before he posed his next question. As though he could see the images of the night before flashing inside of my mind.

"Did any of you leave the apartment last night?"

"Yeah, all of us were out last night," Cat responded. "But we didn't see anything unusual."

Good girl, the demons purred. *She might be worth keeping, after all.*

"What's going on?" Evan waltzed into the living room, a cloud of stale sweat and brown liquor fumes punching each of us in the face with his presence.

"We're from the Green Valley Police Department," Officer Gildan explained. "Your neighbor, Mia Davis, was found dead this morning in an apparent suicide. We're just trying to get some information."

"Why the hell would we know anything?" I fought the urge to smile at Evan's combative response. Any ounce of suspicion that had been hiding in Officer Michael's eyes would surely be redirected at the surly string bean now that he had been so uncooperative.

"It's just a follow-up, Mr. ...?"

Evan folded his arms across his chest, further accentuating his defensive attitude as he issued his response with reluctance, "Summers. Evan Summers."

"Oh, so *you're* Evan," Officer Gildan nodded with secret understanding. "We have a witness who claims they saw you by Ms. Davis's car in the parking lot last night. Can you tell us why she might have seen you there?"

My eyes widened, heart hammered against my chest with such force that I thought for sure the entire room could hear the sound of my ribs cracking beneath the pressure. The fact that they were interested in Evan potentially being by Mia's car told me several things: They had found the suicide note. They didn't buy it. They were looking for someone to blame.

Calm down, the voices urged. *You don't know anything for sure, and neither do they. Just let Evan keep digging his own grave.*

"I fucking live here, don't I?" Evan fumed as though he had heard the demons in my head and was determined to prove them right. I kept a straight face, not daring to reveal how delighted I was at how the conversation was unfolding.

"There's no need to get angry, Mr. Summers," Officer Gildan assured him, not giving Evan the satisfaction of being perturbed by his inflammatory behavior. "When you were by the vehicle, did you notice anything unusual? Did you happen to see Ms. Davis at all near the parking lot?"

They have definitely found the note.

"Look, I don't remember much of anything from last night," Evan said. "I was blackout drunk—ask anybody here."

The officers turned their attention to me and Cat, seeking confirmation of his claim. We each nodded in silent solidarity. Before the officers could say another word, Elaine stepped out of her bedroom and joined the five of us in the living area. At the sight of the officers, she came to an abrupt halt.

"Is everything okay?" Her eyes darted from Cat to Evan, then to me, searching each of our faces for answers. The officers were quick to supply them.

"Oh my God!" She clutched her chest at the news of our neighbor's sudden death. "That's so awful."

As if Evan's demeanor wasn't reason enough for the cops to be suspicious, Elaine cast a furtive glance in her boyfriend's direction, like even she had reason to believe he could have been involved.

This is perfect, the demons voiced their approval. *You won't even factor as a person of interest so long as Evan is around.*

The officers peppered Elaine with the same questions we had just answered. She explained that she didn't know Mia that well, she didn't return to the apartment until eleven o'clock the previous night, and she hadn't seen anything unusual during the time she was away. When she was finished answering their questions, the officers gave each other a satisfied nod.

"Alright, well, that should do it," Officer Michaels announced, rolling back on his heels as he prepared to leave. "We'll be in touch if we have any further questions. Thank you all for your time."

A heavy silence fell over the apartment after the officers left as the gravity of the situation began to sink in. It was odd to me to see the profound despair etched into my roommates' faces, as though any of them had known Mia well enough to feel her loss. The sight of it repulsed me. They didn't have the right to grieve her. They didn't know her the way I did. Didn't hold a piece of her inside of them the way I had. The way I always would.

A piece of her.

My palms went clammy as I thought about Mia's car keys. I had thrown on the first pair of jeans I could find on the floor when the cops showed up that morning, the pant legs still damp from having been knee-deep in the river the previous night. I reached inside of my pocket, felt the hard plastic key fob press against my fingertips.

You have to get rid of the evidence, the voices urged. *If they come back and find those keys, we're done.*

"I'm going for a walk," I blurted out. Cat snapped her head in my direction, concern forming a deep crease in her forehead as she faced me.

"I'll come with you," she said. My fists clenched. *Damnit.* Ever since the night I had tried to confide in her about my darkness, she had developed an irritating habit of not letting me out of her sight. She was so convinced that I wanted to harm myself, at times the misunderstanding felt like a curse rather than a blessing I could take advantage of. With the news of Mia's supposed "suicide" fresh in her mind, I could only imagine what dark possibilities were swirling around in her impressionable little head. It would have been endearing if it weren't such an inconvenience.

"No," I told her. "I really just... need to be alone right now."

"Please, just let me come with you," she insisted.

"I said no!" I hollered too forcefully. Her face crumbled at the sound. But I didn't care. I couldn't let her follow me. Not now.

I bolted from the apartment before she could try to convince me otherwise and headed straight for the Greene Street Bridge. The police had already driven away, giving me complete privacy as I jogged the short distance from the edge of the duplex parking lot to where the stone wall of the bridge stood. I hopped onto its surface, the toes of my sneakers teetering over the edge as I dove my hand into my pocket and extracted the car keys.

"TIM!" Cat's piercing scream was quickly followed by the sound of her footsteps pounding against the pavement as she raced to join me at the bridge. "DON'T!"

I refused to acknowledge her. Without another moment's hesitation, I extended my fingers past the edge of the bridge and dropped the keys into the river below, watching as they sank to the bottom.

"NO!" she shrieked as I momentarily lost my balance, arms flailing for stability. As soon as I regained control, I jumped down from the stone wall onto the sidewalk. Within moments, Cat crashed into me, beating on my chest with her tiny fists, tears streaming uninhibited down her cheeks.

"What the fuck are you doing?" she yelled. "Don't you ever scare me like that again! What were you even thinking?"

She thinks you were trying to kill yourself, the voices mocked. *How sweet.*

I knew I couldn't tell her the truth about what I was doing at the bridge. So, I leaned into what she already believed.

"It's no use." I hung my head in feigned despair. "I thought this would work, but it only made everything worse. I can't control it, Cat. I want to kill m—"

"I know," she interrupted me. *Always with the fucking interruptions.* "I know you want to, but that doesn't mean this can't still work. We can still work, I promise. It's not your fault you can't control it. You're just sick, but you can get better. I can help you get better, I promise. Please just let me help you."

Her eyes swam with worry, heartache catching in her throat as she choked out each word, desperate and terrified. The sound of her pleas should have made me feel guilty, should have planted an ounce of remorse inside of me. But it didn't. All I could think about was how good it felt to be rid of those car keys. How easy it was to manipulate her into believing I was nothing more than a troubled soul whose desire to inflict pain would only ever be turned inward. It didn't matter to me anymore that she cared for me, that she loved me. All I could focus on was the satisfaction that had come from the night before—and how soon I could feel it again.

Something changed inside me when I took Mia's life. No, it was before that. The moment I realized she was pregnant, that she had gone back on her promise, that there was never a promise in the first place, I became someone else. Became *something* else. Because it was then that I realized the truth: They were all the same—all women. Every last one of them. Mama's greed and abandonment, casting me aside like trash only to use me when she thought I could give her money. Those girls in my motel room, lustful and lonely. Pathetic. Elaine and her constant need for attention, her blackmail. Mia's carelessness, her outright rejection, like I meant nothing.

All of them selfish. All of them pitiful. All of them deserving of punishment.

And I wanted to punish them. Wanted to hold them prisoner inside of me. To devour them.

Cat gripped my hand, her fingers trembling around my knuckles. I had to fight the urge to smile at how frightened she was. She really did believe I was on the verge of some mental breakdown, triggered by another person's decision to end their life. And why wouldn't she have believed it? As far as she knew, that was the truth. But even if she did suspect that something more sinister had happened to our neighbor, I had never given her a reason to think that it was me who could have harmed the girl. Especially not when there was another person who had shown such open hostility towards her. Someone who had acted defensively when met with the police.

Evan provided the perfect cover for me—his moodiness and volatility functioned like an umbrella, diverting the rains of doubt from washing over me. As long as he was around, no one would ever pay me any attention.

But I needed to be careful. I could feel a difference in myself since taking Mia for my own. Darkness blossomed in my chest, seeping into my veins, spreading like a cancer throughout my body. Though I could feel her soul belonged to me now, it didn't satisfy me. I still felt empty. I still felt angry.

I still felt hungry.

"Tim, please say something." Cat pulled me away from my thoughts as she twisted her dainty fingers in between my own. I stared down at our intertwined hands as flashes of Mia's body twitching beneath the water danced before my eyes. A wave of catharsis surged through me at the memory. Everything inside me ached to do it again, longed to live in that moment of peace as Mia's essence left her body, merging itself with the shadowy depths that undulated like an inky ocean inside me.

Soon, Michael, the demons reassured me. *You must be patient now.*

"Tim?" I lifted my eyes up from Cat's hand and focused on her tear-stained cheeks. She really was beautiful with her big brown eyes swimming in terror, the previous night's mascara smudged beneath her long lashes. Her malleability would have made me smile if I hadn't been so concentrated on containing the mounting desire within me to seize her by the shoulders and shove her over the bridge. Add her to my growing list of victims. But she wasn't the same as the others. Somehow Cat was different—less deserving, albeit not by much. Like the spider that gets spared in a house infested with flies, a necessary cohabitant in the mission to exterminate the greater pest.

"I don't know what you want me to say," I said to her. My voice quaked around every word like my vocal cords were bark splintering away from tree trunks stripped bare from a hurricane. Cat misinterpreted the waver in my words as a betrayal of the misery I was trying to disguise rather than the war that was raging inside me.

"Say you'll let me help you," she begged. "Please. Please just let me help you."

"*You can't help me,*" I wanted to say. "*No one can help me. I'd be better off alone.*"

But the voices were quick to disagree.

You need her, they asserted, the hoarse, discordant whispers suddenly a singular, strangled screech in my ear. *Look at how she worships you. If you keep her around, you'll always have an alibi. You'll always have her blind belief. Her adoration. Her word against everyone else's.*

I couldn't argue with that. It was the same logic that applied when I moved into the apartment in the first place. A man living in solitude is a walking red flag. But if I had Cat by my side, there was less of a chance that I'd be perceived as a threat. I couldn't risk giving the world a reason to look at me as anything other than benign, not when the police were already suspicious of foul play. Not when I could feel the inevitability of my darkness falling upon me, already hungry for a repeat performance. If I was going to keep doing this, I needed to appear normal. I needed to be patient. I needed to be methodical.

"I know it seems hopeless right now, but we can do something about this," Cat promised as I contemplated how I could use our relationship to my benefit. "We can find you a doctor. Someone you can talk to about what's going on inside you."

"I don't know," I hesitated. Maybe I had let this charade go on too long. I couldn't end up in a therapist's office. It wouldn't take long for them to see through my façade. To find the monster lurking beneath. How soon afterward would they be forced to turn me in?

"I'm not taking no for an answer," Cat insisted. "You need to talk to someone, Tim. Maybe they can even put you on some kind of medication or something to help you through this."

Medication.

A vision of Kyle in the motel room flickered in my mind. The orange prescription bottles hidden in the bureau.

Just a little Valium, he had said. *Who knows? Might help with whatever you got goin' on up there.*

Something sparked inside me as an idea began to take shape in the darkness within me. It was clear that Cat was not going to let this go. My stunt at the bridge had scared her too much for me to convince her that I would be fine without professional intervention. I thought back to those dresser drawers packed with orange bottles full of little blue pills. Maybe I didn't need a doctor to get Cat to look the other way. Maybe all I needed was a prescription. Or, at least, what looked like one.

"Okay," I agreed. "I'll find a doctor."

Her face lit up with relief, the tears instantly absorbing into her skin. "Really?"

"Yeah," I lied. I had spent enough time in Green Valley's seedy underbelly to know where I could get my hands on a stash. Cat would get off my back about being in therapy, the orange bottles all the proof she'd need that I was on the path to healing.

And I would be—in my own way.

***

May 12, 2013

The bar was packed that Friday. Normally such a setting would have annoyed me, the buzz of idle chatter and sea of smiling faces enough to set me on edge and make my fingers tremble with the need to inflict pain. But as I sat across from Evan beneath the glow of red lampshades spilling down from the dark wooden ceilings that hung above us in our booth seat at Lucky's, I welcomed the cacophony of the crowd. It would provide the perfect cover for my next move. One that had been brewing since the moment I took Mia's life.

The waiting was torture for me. My darkness tugged at my insides, an itch at the back of my throat that I didn't dare scratch. But I had learned from my past mistakes. I knew that if I bided my time, waited for the perfect opportunity, I could give the voices what they wanted—what I wanted. And, after years of denying myself what I craved, it was finally time to reap my reward.

It was time to kill again.

"Congratulations, man!" Evan raised a glass of whiskey, waiting for me to do the same. I reached for the tumbler full of brown liquor that our waitress had placed in front of me and completed the toast. Though I normally wouldn't have indulged, I knew that refusing a drink during what was supposed to be my bachelor party would have raised suspicion. Besides, I had worked hard to find a way to feed my darkness. I was entitled to a celebratory drink if I wanted one. A single glass of whiskey wasn't going to ruin what I had planned.

"Thanks," I grimaced as I swallowed a generous sip, "and congratulations to you, too."

"Don't even mention it." Evan waved a hand through the air, dismissing the praise as he gulped down the entirety of his glass. "We celebrated plenty last night. Tonight's all about you. Hey, I'm happy for you and Cat. Really."

"I am, too," I agreed. And I meant it. Not because I was in love with her, but because marrying Cat was the final step in securing my lifelong alibi for the career of crimes I'd been shaping in secret ever since the day she found me at the Greene Street Bridge. As though reading my mind, the petite blonde waitress in the dining section adjacent to where Evan and I were seated lifted her gaze to meet mine across the room. The instant her eyes landed on me, her lips quirked up in a smile, recognition lighting her features as she wiggled her fingers in a coy greeting.

Very soon, Michael, the voices assured me. I turned my attention away from my target, not wanting to give her an excuse to come to our table lest she make it known to Evan that we were already acquainted. Her stare lingered from across the crowded bar, the feel of her eyes on my body like a colony of ants parading through an abandoned picnic. If I continued to ignore her, she would come over to us, and everything I had worked towards would implode in on itself. I needed to act.

"I'm gonna get us some refills," I announced, sliding out of the booth. Evan raised an eyebrow in confusion.

"Don't you just give the order to our waitress?"

"Look around, man." I motioned toward the busy dining area. "This place is a mad house. It'll be quicker if I just get us some drinks at the bar."

"Well, here let me—"

"Don't worry about it," I put up a hand, gesturing for Evan to stop as he attempted to shimmy out of his seat. "It'll only take a sec. Be right back."

I turned to leave before he could protest any further, snaking my way through the throngs of diners and drunkards occupying the space. Though I detested crowds and all the people in them with every fiber of my being, it was good to see a sense of normalcy had been restored to Green Valley since the last time I had been there. Students chatted with easy smiles stretched across their faces, a palpable feeling of invincibility radiating off their skin, taunting the monster they had no idea was hiding in plain view. The calm that hovered in the air was a far cry from the disquiet I had left behind during those final semesters leading up to graduation.

After everyone learned about Mia's sudden passing, the atmosphere on campus shifted. Security guards were ever-present. Girls traveled in pairs, as though increasing the number of potential victims could prevent them from becoming one themselves. The police had called Evan in for additional questioning in the days following their initial visit. Though I was delighted by the elevated interest the cops had shown in my temperamental roommate, part of me was disappointed that they were conducting any kind of investigation at all. If I had done my job well enough, they would have chalked Mia's death up to a suicide—nothing more.

While that's eventually what they concluded to be the case, the increased scrutiny from the police department had made everyone uneasy. Even though Evan was the one who had been placed under the microscope, it seemed that the other students were happy to cast an equal shadow of incredulity over anyone who socialized with him, which of course included Cat and Elaine. And me. The heightened sense of unrest and uncertainty made it more difficult for me to tend to my unanswered cravings without being detected.

But that was then, and now it seemed enough time had passed to dissipate the veil of suspicion that once enveloped me. I was free to walk among the herd, my lupine features imperceptible beneath the layers of wool I had carefully stitched into my skin. Not even the most discerning little lamb would be able to recognize the threat that my existence posed to her—until it was too late.

"Hey there, stranger."

A sweet southern drawl bleated through the crowd as I inched closer to the bar. The syrupy twang settled in my chest, its warmth spreading into the cavernous depths of my soul, instantly calling forth the memory of my sleeping angel. I looked down at the source of the noise to see two bright blue puddles glimmering up at me from above the waitress's perfect pixie nose. If I closed my eyes, I could almost see her sitting on the rocks beside the riverbed. Could almost hear the crack of her skull against the rock in my hand. They looked almost identical.

That's why I chose her.

"Hey," I said finally, the reflection of Mia rippling away as I shook her image from my mind. I looked over at the table where Evan was still seated, double-checking that he wasn't watching the conversation from afar. She followed my gaze.

"You two out celebrating something?" she guessed.

"Yeah, you could say that," I answered. "Just landed our first big client."

It wasn't entirely a lie. After the final year at Green Valley University, I didn't know what the future held for me. Unlike Cat, Elaine, and Evan, I didn't have a degree. I hadn't studied anything during my time on campus other than how to get away with murder—and whatever books I could get my hands on in the library. With Cat planning a return to Williamsburg to live with her parents following graduation, I felt certain that meant I'd be forced into living out of my car once again. But it turned out better than I'd imagined; I didn't need to suffer a return to homelessness after all.

On the night of graduation, Cat's parents were killed in a car accident on their way home from a celebration dinner to honor their only daughter's accomplishment. Their death meant that Cat was the sole heir to their fortune, which of course included their enormous estate. What kind of boyfriend would I have been if I had just let her live there all alone to wallow in her grief? It was only right that I should be the one to fill the void their absence left behind.

For a while, I enjoyed my unexpected landing in the lap of luxury, even if it was punctuated by irritating sobs from my sniveling girlfriend. With its acres of lush greenery, ornate Victorian architecture, and maze-like expanse of rooms wrapped in warm wood and fine furnishings, Cat's childhood home was the culmination of impeccable taste, no doubt informed by her mother's strong design sensibilities.

The sudden thrust into affluence had even been enough to quell the hunger that had been threatening to overtake me since the night I laid Mia to rest in the Tar River. I'd spend my days relaxing by the pool, counting and recounting the mountain of wealth that Cat's parents had left her while she was busy sleeping off the effects of whatever liquor I had fed her to put an end to the constant crying. She didn't even notice that a large sum of her inheritance had been siphoned off and stashed into a secret bank account that I'd established in my true name. How else was I going to pay off the credit card balance I planned to accrue in the years to come? Whenever I felt she was getting close to catching on to my deceit,

I'd crush up a Valium or two in her drink, just to keep her deeper in the dark.

It was fun for a while, languishing among the idle rich, but by the time six months had passed, I was bored and agitated. Williamsburg was a close-knit community where everybody knew everything about everyone—not exactly an ideal environment to feed the darkness inside me. Though the memory of Mia had helped stave off starvation, I still felt ravenous. If I didn't find a way to feed the demons clawing at my insides, I wasn't sure what I would do. But it wasn't as simple as finding a suitable victim. The more time I allowed my demons to hibernate, the more I realized how lucky I had been to get away with my crimes until that point. From the house fire to killing Kyle to the fake IDs to Mia's murder—it was a miracle that I had been able to fly under the radar for as long as I did. If I was going to keep up with my extracurriculars, I needed to be smarter. I couldn't allow my decisions to be dictated by emotion. There would be rules that I'd need to follow.

First, I could never act in the town where I lived. There was too much of a chance that doing so would eventually lead back to me, no matter how careful I had been. Next, I would never kill in the same town twice—unless, of course, enough time had passed between each victim that it would no longer alert the police to a possible pattern. Last, I would never give the cops a reason to suspect anything other than suicide or an accidental overdose had been the cause of death. The less gruesome my crimes could be, the less likely I was to sound the alarm that a serial killer was on the loose. With my rules in place, I felt confident that I could satisfy my hunger without ever getting caught. There was just one problem:

I didn't have an excuse to travel from town to town, leaving a trail of victims in my wake.

But Cat did.

She had followed in her mother's footsteps at school, pursuing a degree in interior design, even forcing me, Evan, and Elaine into conducting a mini-renovation of our apartment during our senior year. After rumors of Evan's possible involvement with Mia's death took its toll on our social lives, the place started to become a tattered testament to our shared misery. With a hole punched through the wall by the door and trash strewn across the floor, it had started to resemble one of the mobile homes in Mama's trailer park community. After we returned the apartment to its pristine condition, Cat would often dream aloud about what an impressive team we all made and didn't we all work so well together and how fun would it be if we all owned a design firm and blah, blah, fucking blah. Even her mother added fuel to the fantasy, spouting off advice about getting into commercial design during that final celebration dinner before her fateful car ride back to Williamsburg.

"Get your feet wet with home renovations first, sweetheart, but don't settle like I did," she had advised her daughter. "If you really want to rise to the top, commercial design is where it's at."

I had barely registered the words when she uttered them, but now as I contemplated how to build a life that would allow me to act out my fantasies, her wisdom flooded me with an ocean of possibilities. I'd convinced Cat to use her inheritance to create a commercial design firm with Elaine, Evan, and myself as partners so we could travel all over the state constructing projects. Of course, we'd need to vet our clients carefully, which would mean weeks of on-site research. Always in a new town. Always surrounded by fresh faces. If one of those faces just happened to disappear by the time our projects were completed, who could shift the blame on us? How could we be held responsible for the sudden rise in suicides and drug addictions? It was an epidemic. A downright shame. Nothing that could be helped.

After some convincing, Cat agreed to get the company started, but it still took three years of grunt work to land our first gig in commercial design. As fate would have it, we were commissioned to build a student housing center for none other than Green Valley University, giving me the perfect opportunity to put my rules to the test. Five years was long enough to get away with striking in the same town again. No one at the university even remembered Mia Davis or any of the details surrounding her death. Least of all the blonde-haired, blue-eyed clone of her ghost whom I'd been tracking for the past three weeks.

"Congratulations on the new client," she beamed at me. "Does that mean you need to cancel our plans?"

A storm of excitement brewed in my gut at the mention of what I'd been waiting for years to unleash.

"Not at all," I assured her. "He'll be leaving soon."

"Oh, alright then," she smiled. "My shift ends at ten. Meet me out front when it's over?"

"Perfect," I told her, glancing at my watch. It was a quarter to nine, which meant I had a little over an hour to get Evan blackout drunk. I reached inside my pocket, wrapping my fingers around the prescription bottle full of crushed-up Valium tucked away within. Maybe I could speed up the process a little. I wouldn't need the full bottle to put the waitress to rest.

"Laura!" One of the waitress's coworkers hissed at her. "Get your ass back to the kitchen, girl. Your table's food is gettin' cold."

Laura gave me an apologetic smile and excused herself. I didn't mind the abrupt departure. Soon enough, she'd be back in my clutches. And I'd never let her go.

I found a small opening at the bar between the masses and flagged down the bartender to order another round of drinks for me and Evan: one double shot of whiskey for him, a plain iced tea for me. It was time to focus. No more alcohol. Within a few moments, the bartender placed the drinks down on the sticky wooden countertop. I explained to her that I already had a table, pointed to where it was, and asked if she could add the beverages to our tab. She nodded and turned away to punch the orders into the computer. With her back facing me and the surrounding barflies distracted by the basketball playoffs on TV, no one noticed when I extracted the pill bottle from my pocket and shook some of the ground-up contents into Evan's drink.

"Well, *that* took fucking forever," Evan griped as I found my way back to our table. "Was starting to think you just left me here."

"Leave you here? I wouldn't do that," I assured him.

Not yet.

"A toast!" I lifted my glass, eager to get the cocktail into Evan's system. He raised his tumbler and clinked the glass against mine. "To the future."

"To the future," he echoed before downing the contents in one long gulp.

Nighty night, Evan, the demons cackled somewhere in the distance. I couldn't help the grin that spread over my face.

"What's so funny?" Evan asked.

"Nothing," I assured him. "Just thinking about what Cat and Elaine are up to right now."

"Ah, don't worry," Evan snickered. "I don't think there are any male strip clubs in Green Valley. I'm sure they're just out getting drunk somewhere... speaking of, you ready for another round?"

I tossed back the rest of my iced tea, grimacing for Evan's benefit around the nonexistent sting of alcohol. "Sure thing, bud," I told him. "I'll head back to the bar right now."

"No need," he said, flagging down the waitress who had been serving us beforehand. I waited for him to finish ordering before excusing myself to go to the restroom. On my way there, I made a pit stop at the server's station to correct my drink order before the waitress had time to enter it into the system. I needed a clear head for the remainder of the night, and another glass of whiskey would ruin that possibility for me. With the order amended, I went back to the table, ready to watch Evan fade away into delirium.

"So, you ready for tomorrow?" Evan lifted his gaze from his empty glass as I took my seat across from him. It had only been five minutes since slipping him the Valium but already his eyes were unfocused, his speech slurred around his thickening tongue.

"More than you know," I answered.

"I think it's cool you guys are just going for it." He nodded, resting his chin in his palm to keep his head from drooping. "But won't your parents be made about being left out? Do they even know you proposed to her today?"

I stiffened at the observation, flashes of Mama's melting flesh burning into my mind. Somewhere in the corner of the bar, Sir's belt buckle played off the light from the lampshades. And my father? His absence felt like a vice grip, squeezing around my throat, making it impossible to articulate the emptiness he left behind.

"I don't have parents," I heard myself say. Evan's eyes widened as though he were seeing me for the first time. As though he understood me. The waitress came with our drinks before he could respond. He waited until she was gone to speak.

"Fuck parents," he announced, holding his fresh glass of whiskey up for a toast.

"Fuck parents," I agreed. We brought our glasses together to complete the now-familiar ritual, then drained the contents in unison.

"Big weddings are overrated anyway," Evan hiccupped, his speech becoming more muffled and incoherent by the second. "I'm sure Elaine'll make it real nice for y'all tomorrow. She's good at that stuff."

I nodded my agreement. Elaine's propensity for party planning was one of the reasons why I decided to pop the question and demand a next-day wedding. I knew she'd whisk Cat away for a night on the town, eager to fulfill her duty as maid of honor—or matron, I suppose, since she had already been married to Evan for years by that point. That was fine by me. It freed up my time so I could focus on more pressing matters.

Like adding Laura to my collection of victims.

The only thing that stood in my way was Evan, but the Valium was taking care of that. Before long, his eyes were dilated, lids heavy with inexplicable fatigue that he struggled to disguise. He sat slouched against the wood-paneled wall, his long, thin legs stretched out beneath the booth like a spider inching out from a darkened closet. It was nine forty-five when he tilted forward in his seat, his lips shiny with drool. Perhaps I had given him too much...

"I gotta go to the bathroom," he mumbled, stumbling to get up from his seat. He tripped and teetered on his way to the corridor beside the bar that led to the restrooms. I let five minutes pass before I followed in his footsteps.

"Evan?" My voice echoed off the grimy tile as I entered the empty bathroom. "You in here?"

At the far end of the room, I could see a pair of sneakers poking out from beneath a stall door. I locked the bathroom door behind me before making my way to the stall where Evan's body lay in a crumpled heap on the floor. The stall door was left slightly ajar in his haste to make it to the toilet. I pressed inside the stall and stepped over his unconscious body. Vomit swirled inside the toilet bowl, tinging the water brown with remnants of whiskey. I crouched down beside Evan and reached for his neck, feeling for a pulse.

He's alive, the demons confirmed it. *Prop him up so no one finds him.*

That seemed like a good idea. I hoisted Evan up into a seated position on the floor against the back wall beside the toilet, ensuring that his feet were contained within the stall so no one would come to his rescue. When I was satisfied that he was safe and snug in his corner, I locked the stall door, stepped onto the toilet, and lifted myself over the top of the partition, landing in the center of the adjacent stall. I took one quick glance around to confirm that nothing appeared out of place. If I hadn't just seen him there myself, I would never have known that there was a drunk pile of human filth wasting away in the corner of the last stall on the left. The bar employees would no doubt find him there eventually as they cleaned up for the night. But, by that point, it wouldn't matter. I'd be long gone.

And so would she.

I checked my watch—it was ten o'clock on the dot, which meant Laura's shift had come to an end. My stomach somersaulted with anticipation. It was finally time.

I weaved through the still-crowded bar, careful to avoid the section where I had been seated with Evan in case our waitress noticed that we were missing—and we hadn't paid our bill. No matter. Evan could deal with that whenever he regained consciousness. I had more important things to do.

A thick fog of humidity settled over my skin as I emerged from the bar and stepped onto the sidewalk. The sun had long since set and it was early in the spring season, but somehow the air was humming with heat. It was as though the friction from the blood pumping through my veins had warmed the air around me, radiated off my body enough to send the entire world into a premature summer.

"Hey." Mia's voice slid through the air, nesting in my eardrum. I twisted around to find her face only to be disappointed by Laura's eyes smiling back at me beneath the glow of a flickering streetlamp. "You ready?"

More than you'll ever know.

"Yeah," I spoke over the sound of my demons. "Just need to make a quick stop on the way."

"No worries." Laura flashed a set of white teeth in my direction. "It's really cool of you to do this for me. Been trying to get a fake ID for a while but I could never find anyone who made them. Then you show up at the bar last week and it's like... woah! Totally meant to be. Funny how life works out sometimes, ain't it?"

"Yeah," I grinned despite myself. "Real funny."

"So, where to?" Laura gestured around the lightly populated street, laughter bouncing off the walls of the skyscrapers that surrounded us from the few stray students stumbling along the pavement back to their dorm rooms.

"The Holiday Inn on Green Valley Boulevard," I answered. She lifted a dubious eyebrow in response. "I have to operate out of hotel rooms," I explained. "Makes it harder to get caught, you know?"

She nodded, chewing on her lip in contemplation. "You have a room there already?"

"I made the reservation," I smiled. "But you have to check in."

"Me?" she balked. "I don't have the money for that. Why can't you do it?"

"Don't worry about the money," I told her. "I've got it covered. I just need you to be the face. Gotta cover my bases just in case."

Laura's eyes narrowed as she pierced me with a scrutinizing stare. For a moment, I thought she might back out of our plans. Panic swelled in my chest at the thought. I had waited for so long, spent all my time in the city following her around, dreaming of the day I could absorb her, use her dying breath to revive those final moments with Mia by the river. What would I be forced to do if she ruined my plans?

She clicked her tongue against the roof of her mouth and shrugged.

"Whatever you gotta do," she decided. "As long as I'm not paying for it, I don't care. I've only got enough money for the fake, so…"

The corners of my mouth flew into my cheeks, relief washing over me like the gentle waves of a river lapping against a rocky shoreline in the moonlight.

"Great," I breathed. "Let's get going then."

It was a short walk from Lucky's to the Holiday Inn. While Laura attempted to fill the silence between us with small talk, I allowed my mind to run away with wild fantasies about her impending death. Would she fade away slow and quiet, the drugs weakening her body until she was no more capable of sitting upright than Evan had been at the bar? Or would it be fast and violent, the sheer volume of Valium in the cocktail I had planned for her forcing her into a state of endless projectile vomit until the only thing left to expel was her stomach lining? Or maybe it would be neither. Maybe she'd refuse the drink and I'd have to get more creative. Maybe I'd have to pin her down on the bed, shove a pillow over her face, feel her body squirm beneath mine until she had no more fight left. It wouldn't be ideal, but at least I could stage it to appear like it had been a suicide. I already had the note written out; all I'd need to complete the picture was a strategically placed pill bottle on her nightstand to make the cops believe—

"Where're you going?" Laura's question interrupted my thoughts. "The Holiday Inn's this way."

"I know," I told her. "Pit stop, remember? All my shit's in my car, which is parked at the Hilton across the street. Why don't you head inside and claim the reservation? I'll meet you in the lobby in a minute."

I turned to retrieve the duffel bag that was sitting in the trunk of my sedan packed full of the things I'd need to make the fake ID, but Laura grabbed me by the wrist before I could cross the street.

"Aren't you forgetting something?" she demanded. I felt the wrinkle in my forehead convey my confusion. She let out an exasperated sigh and held out her open palm. "The money?" she reminded me. "For the room?"

"Oh, right." I fished around in my pocket for my wallet and extracted a credit card. It hadn't been used since that weekend I'd spent with Cat after the Valentine's Day party, but it still worked. I had made sure of it. If anyone bothered to look into who had booked the hotel room, it would be Michael Davies's name on the reservation. And who would suspect him of wrongdoing? After all, Michael Davies had been dead for years.

Laura accepted the credit card and headed into the hotel lobby while I jogged across the street to the Hilton parking lot. Along with the duffel bag, I had a black hoodie and sunglasses stowed away in the trunk. I put these on and slung the bag over my shoulder before making my way back across the street and meeting Laura in the lobby.

"Hey, it's me," I hissed at her when she failed to recognize me. Her lips peeled back into a wide grin after the initial shock of my appearance wore off.

"You look like a burglar or something," she teased. "What's with the getup?"

"I need to lay low, remember?" I reminded her. "C'mon, let's get to the room."

Let's get to the fun part, my demons agreed.

Together, we boarded the elevator and made our ascent to the room on the third floor. Laura led the way with the room key as her guide while I trailed from a safe distance behind, scanning the hallways for cameras. Though I didn't spot any in my immediate line of vision, I kept my head down with my hood pulled tight, just in case I had missed something.

"It's this one here," Laura announced, stopping in front of the door to our room. With a swipe of the key, she unlocked the door and we stepped into the darkness. I could barely hear the hum of the broken AC system sputtering out heated air over the sound of the voices swarming in my mind. As I shut the door behind us, all the impatience and agitation that had consumed me for the past five years seemed to evaporate from my body, replaced by a surge of excitement. Of *knowing*.

She was mine now. There was no escape.

CHAPTER II

March 16, 2023

Eight. That's how many versions of Mia I had acquired for my collection by the time I arrived at the Hilton in Charlotte that Thursday evening. Each one of them had gone down in much the same manner as the waitress, those eager little flies looking for a quick way to grow up only to land smack dab in the middle of my web—too dazed and confused to even notice that I already had my fangs drawn. I'd make the reservation ahead of time, they'd claim it when the time came, and I'd start making the fake IDs to put their simple minds at ease, offering up a drink to pass the time while we waited for the ink to dry, the laminate to cool. None of them ever got to see the finished product, their eyes darkened by the cloud of death before they could ever appreciate what I had done for them.

I'd remove the evidence of my presence, taking the hotel receipts that the receptionist had given each of my little trophies so I would always have a way to remember them. To know that they were mine. It was perfect. It was beautiful.

And it was all ruined the day Elaine came to my hotel room.

No, that isn't entirely the truth. If I had to pinpoint the moment when things started to change for the worse, it was weeks before she showed up to knock down my door. The day she barreled into my office, demanding that Cat get placed into rehab for her drinking problem. A drinking problem I had a hand in creating. A drinking problem that I didn't want corrected as it had served me so well over the years. The more intoxicated my wife was, the less likely she was to take notice of all the things I did while I was off scouting new business for the firm. But Elaine was adamant that Cat needed help, and even though I didn't want to, I had to concede to placing her in rehab.

Part of me had to admit that Elaine was right. Cat's drinking had gotten out of control, so much so that her alcohol-induced antics had threatened the firm's reputation. After her most recent bout of negligence had resulted in a massive delay on a client's project and placed us in breach of contract, we were at risk of being sued. A blemish like that had the power to keep us from securing future business. But it was more than that. Without the business kept afloat, I wouldn't have a cover to disguise my occasional feasting. And I couldn't have that. I needed to eat.

Cat had been the perfect wife to me over the years, her constant state of delirium providing the perfect distraction from my double life. But I was nervous about what the change in her drinking habits would mean for my appetite. If she sobered up, how soon would it be before she started to ask questions? Before she realized who I really was? These were the fears I carried with me as I stepped into the lobby of the Charlotte Hilton.

"Hey, man." Evan greeted me with a hesitant smile while Elaine busied herself at the front desk collecting our room keys. "I heard about Cat. Sucks she's gonna miss the presentation tomorrow, but I'm glad she's getting help."

My jaw clenched at the mention of Cat's impending sobriety. I wanted to scream. Instead, I swallowed down the fire in my throat and gave a solemn nod.

"I'm sure she'll be alright."

"How was she when you dropped her off today?" he pressed. Memories of Cat's big, brown eyes engulfed in hurt as she exited the passenger seat of my sedan and checked herself into the Green Valley Recovery Center floated to the surface. I hadn't said a word to her the entire ride there, too fraught with worry over who she would be when I went to pick her up once twenty-eight days were over.

"Fine, I guess," I shrugged, wanting nothing more than for the conversation to be over. Evan seemed to take the hint, clapping a friendly hand on my shoulder. The gesture sent an unexpected jolt of rage spiraling through my body as visions of snapping his bony fingers overtook me. Ever since the threat of Cat's sobriety had been placed in my mind, the impulse to act on my anger and aggression had become increasingly unpredictable. Unmanageable. It was becoming more difficult to contain.

Focus, Michael, the voices whispered in my ear. *It's almost time.*

I took in a deep breath, lifted my trusty prescription bottle out of the breast pocket of my blazer. It wouldn't be long now. In a few hours, I'd have my release. I'd—

"What're those?"

I hadn't noticed Elaine standing beside me until her nasally voice broke through the darkness. Her presence must have been enough to send her now ex-husband skulking off on his own; a quick glance toward the elevators confirmed this as I saw him several yards away from where he had just been talking my ear off. Elaine nodded at my chest, motioning toward the place where I stashed the pill bottle back inside my breast pocket along with the room key that she had managed to give me while I was still stuck in my daydream.

"Just something I take when... when I can't take it anymore," I answered. With all the time they spent together, I was sure that Cat must have mentioned my "mental breakdown" to Elaine at some point. That was fine with me. The more people who believed that I was incapable of hurting anyone other than myself, the better.

I fixed a tight smile to my lips and attempted to join Evan at the elevators, but Elaine wrapped her wretched hand around my wrist before I could make my escape.

"Hey, you know you can talk to me, right?" The way her blue eyes glimmered with fear reminded me of the way Cat had looked at me that day at the Greene Street Bridge. I had to tame the spasm in my lips that wanted to morph into a maniacal grin. My demons were right about women—they all wanted to be the hero. They all wanted someone to save.

"Thanks, Elaine," I said. "I'll be okay."

"Okay, well, if you need somebody to talk to, I'm just a room away." She held up her room key with her free hand, the fingers of her other still wrapped firmly around my wrist. As soon as the words left her lips, her cheeks dotted pink and she ripped her hand away.

Oooh, very interesting, the voices observed. I didn't need to ask them what they found so compelling. It was obvious from the way Elaine refused to meet my eyes that she was infatuated with me. I logged the thought for later reflection. It could prove useful, though for what was yet to be seen. For now, I seized the opportunity to torture her a little.

"You coming up?" I motioned toward the elevator, enjoying the way my question deepened the redness in her cheeks. She became instantly flustered, spouting off a lie about needing to retrieve her phone from the car when I could hear it vibrating around in her purse, betraying her deception. I decided to play along with the ruse and let her off the hook. Though it was fun to toy with her, she wasn't the meal I craved. There was real work to be done before I could sink my teeth into what I truly desired.

As I turned to leave and begin my preparations for the night ahead, she stopped me yet again. *What the fuck does she want now?*

"And Tim?" she called after me, halting me in my tracks. "I really am sorry. About Cat, I mean. You don't deserve all this mess."

Part of me wanted to reach out and grab her by the throat for the comment. *This is all your fault, you fucking bitch*, I wanted to scream into her face. *If it weren't for you, I wouldn't have to worry. I wouldn't have to deal with a clear-headed wife.*

But instead, I placed a gentle hand on her shoulder and spoke in a slow, steady calm, "It's not your fault. It had to be done. And now thanks to you, she'll be all better when she gets out."

"Yeah, *right*," she shot back, the sarcastic bite of her words catching me by surprise. She seemed to detect the curiosity in my stare. "Sorry I... my mom had a problem, too. Still does. I know how tough it can be to get ahold of."

Though I felt my face relax, something about her explanation felt insincere. I couldn't put my finger on the reason why, but I felt as though she was hiding something from me. If I hadn't felt the pangs of hunger quaking through my veins, I probably would have confronted her about it. Instead, I responded with the only thing a normal person would have said under the circumstances.

"I'm sorry," I said. " I didn't know that."

"It's fine," she assured me. "I'm sure you're right. Cat will be okay."

I patted her on the shoulder and left her standing alone in the lobby, my suitcase full of fake ID paraphernalia rolling closely behind me as I boarded the elevator and made my way to the fifth floor. Without Cat in the hotel room, I didn't have to worry about her snooping through my luggage and discovering what was held inside. Maybe it wasn't such a bad thing that she was in rehab after all. It would certainly make the night ahead easier to manage without her there.

Dark smudges streaked across the sherbet-colored sky through the windows of my hotel room, the smoky clouds an identical match to the shadows edging closer to my mind. If it had been my first time in the Queen City, I might have stopped to appreciate how the skyscrapers looked like giant tombstones clawing at the heavens. But the sight of the city skyline made little impression on me now that I was well-acquainted with its predictable silhouette.

Elaine and I were the sole project managers for the firm, which meant that the task of fielding new business fell squarely on our shoulders. As such, we'd spend the first few weeks on-site with our prospective clients gaining as much information as we could about their projects before it was time to return with the full team in tow to deliver our presentation. My initial visits to our next target location almost always required a meeting with members of the school board where our next student center was meant to be built, and those meetings were almost always held on campus. That's where I found them—my delectable little morsels—waiting to be devoured. After suffering through a mind-numbing meet-and-greet, I'd plant myself in the middle of the campus courtyard and watch the crowd of collegiate faces pass me by until I found one that called to me, begged me to make her another trophy in my collection.

The world was full of Mia Davises, each blonde-haired, blue-eyed temptress adding fuel to the fires I wanted to ignite on every college campus I touched. Once I found the one I wanted, I'd follow her around, commit her schedule to memory, find an excuse to inevitably bump into her. They were all the same with their giddy smiles and flushed cheeks betraying a deeper desire to captivate the attention of the older man in their presence, who already found them far more entrancing than their wildest imaginations could even begin to fathom. It didn't take more than a brief mention of my ability to craft a fake ID for them to agree to meet me in a more private setting, their hearts so set on diving head-first into adulthood that they would have done anything to get their hands on what I had to offer. We'd make arrangements to meet up, always during those trips to deliver the client presentation. It had to be that way. Just like the demons had said when the cops arrived in our apartment the day after I took Mia.

You won't even factor as a person of interest so long as Evan is around.

I set my suitcase at the foot of the king-sized bed in the center of the room and took a seat at the computer desk in the corner. It was time to put the finishing touches on my plan. After all, nothing sold the concept of suicide more than a letter resting on the nightstand beside an empty pill bottle. But the letters were more than just a way to convince the cops that the scene they discovered had been the result of irreversible self-harm. They were my ode to the darkness within. To the person I could have been. To Mia. Each sentence was carefully constructed to spell out what had really been responsible for all the death and destruction, an immortalization of the version of myself I could never expose. If anyone had bothered to look close enough, they would have recognized the pattern, would have seen the name of the monster they had conveniently forgotten about until it was too late: *Michael Davies*. It was my way of letting Mia know the inevitability of our togetherness. I would always be hers.

She would always be mine.

I glanced at the alarm clock on the nightstand, pulse electrifying at the realization that it was already somehow nine-thirty. How long had I been writing that letter? Good thing I didn't have far to travel. The Holiday Inn where I had instructed my latest version of Mia to meet me shared a parking lot with the Hilton where I was staying. All I had to do was head downstairs and cross the pavement to find her. I dug around in my luggage for the black hoodie and sunglasses that I always wore for such occasions. Removing my blazer and placing the prescription bottle in my pants pocket, I threw the getup over my button-down before zipping up my bag and hoisting it onto my shoulder. Within ten minutes, I was walking up to the Holiday Inn, excitement thrumming through my veins, warming my blood despite the wintry chill biting at my cheeks through the mid-March evening.

As I reached the sidewalk outside the hotel lobby, a wave of panic nestled in my gut. There was no one else around that I could see.

Had she forgotten about our arrangement? Had something else come up? There was no way of me knowing either way. It's not like I could have called her up on my cellphone. Aside from the few face-to-face encounters I shared with them before our final night together, I never allowed any version of Mia to make contact with me in any capacity. The last thing I needed was a phone call or a text message pointing back to me as the last person contacted before the light in their eyes was extinguished. But, as I scanned the empty sidewalk in frustration, I started to wonder if I needed to change tactics. Maybe I needed a burner phone or something so I could keep better tabs on them. But the realization did little to help me in my current situation. Emptiness ripped at my stomach lining. If I didn't fill the void, there was no telling how the night would end.

"Tim?" Mia's voice sang out from behind me, flooding me with instantaneous relief. I turned to face her, but it was only the cheap lookalike I'd been targeting. "It's Tim, right?" she repeated cautiously. "Stacy, remember? We were supposed to meet here for the... y'know?"

A moment passed in awkward silence as I inwardly fought to compose myself.

"Yeah," I said finally. "Yeah, it's me. Sorry about the getup. Gotta keep a low profile."

Her smile erased the uncertainty in her features as she breathed out a sigh of relief.

"God, I was nervous there for a second," she admitted. "Thought I had the wrong guy."

Oh, but you do, the voices mocked from within. *So very, very wrong.*

"So, are we going somewhere or... how exactly does this all work?" Her question cut through the chorus of cackling demons in my mind.

"Oh... right." I patted down my pockets in search of my wallet, extracting the credit card held within and handing it to Stacy. "Just go inside and tell them you're here for the reservation under the name on that card. I have to operate out of hotels. Makes it harder for the cops to catch on."

She hesitated a moment, trying to decide if that was the truth. I flashed her a reassuring smile, pushing the credit card closer to her outstretched fingertips. Finally, she gave in and accepted the offering. I told her that I would wait outside and to come collect me when she was finished. Ten minutes later, she was back on the sidewalk with a room key in hand and a confident smile on her face.

I liked the Holiday Inn. It was dated and unimpressive with drab, beige interiors and a notable lack of security compared to the likes of the Hilton or the Marriott. The maids frequently abandoned their housekeeping carts in the hall while they cleaned each room, which made it easy for me to keep a stockpile of powerful cleaning supplies handy for the inevitable crime scene cleanup my work would require. Or to mix the occasional knock-out concoction to more easily subdue a willful victim. Though there were cameras interspersed throughout the building, they were easily spotted and avoidable, allowing me to navigate the halls virtually undetected. Unimpeded. Free to lead my little lambs to the privacy of the slaughterhouse I had prepared for them.

Stacy entered the room first, propping the door open for me as I filed in after her. I never touched the handle, or anything in the rooms for that matter. If the cops were going to dismiss the crime scene as a suicide, I couldn't leave behind any trace of me having been in the room with the victims.

"We have to take a picture first," I informed the wannabe Mia as we settled into her final resting place. "The bathroom has the best lighting if you wanna head in there. I'll be right in."

Stacy nodded her understanding, shrugging her shoulders casually as she headed into the bathroom to await her photoshoot. I laid my luggage down in front of the bed across from the computer desk, fished out the camera packed inside, and joined her in the restroom. When we were finished, we made our way back to the main living area and I pulled out the rest of the tools of my trade. There was the laptop, the laminator, the printer, the Teslin paper, an X-acto knife for trimming, and—most importantly—a box of rubber gloves. I reached for these first before extracting anything else.

"To keep from smudging the ink," I explained when Stacy's eyebrows shot up as I snapped the gloves over my hands. She was satisfied with the explanation. They always were.

"How long does this usually take?" she asked, taking a seat on the edge of the bed behind me while I uploaded her image to the laptop.

The rest of your life, the demons snarked. I fought the urge to smile in response.

"A few hours," I answered. Her dismay was made evident as an audible sigh deflated from her chest. I twisted around in the boxy, wooden computer chair to face her. "Don't worry," I assured her. "I've got a way for us to pass the time."

I gave her a wink, the gesture turning her cheeks a vibrant pink as I lifted myself from the desk chair and sauntered over to where she sat on the bed. She tilted her head up at me, a shaky hand snaking up to her neck as she tucked her hair behind her ear. I could have done anything I wanted to her in that moment, and she would have let me. I hovered over her, allowing her to explore the possibilities of exactly what it was I had in mind. As I bent down to retrieve my luggage at her feet, the smallest gasp escaped her lips, an almost imperceptible pout pillowing her mouth as she prepared herself for what she thought was going to be a kiss. I smirked at the noise, at how easy it was to disarm the women in my presence with the simplest of gestures. It was almost as fun as watching the disappointment cave in their faces as they realized that I had no intention of fulfilling their sexual fantasies.

When she understood that I wasn't going to touch her, Stacy's expression grew sour, her arms hugging her torso as though she were trying to keep her chest from cracking open from sheer embarrassment. Her demeanor changed again, however, when she saw me remove a bottle of cola and two Solo cups from my bag. The corners of her mouth curled up despite her lingering mortification.

"Want a drink?" I offered as I turned toward the mini-fridge beside the computer desk.

"Sure," she said.

"What's your poison?" I tried not to laugh at my own joke as I reached inside my pocket and wrapped my hand around the prescription bottle within. When she indicated that she preferred whiskey, the response sent an unexpected pang of guilt through my chest as images of Cat rushed to the surface.

Don't think about her right now, the voices urged. *You need to focus.*

I shook the thoughts from my head, looking back at Stacy to give her another disarming wink as I switched on the TV. She blushed in response, diverting her eyes to the screen and giving me the needed opportunity to remove the pill bottle from my pocket without her knowledge. I uncapped the bottle and poured the crushed-up contents into the bottom of the plastic cup, followed by the whiskey and cola. After pouring some soda into my cup and placing the empty prescription bottle back in my pocket, I turned around and handed her the drink.

"To being twenty-one," I announced with a grin, holding up my cup for a toast. Stacy raised her glass in response and flashed a smile.

"To being twenty-one," she echoed, taking a hearty swig from her cup. Her eyes bulged as the mixture hit her tongue, flecks of spit flying out of her mouth as she coughed around the bitterness. "Wow, that's strong!"

"The more you drink, the smoother it gets," I promised. Her lips quirked upward in defiance of her unease as she tilted the contents of the cup into her mouth once more. She grimaced, her mouth puckering with unfettered revulsion at the taste. I set my cup down on the desk and proceeded to go through the motions of creating her fake ID—my parting gift to all my victims as a thank-you for their sacrifice. Their naivety.

Stacy got up from the edge of the bed and placed her drink on the nightstand, choosing to prop herself up against the headboard with her legs extended in front of her overtop the comforter. We filled the silence with small talk while I worked. Every so often, I'd twist around in my chair to face her while delivering my response to whatever trivial question happened to leave her lips, just to make sure she was still sipping from her cup. It was a little after ten when I first handed her the concoction. From past experience, I knew it would only take a half hour or so for her to become completely incapacitated. But as the clock on my laptop crept towards eleven, I became concerned. And I wasn't the only one.

Why is she still conscious? I didn't have an explanation that would calm my demons' panicked whispers. *She should be out cold by now.*

I turned back toward Stacy, searching for a possible reason for her lucidity. Her cup was on the nightstand beside her. From the way the lamp illuminated the plastic from above, I could see the darkened outline of the liquid contained within. It was still over halfway full. *Fuck.* This had never happened before. The other girls had all but guzzled the contents of the cocktails I prepared for them, slipping into their forever slumber in no time at all thanks to their gluttony. But Stacy remained stubbornly awake, albeit several shades paler than she had been when we first arrived in the room. Her eyes were hazy as she peered at me, the fog of intoxication thickening in her veins despite the meager amount of alcohol she consumed. She lurched forward, her skin ashen as she clamped a hand over her mouth.

"I thi—" she gagged, then tried again, "I think I'm gonna be sick."

Do not let her throw up, the voices urged. I stood at once, my sudden movement knocking the X-acto knife off the edge of the desk. I bent down to pick it up and placed it in my pocket before tending to Stacy.

"Just lie down," I told her, placing the cup in her hands. "Drink more of this. It'll pass."

She pushed my hand away, nearly spilling the drink as she moved to get back up.

"I need to go to the bathroom," she insisted. This wasn't good. If she threw up the drink, she might get better. She might survive. And I couldn't have that.

"I'll help you," I heard myself say, still trying to formulate a plan for what to do next. I hoisted her off the bed and helped her over to the bathroom, her head lolling to the side, legs wobbling as she stumbled across the room. She was cognizant, but she was fading fast, though not enough to suggest that she would have done anything more than pass out for an extended period. If I wanted her dead, she'd need to drink more. That clearly wasn't going to happen.

"I feel funny," she slurred. "What did you do to me?"

"You're just drunk," I assured her. "The whiskey was too strong. But I know what will help."

Atta boy, Michael, the demons voiced their approval as I sat Stacy down by the toilet and started to fill the bathtub. *Be resourceful*.

As the water filled the tub basin, Stacy's moans bounced off the tile. Though she made a few gagging noises, the vomit remained trapped in her throat, nothing but a string of drool dangling out the side of her mouth to suggest that she was on the verge of expelling her stomach contents. When the tub was full, I lifted her off the floor and began to remove her clothing, her eyes barely able to remain open as each garment was pulled from her body.

"What's happening?" she mumbled.

"Relax," I hushed her. "Very soon, it'll all be over."

In one swift movement, I swept her legs out from beneath her and cradled her naked body in my arms, carrying her over to the tub. Her head dropped back like an unsupported infant, eyelids like finely veined tissue paper draped over the crystal pools beneath. I half expected her to begin flailing when the water touched her skin, shocked into consciousness by the sudden shift into submersion. But she remained limp and languid as I placed her into the water.

"That's nice," she muttered, the words soft as a lullaby despite the echoing tile. Her head rocked back, resting on the lip of the bathtub. She looked serene with her limbs floating in the bathwater like strands of seaweed curling up from the ocean floor, swaying through the current. I slid my gaze from her bare legs to her delicate arms until I came to a stop at her face, fixating on her lips. Flashes of Mia surged to the front of my mind, the memory of that single kiss we shared weakening me at the knees. If I closed my eyes, I could still taste her strawberry lip balm, still feel the soft pull of her lips on mine just before she—

Smack!

"Stay the hell away from me!"

The memory set me on edge. As I knelt beside the bathtub where Stacy remained submerged beneath the water, I could feel the heat of Mia's palm burning across my cheek as though it had just happened. But it wasn't the slap that angered me so much as it was the sickening realization that this might be the final time that I'd get to give my demons what they wanted. What they *demanded* from me over and over again. The threat of Cat's sobriety loomed overhead, promising to put a stop to my illicit activities. I couldn't take it. If this was going to be the last time that I'd see Mia, then I needed to make it count.

A burning sensation swelled inside my gut, building in my veins until I was sure my entire body was on fire. My mouth filled with copper, the taste of blood sliding over my tongue like satin. At first, I thought that I had bitten my cheek in a fit of rage, too numbed by the comfort of darkness to notice the pain of my self-inflicted injury. But I hadn't. The metallic taste in my mouth didn't belong to me at all. It was different. Sweet.

Because it was Stacy's.

Part of me knew that I should have felt horrified by the impromptu mutilation. It went against every sensible precaution I had put in place since devoting myself to the darkness. But as the blood squirted out from Stacy's mangled wrist and into my mouth, I felt... relief. Ever since that night with Mia in the river, I felt as though I'd been chasing an impossible dream, longing to recreate a moment of release that could never be attained through the level of meticulous planning my alternate existence required to remain hidden. As I dug the X-acto knife deep into her wrists, dragged the blade up her papery skin, I felt as alive as I had the instant I plucked the rock from the shoreline and drove it into Mia's skull.

Then the panic came.

"Fuck," I hissed. "Fuck, fuck, fuck!"

I leaped back from the tub, watching crimson swirls bleed into the bathwater as Stacy's life drained from her body. Small fires ignited in my chest as anxiety slowly replaced the initial bliss that had come from admiring my handiwork. Pink water dripped from my gloved hands onto the tile floor, my grip still firm around the hilt of the X-acto knife. What had I done? In ten years of dedicated service to my demons, I had always done everything in my power to ensure there was no chance that my feedings could be deemed anything other than an accidental overdose at best, an intentional suicide at worst. Now, one moment of weakness, one burst of unbridled violence, had the power to destroy everything.

A surge of determination swept through me. There was nothing I could do about Stacy but hope that the cops who inevitably arrived at the scene would dismiss her death as a suicide as easily as they had with all the other victims I had claimed over the years. Lots of people slit their wrists in the bathtub. It wasn't so outlandish to believe that Stacy could have been one of those people.

"You're just being paranoid," I told myself. "Get your shit and get out of here."

I exited the bathroom and began gathering up all my belongings as fast as I could, all the while trying to ignore the panicked thoughts racing through my head. Why had I deviated so far from the plan? Why hadn't I paid closer attention to Stacy's drink? Why couldn't I get the taste of her blood out of my mouth?

Why did I already want more?

With my mind so preoccupied, I almost neglected the most important part of my ritual. The Teslin paper with Stacy's portrait and personal details mocked me from its place in the laminator, waiting for its final trim. I wiped the excess blood from the X-acto knife on my jeans and proceeded to carve into the plastic, placing the final product into Stacy's abandoned wallet where she would never get to see it once I was finished. The task helped calm my nerves, sharpen my focus somewhat so I at least remembered to place the suicide note on the bathroom counter before darting out of the hotel room with my luggage in tow.

I kept my head down, hood pulled tight around my face, sunglasses planted firmly on my nose as I half-jogged the short distance from the Holiday Inn back to the Hilton across the parking lot. It was almost eleven o'clock by the time I made it back to the safety of my hotel room, my heart racing with adrenaline as I threaded the security chain through its track and leaned against the door.

My hands shook as I tried to steady myself. When I looked down, I realized they were still gloved, the blue rubber streaked with blood splatter. I darted into the bathroom and ripped the gloves from my hands, shoving them into the trashcan beneath a wad of toilet paper. Before I left the room, I caught sight of my reflection in the mirror, flecks of Stacy's blood drying in the corners of my mouth, along my forehead, down the sides of my temples. It was a miracle no one saw me, though I suspected my luck had more to do with the thick sunglasses and black hoodie than any sort of divine intervention.

I stripped down naked and stepped into the shower, cranking the faucet on high heat as I stood beneath the showerhead. The boiling water melted down my back, and I had to fight the urge to scream at how it seared into the scars that decorated my skin, choosing instead to focus on the pink swirls of blood that circled the drain as remnants of Stacy slid off my body. I scrubbed myself raw, determined to eliminate all the evidence of what I had just done yet simultaneously longing for the taste of her blood in my mouth, the feel of her limp wrists in my hands as I glided the blade along her skin. Only when my skin turned to fire from all the rubbing did I shut off the water and release myself from the shower. Just as I placed my hand on the complimentary bathrobe hanging from the towel rack, I heard what sounded like a frantic drumbeat banging against my hotel room door.

Despite the steam rising from my skin, the noise formed an icy pit in my stomach as thoughts of uniformed men swarming my hotel room ran wild through my mind. I hadn't been back in my hotel for more than twenty minutes. Was it even possible for them to have discovered Stacy's body and locate me as the killer in such a short amount of time? I didn't think so, but the knocking at my door suggested otherwise.

Snaking my arms through the sleeves, I draped the bathrobe around my body and reluctantly made my way to the door, peering through the peephole to see what awaited me on the other side. My heart sank. It was worse than the cops.

It was Elaine.

Part of me wanted to ignore her, pretend that I had been in the throes of a deep slumber if she asked me why I hadn't answered her during our presentation the following morning. But if there was one thing I had learned about my wife's best friend over the years, it was that she didn't take no for an answer. I hung my head, sucked in a deep breath, and cracked the door open as wide as the security chain would permit.

"Elaine? What're you do—"

"I need to talk to you," she interrupted. Her voice was razor-sharp. Piercing. The longer I stood there in silence, the clearer it became that she wanted to be let inside. My mind drifted to the rubber gloves in the bathroom trashcan, the bloodstains on my discarded clothing lying in a heap on the tile floor. I'd need to at least get those out of the way before I let her inside—just in case she decided to poke her nose where it didn't belong.

"Okay just... give me a second," I told her, closing the door in her face. I raced back into the bathroom, placed my clothes into my luggage, and shoved my bag in the cabinet beneath the sink before finally answering the door and letting Elaine inside. She pushed past me in a flurry, making a beeline for the chaise lounge in the corner of the room beside the windows that overlooked the city. I stepped into the main living area cautiously, peering out through the glass to make sure there were no blue and red lights flashing among the sea of white spilling out from the skyscrapers beyond.

"Elaine, is everything okay?" I pressed, wanting nothing more than for her to leave me in peace to reflect on the night's events. She fidgeted in her seat as I crept closer to her. "You seem tense," I observed. "Did something happen?"

"I need to tell you something," she blurted. "It's about Cat. And—"

She stopped herself mid-sentence, chewing on her lip as she debated whether or not she should continue. I didn't appreciate being kept in suspense, especially when I had so much else to think about as it was.

"And what?" I urged when she didn't speak.

"And Evan!" The answer took me by surprise, effectively erasing all thoughts of Stacy from my mind.

"What about Evan?" I probed. She wasted no time delivering her response.

"They've been sleeping together behind our backs."

A strange pulling sensation tugged at my chest, as though my ribs were being pried apart by a pair of metal claws. Elaine continued to prattle on about the accuracy of her revelation, but I hardly registered a word. It was as though I had been sucked into a vacuum, the only sound permitted to invade my thoughts that of the blood rushing over my eardrums as my veins throbbed with fury.

My marriage to Cat had always been part of a greater desire to feed the darkness inside of me, but I had to admit that my fondness for her never truly dissipated. Even though she was more of a convenience to me than anything else, I couldn't ignore the fact that she had been the only woman in my life who ever showed me an ounce of genuine kindness. I knew she cared for me. She loved me. I depended on those facts. But now she had turned me into a fool, abandoning me for another man just like Mama and Mia had done. My vision turned red.

I sank into the bed across from Elaine and covered my face with my hands.

"How long?" I don't know why I asked the question. It wasn't going to change anything. It wasn't going to lift the shadows that were encroaching on my mind.

"I'm not sure exactly," Elaine answered, "but I think it's been going on for years."

I dropped my hands into my lap. *Years?* I couldn't believe what I was hearing. My insides trembled as rage and anguish fought to overtake me. A parade of women danced through my mind, each one of their smiling faces like a fresh dagger in my gut. Mama was just the first. The best (and quite possibly the only) lesson she ever taught me was what to expect from the rest. Mia, Laura, Stacy, and all the other women I had murdered—all of them bled together until they were one, indistinguishable conglomerate.

They're all the same, Michael, the voices reminded me. *They all deserve to die.*

The feel of Elaine's body next to mine on the bed pulled me away from my agony. She took my hand in hers, and I had to fight to keep myself from squeezing until her bones popped inside my palm.

"I'm sorry I have to be the one to tell you this," she whispered. "You're such a good man. You deserve so much better."

"No, I don't," I told her, flashes of the blood-filled tub basin filling my mind.

"Hey, that's not true," she insisted. "This isn't your fault. It's *hers*. It's *both* of theirs."

"No, it isn't," I admitted, unable to shake the feelings of inadequacy from my mind. It was ridiculous, I know, but the thought that the woman who had once worshiped me was now engaged in an affair made me feel uneasy. Just like I had when Mama drove away from the ranch the night that Sir beat me senseless in the slaughterhouse. No matter how much of a sham our marriage had been, on some level, I wanted her to want me. I *needed* it.

"I'm not good enough," I whispered. "I'll never be good enough."

"Don't say that," Elaine inched closer to me on the bed, her soft hands enveloping either side of my face as she tilted my head to meet her gaze. Maybe it was the nostalgia that came rushing back with a fresh kill or maybe it was the way her damp, blonde locks reminded me of the golden strands I had seen floating in the water that night in the Tar River, but as I peered into Elaine's face, all I could see was Mia staring back at me. When she spoke next, I swore I heard that sweet, southern sing-song dripping out of her mouth as she said, "You *are* good enough, baby."

A deep ache ripped through my chest at the words. It was all I ever wanted to hear, the only thing that mattered—and it was coming directly from the mouth of the woman I wanted more than anything. Before I could say anything in return, Mia jumped from the bed, her cheeks flushed pink with embarrassment as she looked down at me.

"I'm sorry," she stammered. "I'm sorry. I should go. I should—"

"Stay," I begged her, grabbing her hand and pulling her back down to the mattress. Deep down, I knew it wasn't her, but I wasn't ready to let the illusion go. I needed it to last. "Please stay."

"Okay," she murmured. "I can do that."

"Thank you," I whispered. She scooted herself closer to me, resting her head on my shoulder with our fingers entwined in my lap. I laid my head on top of hers, savoring the sweetness of her hair, the warmth of her skin, the trail of goosebumps that slid up her dainty arms as I traced circles into her palm with my thumb. When I closed my eyes, I was back on that rocky shoreline, moonlight sparkling in the river while Mia pressed her face into my chest and sobbed. This was how it was always supposed to be. Me and my Mia Davis.

"I should have thrown scissors," she said miserably.

"What do you mean?" I mumbled into her hair.

"Cat never told you?" My stomach lurched at the mention of my wife's name, the sound of it enough to chip away at the illusion I clung to with every fiber of my being. Mia continued, "We both saw you at the Sig Nu house one night, so we played Rock, Paper, Scissors to see which one of us would be lucky enough to take a shot with you. I felt sorry for her, so I threw the game on purpose. I wish I hadn't. I…"

With my eyes shut tight, I forced the memory of that night to change. In my mind's eye, it wasn't Cat and Elaine. It was Cat and

Mia battling it out for my affection. There was no doppelganger. There was no mad dash through the frat house. There was only one Mia. And I had her now. She was mine. Finally, she was mine.

"You what?" I urged her to keep talking when I realized she hadn't finished her sentence.

"I wanted you." Her voice hitched on the words. "I still want you."

All at once, her body turned into mine as she tilted her head up and placed her lips on my own. Keeping my eyes closed, I imagined that it was Mia's lips pressed against mine, her tongue prodding deeper into my mouth, her hands hungrily tearing the robe from my torso. I pulled her closer, which sent a gentle moan rumbling through her throat as my teeth grazed her neck. She ran her hands along my back and gasped, pulling away in an instant.

"Tim, what happened to you?" Her eyes were wide with horror as she raked them over my battered body. I cowered away, pulling the bathrobe up as I tried to shield her from my scars.

"Shit," I grumbled. Cat was the only person who had seen me for who I really was. The thought of what Mia might think of my mangled form was almost too mortifying to imagine. "I'm sorry," I stuttered. "I... I'm so fucking ugly."

"No, no, no," she assured me. "You're not ugly, I promise. I just was... surprised is all."

She reached her hand around the back of my neck and pulled me down to her, removing the robe from my body once again.

"Don't stop," she whispered. "Please don't make me stop."

"I won't," I told her.

I laid her down on the bed, her naked body writhing beneath me as I thrust myself deeper into her, never once admitting to myself the truth of what was happening. I couldn't. To do so would have been to admit that none of it was real. And I couldn't entertain that possibility. Couldn't face the fact that it would never be her. It would never be us, the way it was supposed to be. The way she had promised it would be. But maybe if I pretended, that could be good enough. It needed to be. Because the moment it wasn't was the moment I'd slip back into that terrible darkness.

And this time, I didn't think I'd ever make it out.

CHAPTER 12

May 6, 2023

I woke up to an empty bed, the absence of Elaine's body next to mine simultaneously comforting and alarming. Comforting because the expectation of sex always weighed too heavy over each of us whenever we were in her house in Williamsburg, and I couldn't bring myself to touch her—especially not when there wasn't an express purpose to do so. Alarming because I couldn't shake the nagging feeling that she knew what I had done to her while we were still in Charlotte. What I had done afterward.

We need to do something about her, the voices warned.

"Like what?" I muttered bitterly to myself. "She's already talked to the fucking cops. It's only a matter of time before—"

Don't think like that, they snapped. *You heard her the other night in the hotel. She thinks Evan is to blame for all this. You just need to—*

"Shut up!" I hissed. "I don't want to hear any more about what you think I need to do. Every time I listen to you, things just get worse."

The only reason you have survived for as long as you have in this disgusting, shit-stained world is because of what we have done for you. Don't you ever forget that, Michael.

"But you aren't helping me anymore," I whispered. "Ever since Stacy, you've been reckless. What happened to planning? What happened to not getting caught?"

You're being paranoid, they argued. *There's nothing that can trace this back to you. As long as Evan is around, you won't—*

"But he wasn't around for this!" I shouted. The sound of my voice bounced off the uncluttered walls of Elaine's bedroom with a horrible ring. "What I did to her... what I did to that girl... and it all happened so fast. There wasn't even a plan! I didn't even have time to—"

I stopped suddenly, an icy deluge of dread pooling in my gut as flashes of that night flooded my mind. It wasn't supposed to happen this way. Enough time hadn't passed since killing Stacy to justify a second feeding so soon in the same city. But between finding out about the affair, breaking up with Cat at the rehab center the week afterward, and shacking up with Elaine, trying to convince myself that she could somehow replace Mia—my sanity was slipping. My hunger was at an all-time high. I knew I needed to eat. I had every intention of doing so even before Elaine had come back to the hotel room that night. But once the confessions started spilling from her lips, it was like a veil had been dropped over me. Any semblance of light, of reason, that I had left was eclipsed two nights ago when we were back at the Charlotte Hilton.

***

May 4, 2023

I knew there was something wrong the instant she refused my advances when she sauntered into our hotel room. Elaine was normally an insatiable creature, her need for sex almost as urgent as my appetite for killing. And I was more than eager to appease her cravings; it offered me a convenient way to disarm her, fatigue her to the point of exhaustion so she wouldn't leap out of bed in the middle of the night wondering where I had gone.

The darkness had been blinding since that first night we spent together back in March; I knew that I wouldn't be able to resist temptation for much longer. We went back to Charlotte two more times to meet with the stakeholders on the upcoming student center project, and while I had ample opportunity to select and track my target during the day at the insistence of my demons, Elaine's presence in my hotel room made it nearly impossible to do any meaningful work at night. She didn't have the same addictive personality as Cat—at least not when it came to alcohol. I figured between the rough sex and the small amount of Valium I was able to mix into the few drinks she did consume, it would be enough to keep her fast asleep well into the early morning hours. Plenty of time for me to do what needed to be done in preparation for my next meal. But when she returned from her client meetings that evening and showed no interest in having sex with me, I started to grow impatient.

"What's wrong with you?" I demanded, trying (and failing) to temper the anger in my voice. The hunger inside me was palpable, insistent, but she had only taken one gulp of the gin and tonic I had prepared for her and now she was rejecting my advances.

If her stubbornness kept me from fulfilling my obligation to the darkness, I wasn't certain that I'd be able to feign control.

"Sorry," she grumbled, pushing past me to take a seat on the chaise lounge. "I've just got a lot on my mind."

"Then let me help take it off." I bent down at her feet and tried to pry her legs apart, but the dumb slut wouldn't budge. She clamped her knees together and grabbed me by the wrists, wrenching my hands away before I could force myself on her any further.

"Tim, stop," she reprimanded me. She actually *reprimanded me*. "This isn't funny."

For a moment, I thought about overpowering her. It would have been easy enough to pin her fragile little arms down at her sides, hike that flimsy skirt of hers up to her torso, tear off her panties, and—

Breathe, Michael, the voices whispered. *Calm her down, soothe her. Then you can do what you want with her.*

I swallowed down the bitter taste of acid biting at my throat and focused all of my attention on softening my features. As I cupped her head in my hand, I tried not to think about how wonderful it would feel to grab a fistful of her hair and ram her head into the computer desk beside her. I tried not to think about how close my thumb was to her eye sockets as I stroked her cheek. I tried not to imagine the warm suction on my nailbeds as I pushed them deep into her skull until the blood oozed out of her nonexistent eyes.

"What's the matter?" I spoke in the gentlest voice I could muster. "You're not yourself. I know there's something you're not telling me."

"You're right," she confessed. "I'm just... distracted, I guess."

"By what? The project?"

She fell quiet, her gaze landing in her lap with the tears that started to fall down her cheeks. *Shit.* This wasn't supposed to happen. I was supposed to be calming her down, not working her into a tear-filled tantrum, making it even more impossible for me to escape into the night. But there she was, blubbering and sputtering until snot dripped from her nose as freely as the saltwater staining her reddened cheeks. *Perfect.* If she kept this up, I'd have to spend the night playing concerned boyfriend instead of sinking my teeth into that tasty little morsel I had stalked all day and reserved a grave for at the Holiday Inn later. Maybe if I did a good enough job of soothing her, I could still tire her out with some consolation sex and count on the post-crying crash of emotions to be enough to subdue her for the night.

I folded her in my arms and ran my hands through her hair, shushing her as she sobbed into my shirt. Again, I was reminded of Mia as I held her against me, absorbing her sadness. The similarities between the two had given me comfort at the beginning of our affair, but as time wore on, it became sickening. Taunting in a way. Because no matter how much I tried to pretend that she was, she would never be my Mia. And I hated it. I hated her for it. It made me want to—

"It's Evan," she wailed suddenly into my chest. The way she was carrying on, I assumed that he must have done something terrible to her. I had to respond appropriately, summon the affection that a protective lover would possess.

"What did he do to you? Did he say something? Did he hurt you?"

"No, but he..." She trailed off, fresh tears glistening in the corners of her eyes as she bit down on her bottom lip to keep it from trembling.

"He what?"

"I think he might have hurt somebody else," she cried, burying her face back in my chest. I shushed her, smoothed her hair, tried not to listen to the hammering heartbeat in my ear.

What was she talking about?

Why did she think Evan had hurt somebody?

What did she know?

"Who did he hurt?" The question burned from my lips, blistering my skin as it left me. As though I already knew how much the answer would make my blood boil.

"Mia!"

A fire ignited in my gut at the sound of Elaine's response. I couldn't move. Couldn't breathe through the smoke curling up from my insides, suffocating me where I stood. Despite the endless fighting between the two during our years at Green Valley University, Elaine had never given in to the rumors that her boyfriend had somehow been involved with Mia's death. It was almost admirable the way she stood by her man—a rare display of altruism from an otherwise self-absorbed, insufferable woman. Though I should have felt comforted by the fact that she had changed her tune fifteen years later, I didn't. Since the group of us left Green Valley, Mia's death wasn't mentioned a single time. I was the only one who carried her with me, who held her inside of me, who devoted my entire existence to her and her alone. There was only one reason why Elaine would think to mention Mia's name all these years later.

She learned something new. And I needed to know what it was.

"Why do you think that?" I pumped her for information, the edges of my vision blackening before the response even left her lips.

"A detective came to the office a few weeks ago," she stammered. "You remember that girl, Rachel, who lived in the apartment below us? Mia's friend? Well, she's a cop now, I guess, and she cornered me and—"

"Wait a minute, the cops came to talk to you?" My hands gripped her shoulders hard. I had noticed a blue Honda lingering around the office back in Williamsburg over the past few weeks. The sight of it made me nervous for reasons I couldn't understand—not until Elaine admitted that she had spoken to the driver. "What the fuck, Elaine? Why didn't you tell me this?"

She tried to apologize, but I wasn't interested in her half-hearted concessions. I needed to know what the fuck that cop wanted to talk to her about, and why it all of a sudden had her convinced that Mia had been murdered.

"She started asking about when we first came to Charlotte, if Evan was there and all that," she rambled. "Then she started talking about dead girls showing up at Holiday Inns near all the student centers we've built, and that's when I knew."

My palms began to sweat, mouth turned so dry that I could barely feel my tongue press against my teeth to form the words to speak.

"That's when you knew what?"

"That she was right." Little red veins snaked at the edges of her eyes as tears threatened to spill down her cheeks. "Evan's been booking rooms at the Holiday Inn for years without our knowledge."

I felt my eyes bulge from my skull before I could stop it from happening. Whatever composure I had managed to hold onto up until that point slipped away from me completely as I struggled to find the words to say next.

"H–how do you know that?" I whispered.

"Because I found the receipts in Cat's office," she answered. "I thought it was just evidence of their affair, checking in under a different name using that fake ID you made him back in college. You remember, right? Michael Davies?"

The earth shifted beneath me, stomach dropped to my feet as a terrible understanding gripped at my insides. *How did she find those receipts?* I had been so careful with my hiding place. Okay, maybe *careful* was the wrong word to use, but I thought that it was a clever thing to do, taping my folder full of trophies to the bottom of Cat's desk drawer. I didn't want them hanging around in my office, after all, and though I contemplated hiding them among Evan's belongings, I decided against it. They were too important to me; I wanted to be able to visit them as often as I liked, and that opportunity wouldn't be possible if they were tucked away in Evan's office. It had to be Cat. But how did Elaine discover them? How did she—

That's when it hit me. If I closed my eyes, I could almost see it happen. She had been so adamant about Cat going to rehab, so insistent that her friend was fighting a losing battle against alcoholism, that she had even gone so far as to convince me to get a lawyer involved. As equal partners in the business, it wasn't possible for us to simply fire Cat for her antics—not that I'd ever want to, but the thought had definitely crossed Elaine's mind, of that I was certain. The lawyer had advised us that unless she was a danger to herself or to others, there was no way that we could take action against her. I thought that would be the end of it, but Elaine was too stubborn. She wanted Cat gone, but without any real proof of wrongdoing, it wasn't going to happen—so she went looking for the evidence in Cat's office. I could picture it clearly, how she hunted through each drawer in search of a damning liquor bottle—the one that was hidden away in that last desk drawer. Maybe she ripped the drawer open too hastily, loosening the folder from its place secured beneath the second drawer, spilling all the contents on top of the whiskey bottle.

"*I thought it was just evidence of their affair.*"

"*They've been sleeping together behind our backs.*"

"*It's been going on for years.*"

My fingernails dug into my palms as echoes of Elaine's lies rattled around in my skull, my vision narrowed to a pinhole through the blackness invading my peripheral. She had it all wrong—all of it. Cat and Evan weren't having an affair. That's just what Elaine assumed based on what she had found in my trophy case. And I listened to her. I actually *believed* her. And because of that, I lost my wife, I lost the one person tying me to any semblance of normalcy, the one person who would vouch for me no matter what. I lost my ability to dine without consequence.

And it was all her fucking fault.

"Well, whoever's been killing these girls has been using that name to check in, I guess." The sound of Elaine's voice persisted through the darkness, tethering me back to my dismal reality.

"Why do you think that?" I pressed.

"Because Rachel asked me if I ever heard the name before."

"What did you tell her?" I tried to keep my voice level, but the panic was rising in my chest, threatening to drown me. Instant relief washed over me at Elaine's response.

"I told her that I never heard of it. But I'm scared, Tim. What if he really did this? What if he's been hurting people all this time and I've been so stupid that I couldn't see it happening? I'm such a fucking idiot. Oh God, what if he does it again? What am I going to do? I can't—"

"Hey," I took her by the shoulders, snapping her out of her spiral. She was slipping away into hysteria, and I couldn't have that. I couldn't have her mouthing off to the cops, even if she was pointing the finger at Evan. If they continued to poke around, it would only be a matter of time before they figured out what was really going on.

"You're not stupid," I lied. "You did the right thing telling me all this, okay? It sounds to me like Rachel is just trying to put ideas into your head. Make you think things that aren't real. Cops are good at that."

"But what if she's right?" she argued. "What if she's right, and I lied to her, and now someone else gets hurt?"

"That's *not* going to happen," I insisted, grasping at straws to get her to stop entertaining the idea of going back to that fucking detective.

"How do you know that?"

"Because I just know," I assured her. "Evan is a creep, there's no doubt about it. But he's not a killer. I mean, c'mon. He doesn't have it in him. He's not that smart."

I thought that appealing to the hatred I knew she harbored towards her ex-husband would give her a reason to doubt his involvement, but she remained insistent. Everything was slipping away from me faster than I could hold onto it. There was nothing I could do. There was nowhere I could run. There was no one I could—

We're here to help you, Michael, that familiar numbness tingled at the base of my skull as the demons whispered their reassurance. *Let us take control.*

With that, I felt myself fade into obscurity. It was as though a switch had been flipped, sending me into a blackness so complete, so all-consuming, it was like being sucked into a void, suspended in a state of utter surrender. I don't know how long I lost control; I don't even fully remember everything I did, bits and pieces fed to me here and there over the course of the next few days like clips of found footage haphazardly strung together. The next thing I knew, I was standing in an alleyway somewhere in the city, looking down at Mia's bloodied, broken body sprawled along the concrete. Only it wasn't Mia. It was that girl that I'd been tracking, the one I planned to meet at the Holiday Inn before Elaine threatened to ruin everything.

I didn't even know her name. Didn't remember ripping her flesh open with the X-acto knife. Didn't remember drugging Elaine with the chemical-drenched towel as she soaked in the bath I had drawn for her. Didn't remember leaving her to meet my prey at the hotel across the parking lot so I could do... whatever it was that I had done next. I especially didn't remember pulling Elaine from the bathwater after my return, laying her down on the bed, tearing into her unconscious body until I cried out in euphoria. I couldn't have done these things. It couldn't have been me. Could it have? No. I wouldn't do something so reckless. But the demons would.

They'd gotten a taste of recklessness when we had devoured Stacy together.

And they wanted more.

Elaine didn't say anything to me the following morning in the hotel room that led me to believe she suspected what I had done to her. She didn't say much of anything at all, which was unnerving in its own right. But perhaps even more unsettling than the thought that she might somehow remember what happened was the fact that when I finally did return to the hotel room, something else was missing aside from my memories of what I had done.

I couldn't find my cellphone.

***

May 6, 2023

Thoughts of my missing cellphone clouded my mind as I haunted Elaine's empty house that following Friday, wondering where she had run off to, when she would return. Her black Audi was missing from the driveway, nothing but my silver sedan staring back at me as I peered through the sheer, cream curtains that framed the windows in her bedroom. Maybe I was just being paranoid, and the demons were right. There was nothing telling about Elaine's sudden disappearance. She had simply gone into the office for another day's work like I should have done. It was Friday, after all, and there were clients to take care of, things I could have been doing to maintain the illusion of normalcy that was quickly crashing down around me.

But if she went into the office, why hadn't she woken me first? Why had she slipped out of the house without so much as a note telling me where she had gone? And where the *fuck* was my cellphone?

It's probably under the bed in the Hilton, I could almost taste the boredom lilting from their words as the demons voiced their reassurance while I raced around Elaine's massive home, frantically searching for the elusive device. I ripped the silky bedsheets from her king-sized mattress, flung her expensive dresses and blouses from off their hangers in the walk-in closet, rifled through the maze of linen closets and kitchen cabinets and bathroom vanities and media centers—all to no avail. Deep down, I knew I wouldn't find it in any of these places, but it was all I could do to hold out hope that I had somehow left it at home during our trip. I didn't want to think about what the alternative might be.

When I had run out of places to search, I sank into the cushions of the suede sectional in her living room that could have comfortably devoured the entirety of Mama's mobile home several times over. To my right, I could see the luggage that Elaine and I had discarded on our way up to bed the night before, too tired from the long drive back from Charlotte to unpack them properly. Maybe my phone was hiding out inside, tossed in as an afterthought during my fugue state under the demons' control. It couldn't hurt to look.

There wasn't much to find in my bag aside from the tools that my darkness required. With the printer, the laminator, the cardstock, and everything else I had tucked inside, there was little room left for even a pencil let alone a cellphone. I unzipped the top of Elaine's suitcase, the gaudy snakeskin surface like a scab scraping against my fingertips as I pried it open and shoved my hand inside, desperate to wrap my fingers around the phone I still couldn't find. No luck. Aside from an almost comical collection of high-end clothing packed inside, the only thing resembling anything close to a cellphone was Elaine's razor-thin Macbook. *That* wasn't going to do me any good.

Wait a minute.

I plucked the computer from its place among the threads of silk and cashmere that comprised Elaine's elaborate wardrobe and set it on the wooden coffee table in front of me. Getting an iPhone wasn't something that I ever wanted to do, but it was necessary in order for me to appear "normal." To fit in. I hated the invasive nature of technology, the built-in tracking systems, the complete lack of privacy, the interconnectivity of it all. It made it so much more difficult for me to be unnoticed. Untraceable. But as I powered on Elaine's laptop and logged out of her Apple account to plug in my own information, I couldn't help but feel somewhat relieved. All I needed to do was log into my account and use the Find My app to pinpoint the precise location of my phone. If it was at the Hilton, there'd be no reason to worry. But if it was at the Holiday Inn...

Bang, bang, bang!

The sound of heavy beating against the front door thundered down the hallway into the living room where I sat. Bile burned at the back of my throat at the noise, visions of Rachel flanked by a pair of brawny police officers searing into my retinas as I rose from the couch. I stepped cautiously toward the foyer as the sound of actual thunder rumbled through the home along with the persistent knocking that continued to rattle the front door. Through the frosted glass in the center of the wooden entrance,

I could see the shadowy outline of a single person—no red and blue lights flashing in the background to suggest a greater threat, an impending arrest. I decided to greet the intruder head-on, swung open the door in a flash, nearly catching the full force of Cat's bony fist in my chest as she reared back to thrash her knuckles into the wood once again.

"Cat?" I blinked away my disbelief. We hadn't spoken since the day I went to inform her that our marriage was over at the rehab center. I didn't even know how she made it back to Williamsburg after the twenty-eight days of the program had ended. The sight of her made me ill with regret, anger twisting my intestines with the knowledge that I had ended our relationship, potentially ended *my existence* based on a lie.

"What're you doing here?"

Without any warning, she flung herself at me, melting her lips over my mouth with all the elegance of an untrained Labrador drooling all over their master's face. In the heat of the moment, I felt myself relax against her, almost fooling myself into believing that the past few months had all been some terrible dream. I hadn't lost control. I didn't throw away my entire life. I wasn't on the brink of being found out for all the things I'd done over the past fifteen years. But as quickly as the delusions flooded my mind, they dissipated. Flashes of tearing open Stacy's wrists, of violating Elaine's unconscious body, of mangling that girl in the alleyway threatened to rip me apart at the seams.

I pushed Cat off of me in an instant. No matter how much I wanted to rekindle what we had, to save the life I had worked so hard to maintain, it was too late now. I couldn't give Elaine another reason to doubt me if she decided to return home.

Where was she?

A fog of whiskey stung my nostrils as I untangled myself from my former wife.

"Cat, you're drunk." I kept a firm hand on either shoulder, immobilizing her so she couldn't dive back in for another kiss. "You have to go."

My mind drifted to the laptop on the coffee table. I still hadn't had a chance to use the Find My app to locate my phone and there was no telling when Elaine might return. I'd have to think up an excuse to give her for why I had used her computer, why I had logged out of her account, why I still didn't know where my phone was...

Cat shoved her way past me, stomping through the foyer, down the hallway, and into the living room where the laptop still sat on the coffee table. *Goddamn it!* I needed her gone. I couldn't think with her incessant hollering, her belligerence threatening to crack the foundation from the sheer force of her fury. She kept crying out for Elaine, demanding that she show herself, but no matter how many times I tried to tell her that Elaine wasn't there, that she needed to leave, she wouldn't listen to me.

I grabbed her by the shoulders as she tried to climb the stairs to the second story and attempted to guide her back towards the front door, but she sank to the hardwood like a toddler leveraging her dead weight to keep her parents from dragging her to bed. It was pitiful to watch, the tears and snot dripping from her face as her body shook with sadness and rage. Revolting.

"Why don't you love me anymore?" she whimpered, her question sinking like a stone in the pit of my stomach.

"I don't know how to answer that," I whispered. What would I have said? It's not like I could have explained the misunderstanding. *Oh, sorry, Cat. I only slept with Elaine because she thought you were having an affair with Evan thanks to the receipts she found in your desk, but it turns out she just stumbled upon my trophies from all the women I've murdered under your naïve little nose. Let's just put this all behind us now, shall we?*

"Can you at least tell me what I did wrong? Please! I need to know why you're doing this to me." She wailed, covering her face as she sobbed into her palms. A twinge of guilt corroded my heart as I stared down at her. As malleable and stupid as I thought she was, I couldn't deny the fact that I had a soft spot for the woman groveling at my feet. I empathized with her. How she pined after someone who abandoned her without explanation, doing whatever she could think to do to get back in their good graces. To make them realize what they were missing. To hold them to their promise to be forever hers. We were the same in that respect, haunted by the notion that we would never be good enough for the people we loved.

I bent down beside her, slinging an arm around her shoulders as I pressed her into my chest. Her sadness soaked into the front of my button-down as I rubbed the space between her shoulder blades.

"You didn't do anything wrong," I comforted her. "I wish I could explain it... I didn't want to hurt you like this."

And I didn't. Sure, I thought of her more as a convenience than anything else and yes, I bore responsibility for her addiction and okay, I stole from her during her hour of grief. But I didn't want this. That was never part of the plan. I buried my face in her curls, placing a gentle kiss on top of her head as though the gesture had the power to erase the heartache I had caused. She lifted her gaze to meet mine, mascara forming thick, black streaks down her cheeks. Her eyes were like two bronze puddles threatening to spill out from her sockets. Once again, she folded herself into me, sliding her tongue between my lips, the taste of alcohol sour in my mouth as we kissed in the stairwell.

As I pulled her closer, I couldn't help but wonder why this would never be enough. Why did I have to pretend? There was nothing *wrong* with Cat. She wasn't particularly smart and she had a stick-figure frame that left me searching for something to grab onto, but she was kind and decent enough to look at. Surely, I could have built a life with her. I could have been happy with her. Was I really so stuck on Mia that I could never fully give myself to another woman? Or did it have nothing to do with Mia at all? After all, I had taken her. Over and over again, I had taken her as mine, and each time I did, I got no closer to finding peace. To finding happiness. Would I always be this way?

Was there something... wrong with me?

"We have to stop," I muttered, pulling away from Cat as her lips hungrily searched for mine.

"Don't say that," she pled. "You promised you would never leave me. Please don't do this."

"I'm sorry," I brushed away a stray tear, placed a solemn kiss on her cheek, "it has to be this way."

"What's going on here? Why is Cat's car on the—?"

Elaine's voice cut through the air, the sound striking instant panic into my chest. I didn't hear her car pull into the driveway, didn't hear her enter the house, didn't know how long she had been standing there or if she had time to notice that her laptop was sitting open on the coffee table. I stood at once, wracking my brain for the words that would explain why I had been fiddling around on her computer, why her clothes were ripped from her luggage, why Cat was crying on the floor beside me. But I didn't need to speak.

In an instant, Cat had gone from cowering at my feet to thrashing her fists into Elaine, screaming out profanities as she pummeled the woman she felt was responsible for stealing her husband into the ground. I debated whether or not I should intervene. On the one hand, I rather enjoyed watching Elaine get the shit kicked out of her in the middle of her fancy living room. It served her right for all the meddling she had done in my personal life. But I knew I couldn't just stand there and watch. I couldn't give Elaine another reason to distrust me when I already felt she was on the verge of piecing together the truth. I needed her on my side.

"ENOUGH!" I screamed, grabbing Cat from behind and ripping her off of Elaine. She wriggled in my arms before I placed her down on the ground, her nostrils flaring around deep, angry breaths as she seethed at me. "Get out of here," I growled. "Now!"

Her face disintegrated into a pit of despair, the dejection so palpable in her eyes that I thought her chest might crack open and spit her heart out onto the floor.

"After everything I've done, this is really how you want it to end?" I could practically feel the anguish vibrating through her body as the question left her lips. Everything in me wanted to stomp down on Elaine's skull, grab Cat by the hand, race out the front door back to the life we once had, the life we would never have again. But I couldn't. There was too much at stake.

"Get out," I hissed. The color drained from her face, fists clenched at her side as though she were contemplating another attack but thought better of it. Defeated and deflated, she turned on her heel to leave, staggering back down the hallway on drunken legs. As she inched toward the front door, Elaine stopped moaning just long enough to issue a warning.

"Stay away from him, Cat," she yelled. "Don't come back here again!"

My heart hammered against my chest at the statement, blood ballooning in my veins until I was sure my skin would pop open from the pressure. *Why would she say that to her?* Was she being protective of me? Or was she trying to protect Cat?

She knows, the voices observed. *You need to fix this.*

I scrambled to Elaine's side, quickly adopting my role as concerned boyfriend, hoping it would be enough to quell whatever fears were circling around in her idiotic little brain. She flinched away from me as I assessed her wounds, an unusual display of revulsion that I hoped was more related to the bruises forming on her face than any aversion she had to my presence. I darted off to the kitchen to grab some ice from the freezer, desperate to calm her nerves, to make her see that there was nothing to be afraid of. I was nothing to be afraid of. When I returned to the living room with a paper towel full of ice cubes and tried to press it against her swelling cheek, she snatched it out of my hands in an instant.

"I've got it," she snapped. I ground my teeth together in silence, swallowing down the urge to wrap my hands around her throat, squeeze until her trachea crushed beneath my grasp.

"I'm sorry," I finally choked out. "She just threw herself at me. It didn't mean anything, I swear."

Maybe Elaine's anger was just jealousy. Maybe it had nothing to do with whatever ideas Rachel had planted inside her head. Maybe she just didn't want me running back into Cat's arms. Maybe—

"I think I'm going to go stay with my parents for a bit," she blurted. A cold sweat broke out on the nape of my neck. She wanted to leave her own home. She wanted to escape.

I couldn't let that happen.

"I just need to get away from Williamsburg for a bit," she insisted when I asked if she was leaving because of me. I didn't buy the excuse for a second. She knew something, and I needed to know what it was.

"Are you sure you're okay?" I pressed. "You've been acting strange ever since yesterday..."

"Yeah, I—I'm fine. I just... I'm feeling a little guilty about all this, I think. And tonight didn't help."

Liar.

"You have nothing to feel guilty about, Elaine." I gripped her hand, desperation tugging at my insides as I searched my mind for the words to say that might get her to let go of whatever suspicions were dancing around in her head. "This can work," I insisted. "It has to work. Please don't leave. I... I love you."

I would've said anything to get her to stay. Would have done anything. I kissed her hands, tried to make her believe that what I said was the truth. But she didn't budge.

"I'm sorry," she whispered. "I just need some time."

I lifted my gaze to meet hers, the darkness bleeding out from my brain, staining my insides black with the need to eat. Flashes of unfettered violence goaded me into action, daring me to strike her, to mutilate her, add her to my collection.

But I couldn't.

There was nobody around to take the blame for my actions. Nothing I could do to shield myself from scrutiny if I decided to take her life right there in her living room. I didn't have a choice. I had to let her go.

Without another moment's hesitation, I released my grip around her wrist and allowed her to pack up her things and leave. As I watched her taillights fade into the stormy horizon, an icy knot twisted inside of my gut, leaving me trembling at the front door. I smashed my fist into the doorframe, blood pooling over my knuckles as they cracked through my skin.

"Fuck!" I shouted. "God *fucking* damn it!"

She had the laptop. It was still signed into my account.

***

May 16, 2023

My mind was racing, temples pulsing around the blood that rushed from my skull, carrying the poisonous thoughts that overflowed from my mind like a geyser. It had been three days since I sank that knife into Elaine's chest, the memory of how it had happened still hazy, unclear. But there were three things I knew for certain: Elaine was dead. Cat was in jail. And Rachel was still poking her nose where it didn't belong.

In the moment, I thought that placing the knife in Cat's hand would have been enough to convince the cops that she had been responsible. She was the jilted wife, and Elaine was the other woman who had taken everything from her. What better motive was there than that? But I couldn't get the memory of what had happened the week before out of my mind, couldn't stop feeling guilty about throwing her under the bus even though I knew it was the right thing to do—the only thing I could do to save myself.

To keep eating.

I tried to tell myself that it would pass. I just needed to pretend for a bit longer, play the part of concerned husband, act as shocked as the rest of the world that Elaine had turned up dead in Cat's kitchen. It didn't seem like a difficult role to fill. I even contacted the lawyer that Elaine had consulted with when she was hell-bent on sticking Cat into rehab, partly to quell my guilty conscience but also to keep the shroud of suspicion from enveloping me. After all, what killer in their right mind would get a lawyer involved with the crime that they committed? That was the brilliant line of thinking I had at the time, at least. Fucking idiot. I had lost complete control, forced into the background of my own mind while my demons took the helm. And it only got worse when Rachel showed up at the office the following Monday, demanding to see Elaine.

She didn't stay long, which I had to admit was both a surprise and a relief. I thought for sure that she'd want to pester me with questions, especially after I broke down sobbing in front of her at the very mention of Elaine. If it hadn't been for the fact that the lawyer was there to step in and get her up to speed, I wasn't sure that I'd have been able to keep from telling her the truth of what happened. Of what I had done. But as soon as she found out that Elaine was killed, Rachel fled from the building like her life depended on it, and the lawyer wasn't far behind her.

"I'll be in touch with any information as it becomes available," he assured me before he left, a sad smile crinkling the edges of his brown eyes as he spoke. "Just hang in there, Tim. We'll get through this."

With that, he was gone, and I was left alone in the office with nothing but my demons to console me.

You need to leave this place, they said. *It's not safe for you here—not with that detective around.*

"I can't just leave," I argued. "I'll look even more suspicious than I do already."

There's nothing left for you here, they snapped. *We are in control now. You'll do as we say.*

Something snapped inside me in that moment, even more than it had the day that I let the blackness swallow me and I buried my knife inside Elaine's chest over and over and over again. All this time, I believed that the voices had been there to help me, to give me strength when I needed it. But all they wanted to do was control me, scare me into submission. Mold me into what they thought I should be. And I was tired of it. Tired of being a puppet. Tired of always being told what to do.

"No," I whispered.

No?

"No!" I shouted. "I'm not listening to you anymore. I'm not doing this anymore. It's gone too far this time. I won't—"

You don't get to make that decision, they barked. *When we came to you, we asked for your permission, and you gave it. You don't get to turn your back on us now. Not after everything we've done. Now, get your ass in the fucking car and get out of here!*

Before I knew what was happening, I was sitting behind the wheel of my sedan, car keys plunged into the ignition as I peeled out of the parking lot and turned onto the street. There was nothing I could do. I wasn't me anymore. And they wanted it that way.

"Where are we going?" I asked miserably, not even registering the fact that I was driving.

Where it all began, they answered. *No one will think to find us there.*

I didn't need clarification on what that meant. I just kept my hands on the steering wheel and let them take me back to the place that had kept me prisoner long after I had left it behind. The place where they had found me. Where the darkest parts of me still lived.

The ranch.

PART 2
EVAN

CHAPTER 13

May 28, 2023

I spent so long hearing the entire world tell me I was a monster that eventually, I started to believe it. And why wouldn't I? My conscience was far from clean, the anger inside always simmering dangerously close to the surface, an active volcano waiting to smother my surroundings in lava. It was that familiar sensation of molten rage that bubbled at the back of my throat as I sat on the edge of my mattress in my darkened bedroom, sipping whiskey straight from the bottle, clips of my conversation with Cat from earlier in the day drifting through my mind like ash.

Part of me debated whether I should even visit her at the county jail that day. After our last conversation had ended with her accusing me of murdering my ex-wife, I didn't think I'd ever be able to face her again. I was feeling guilty enough as it was remembering all the terrible things I had put Elaine through, all the drinking and fighting and unchecked anger that comprised our final years of marriage parading through my mind, reminding me that I would never get a second chance to make things right between us now that she was gone.

Getting blamed for her death was the last thing I needed—especially when the accusation had come from the only other woman I had allowed myself to love since our divorce. Suddenly, I was back in those final semesters at Green Valley University, still fighting to prove my innocence for a crime I didn't commit while everyone around me assumed the worst. If all Cat saw in me was a murderer after everything I had confided in her, after everything we had been through together, so be it. I wasn't going to waste my time trying to convince her otherwise, even if I was in love with her. But then the detective showed up at my doorstep, and everything changed.

I recognized her immediately. You don't forget the face of the person who ruined your life. Even if Cat's finger-pointing over Elaine's death hadn't dredged up all the hurt and bitterness I still felt over getting blamed for what happened to Mia all those years ago, I still would have known it was Rachel McGowen standing at my front door. She looked more put together than she had when we were in college, but she still had the same freckles splayed across her nose, the same frizzy hair, the same serious expression engraved on her face that gave her an almost masculine appearance.

Before Mia died, I never paid her roommate much attention, probably because I was too busy actively avoiding anything to do with the blonde-haired bimbo who lived in the apartment beneath us. It wasn't a secret that I hated Mia. Okay, *hate* was a strong word, but I sure as hell didn't like her. Despite growing up in Green Valley, I didn't have many friends when I got to college. Going away to juvenile detention for beating a classmate to a bloody pulp and sending them into a coma would take its toll on anyone's social life, I suppose. So, when Mia struck up a conversation with me in our shared math class during freshman year, I was over the moon.

Here was this gorgeous girl laughing at all my lame jokes, taking what appeared to be a genuine interest in me for the first time in years—how could I be anything but elated? When she asked me to come to a party at some frat house on Fifth Street, I of course said yes despite the fact that I hated everything about Greek life. Imagine my surprise when I arrived at the party only for her to pretend like she didn't even know who I was. It was humiliating.

A year later, I ran into her again at that same frat house and she *still* didn't recognize who I was, even after spending the entire rest of that math class in freshman year sitting in the same lecture hall. The whole thing made me want to scream. I knew it was irrational and maybe even a bit prideful, but I couldn't help it. Anytime I saw her after that, my skin crawled with the urge to shake her, scream in her face, *Do you remember me now you fucking bitch?*

I never told anyone why Mia bothered me so much—it was embarrassing, and I didn't want Elaine to get the wrong idea thinking I still had a thing for her (even though, admittedly, I did). But I guess my mandatory anger management classes following my stint in juvie didn't do a good enough job of helping me reel in my emotions because after Mia died, it seemed the whole world knew that I had a vendetta against the campus "it girl." Especially her roommate, Rachel.

In the weeks and months that followed Mia's death, I could feel Rachel watching my every move. She had even cornered me one afternoon on my way back from the deli across the street from the duplex where we lived, stopping me in the stairwell to interrogate me about my involvement with Mia's death. Rachel didn't keep her beliefs about my guilt to herself, either. Mia had died at the end of our junior year, but by the time senior year started, Rachel had made sure the entire campus knew that I was not to be trusted.

When she showed up at my apartment years later asking questions about the night Elaine was killed, it only amplified my fears that I was reliving my worst nightmare, once again blamed for something I didn't do because it was easy. Convenient. *Of course, it was Evan. He almost killed that girl in elementary school. He still goes to anger management because of what he did. He hated Mia. How could it not be him?* I figured that Rachel's interrogation at my doorstep was just more of the same, another way for her to place the blame on my shoulders, pin me for something she could never prove for certain but that she always suspected I did. Especially when she brought up a name that I hadn't thought about in years—not since the last time the cops had asked me about it.

"The night that Elaine died, she was carrying a bag full of hotel receipts—all with the name Michael Davies on them," she had said. "Do you know why she might have had those with her? Have you ever heard that name before?"

Of course, I had heard the name before, and of course, I told her all about it. Why wouldn't I have told her about it? I didn't have anything to hide. Sure, it was technically a crime to have a fake ID, but I had gotten rid of my "Michael Davies" license after the police started questioning me about Mia during those final days of junior year in Green Valley. Now Rachel was bringing it all up again for reasons I couldn't even pretend to understand. But even though her line of questioning made me believe that I was once again a prime suspect in a murder case, there was something different in her demeanor. Something softer. Almost like on some level, she knew I was innocent—for all of it. Maybe that's why I decided to listen to the final message she left me with before taking off from my doorstep.

"Cat wanted me to tell you that she wants to see you again," she informed me.

"Why the fuck would I go to see her?" Echoes of Cat's accusation stabbed at my insides, stinging me like a swarm of angry wasps fighting to break through my skin from the inside out.

I know what you've done, she had said to me. *I know what you're capable of doing.*

The way her eyes hardened when she looked at me, like I was the ugliest thing she had ever seen, like my very existence was unforgivable—it reminded me of my father, how he never forgave me for what I did to that girl on the bus. How I never forgave myself. The thought of suffering another second of that kind of disdain was almost too much to bear.

"Just talk to her," Rachel insisted. "She really needs to see you right now."

It took me three days to summon the courage to make the trip to the Monroe County jail. But even if I waited three years, it wouldn't have prepared me for what I was about to learn when I finally arrived.

"Evan, I... I need to tell you something," Cat's voice shook as she spoke the words into the telephone clutched in her hands. Even with the Tyvek suit drowning out her slender frame and the red rims circling her eyes from all the crying and sleeplessness, I couldn't help but notice how beautiful she still looked. It made it difficult to stay mad at her.

"Just tell me what's going on," I begged her. "I can't take this anymore."

"I know," she sighed before continuing, "Detective McGowen came to visit me last week to discuss what happened with Elaine. She said she knew who really murdered her, and at first, I... I thought she was talking about you. I was wrong. I know that now. *She* knows that now."

"If she knows that, then why is she still trying to pin this on me?" I shot back, memories of my most recent conversation with Rachel still making my blood boil. "Why is she asking me all these stupid fucking questions like I had anything to do with it?"

"I don't think she was asking you those questions because she thinks you're guilty," Cat explained. "I think she was trying to do her job, get some answers about... about the real Michael Davies."

I felt the icy hand of dread pull the skin of my forehead together in a wrinkle of confusion as the words left her lips. There was that name again. The same name that had been on the fake ID that Elaine had gotten me back in college. The same name that Rachel had asked me about when she had shown up at my doorstep days earlier.

Something wasn't right.

"What do you mean the real Michael Davies?" I pressed her. As Cat struggled to form the answer to my question, the guards announced that visitation was coming to an end and to finish up our conversation. With her window of opportunity coming to a close, Cat raced to get the words out as fast as she could.

"Detective McGowen showed me this high school yearbook page with Mia Davis's photo on it," she blurted. "Right next to her picture, there was a student named Michael Davies. Only it wasn't

Michael Davies in the picture. At least, that's not the name I knew him by…"

I fought the urge to roll my eyes in response.

"Cat, you're not making sense," I griped through gritted teeth. "Who cares about some yearbook with a guy's name you don't even know?"

"Because I *do* know him." Her voice broke as she answered, tears shimmering in the corners of her eyes. "We both do. We just didn't realize it was him."

"*Who?*" I half-shouted into the receiver, tired of being kept in suspense, of being kept in the dark.

"Tim," she blubbered, the sound of her husband's name taking me by surprise. "Tim Clark *is* Michael Davies. Evan, he's not who he says he is. He went to high school with Mia. His fucking name is in her suicide note and everything. I think he… I think he killed her. And she's not the only one."

All the blood in my body evaporated at once as the weight of her words crashed into me. If Tim Clark was actually Michael Davies and Michael Davies killed Mia Davis, then that meant I had spent the past fifteen years of my life working alongside the very person responsible for destroying my reputation. I had been the best man at his wedding. I had delivered countless presentations to clients at his side for a design firm we co-owned together. I had become a slave to addiction, alcohol the only thing strong enough to numb the pain of being falsely accused of murder in the years that followed Mia's death—all while her true killer watched me drown myself with a smile on his face.

My mouth filled with water, the realization turning my stomach sour with the need to vomit. But it wasn't just the knowledge that

Tim Clark wasn't who I thought he was that made me feel sick with rage. The final words of Cat's confession hung in the air like an anvil, heavy with unspoken meaning.

She's not the only one.

"What do you mean she's not the only one?" I croaked.

"I'm not really sure," she answered. "But there were all these receipts in Elaine's bag when she came to my house that night. I thought she was gloating about the affair, but she wasn't. I think she was trying to warn me. And he killed her for it. Oh God, Evan, I'm sorry. I'm so, so sorry."

Tears flowed down Cat's cheeks with such force, I thought the saltwater might burst right through the plexiglass divider, showering me in her grief. Part of me wanted to comfort her, tell her it was okay, she didn't know, it wasn't her fault. But I couldn't speak around the fire engulfing my vocal cords. All I could do was sit there and allow the flames of fury to burn me from the inside out. Whispers of the accusations that had followed me around campus echoed around in my skull like broken church bells clanging through a forgotten tower.

Murderer, they had called me.

Asshole.

Freak.

Monster.

While the name-calling stung, it was the least of my suffering. The thing that hurt worst of all, the one thing I couldn't erase from my mind no matter how many years had passed, was the sheer conviction in the voices of my peers when they'd mutter under their breath as I walked by, *It should have been you.*

There were so many times I wished it had been. So many nights I thought about heading down to that bridge, hurling myself off the edge, giving the world exactly what it wanted. Even after graduation, my life was never the same, the desire to live as elusive to me as the search for happiness at the bottom of whatever liquor bottle I could find. And at the heart of it all, there was one person responsible, one person who had sat idly by and watched as I flirted with death day in and day out, daring the waves of alcohol to wash me away for good.

"Where is he?" I growled into the phone, knuckles burning white as I gripped the headset.

"I don't know," Cat whispered. "I don't even know who he really is."

"You have to know *something*," I snapped, chest heaving around deep breaths as the anger pulsated through my body.

"I th-think he m-might be in Red Rock," Cat sputtered in response. "He mentioned growing up on a ranch there, but I really don't know if that's where he is."

"Red Rock," I echoed, sinking back into the black plastic chair. *Of course.* Images of that fake ID came dancing to the forefront of my mind. It had been years since I last saw it, but I remembered every detail as though it were still sitting in my wallet waiting to be used to score a fresh bottle of whiskey. I had it all memorized; I had to—how else was I going to pass the quiz from the liquor store clerk as she peppered me with questions about my identity. *What's your name? When's your birthday? What's your home address?*

Michael Davies.

October 24, 1984.

813 Albemarle Rd., Red Rock, North Carolina.

"Evan, you can't—"

"Don't worry." I cut Cat off before she could finish, sensing the source of her concern. She had already warned me that she had been sworn to secrecy about everything because of Rachel. "I'm not going to tell anybody," I assured her, but the statement did little to ease the tension in her expression.

"What're you going to do?" she pressed. But I didn't have time to respond. Before I could open my mouth, the guards announced that visitation had ended. It was time for me to leave. But even if we had all the time in the world, I still wouldn't have told her the truth. Even as I sat alone in my room hours later, the sting of whiskey tracing a hot trail of liquid fire down my esophagus as I stared through the shadows at the safe in my closet, I couldn't admit it. Couldn't bring myself to speak the words aloud. But that didn't make them any less true.

I tilted my head back, drained the last gulp of liquor from the bottle, and staggered from the bed to the closet, kneeling down at the safe. My fingers shook as I entered the passcode, the distinct click of the lock opening sending involuntary shivers down my spine. I unlatched the door and pried it open, wrapping my fingers around the grip of the handgun resting inside on the bottom shelf. A surge of adrenaline electrified my senses, sobering me in an instant as I came to terms with what I was going to do.

For fifteen years, the entire world had labeled me a monster. And maybe they were right. Maybe I was nothing more than a killer. And maybe that was okay. It would have to be. Because my mind was already made up. I was going to that ranch in Red Rock.

And I was going to kill Michael Davies when I got there.

PART 3
RACHEL

CHAPTER 14

May 31, 2023

I woke up to the smell of smoke, an orange glow radiating off the wood-paneled walls that surrounded me, a burning sensation stinging at my lips and around my wrists. Panic swelled in my veins as I struggled to make sense of my strange surroundings, the memory of how I arrived in this place evading me like a distant dream that I was too far removed from slumber to recall. Beneath the acrid stench of burning wood, I could smell the distinct scent of gasoline curling up in my nostrils, the odor instantly calling forth the final moments I remembered before everything went black.

The farmhouse at the end of the dirt road. Evan's abandoned Jeep in the driveway. Gaseous fumes mingling with the unmistakable reek of decay. The creak of the floorboards signaling another person's presence. Rough hands snaking around my nose and mouth, suffocating me in a cloud of spiced pine and worn leather. And chemicals.

A low roar tore me away from my disjointed memories, sending fresh waves of anxiety crashing through my chest as I directed my attention toward the right side of the room. My ears pricked as a chorus of crackling popped and snapped beneath the thunderous rumble, suggesting something far more sinister than a freight train barreling down a faraway track. I opened my mouth to scream but was silenced by a mouthful of cotton, coarse fabric pressing into my dried tongue from the cloth that I hadn't noticed was tied around my head. Muffled shrieks saturated the fabric around my face, doing nothing to alert the world to my peril—if there was even anyone around to hear me in the first place. As I wailed into the cloth, desperate to make myself heard, I realized that the fabric in my mouth was the least of my worries.

My wrists were tied behind my back.

The smoke that I had smelled was spilling into the room in thick, black plumes that blinded me where I sat. That song of sparks and thunder had given way to a wall of flames that were inching through the doorway to my right, devouring everything in their path. If I didn't get out of there fast, I would be next.

As the world melted down around me, I couldn't shake the terrible feeling of déjà vu. The fire, that room, the rope around my wrists—I had been there before. I had lived this exact moment, could anticipate what would happen next as though I had done it a thousand times, the memory of my nightmare still so fresh in my mind, it was like I had never woken up from it at all.

But this wasn't a dream. I was wide awake. And I was going to die.

I twisted around, unwilling to succumb to my fiery fate without putting up a fight. If my dream had been some sort of paranormal prediction, then I already knew how to make my escape. Sure enough, I found a stone hearth behind me, the chipped masonry along the base of the fireplace providing a sharp enough edge for me to fray the rope around my wrists as I worked it back and forth along the serrated surface. With my wrists freed, I shook the remaining rope from my hands and ripped the cloth from around my head.

The smoke stung my eyes as I clambered to a standing position, darting my head around to locate the nearest exit. Just like in my nightmare, the entire right side of the room glowed red, not a single avenue to safety in sight. I covered my mouth to keep from gulping down a lungful of ash and ember, backing away toward the left side of the room. There was no time to worry about what had caused that rotting flesh smell, why Evan's car was in the driveway, or where Matt had gone. All that mattered to me in that moment was finding an evacuation route and getting the hell out of that inferno before I was burned alive.

I caught a glimpse of an untouched doorframe through the sea of smoke toward the left side of the room. As I made my way to the door, I nearly tripped over a coffee table, my hands landing squarely on the handle of my Glock as I reached out to steady myself and keep from falling over. Beside the gun was my badge, which I pocketed before plucking the handgun off the table and continuing toward the left side of the room.

You're almost there, I assured myself. *You're going to make it out of this.*

As I approached the door, I placed the back of my hand on the handle to ensure it was safe to enter despite the fact that I already knew it would be cool to the touch. It had been in my dream, at least. Momentary calm surged through me as my hand was met with nothing but cool metal, but the relief was short-lived. Memories of my nightmare clawed at my mind, freezing my feet to the floorboards despite the sweltering heat puckering the nape of my neck.

The stranger's silhouette at the end of the hallway.

The gunshot.

Nick's lifeless body lying in the center of the floor.

I shook the images from my mind, popping flames exploding around me, helping to jolt me out of my trance.

This isn't a dream, I told myself. *Nick isn't here. You need to move.*

Without another moment's hesitation, I pressed through the door and into the hallway that I already knew would be waiting for me on the other side. To my left was a dead end, the darkness lulling me into a false sense of security, promising safety where none existed. At the end of the hall to my right, fire danced along the walls, an angry red glow emanating from the flames that raged beyond. I knew from my dream that there was no other option but to move closer toward the destruction, but that nagging feeling of déjà vu had turned my legs to lead. Everything I had seen in my nightmare was happening in real time. If that was the case, then I didn't want to see what was waiting at the end of that hallway. Couldn't bear to relive the moment when I realized that I had shot and killed the love of my life.

Nick isn't here, I reminded myself again. *This isn't a dream. Keep moving.*

The walk to the end of the hallway couldn't have been more than fifteen feet, but it might as well have been fifteen miles. Every step I took seemed to echo with the same thunderous blast of a bullet exploding through a metal chamber. A sigh of relief rippled through my lips as I approached the end of the hall and peered into the heart of the flames that encircled the living area beyond.

It was empty.

There was no black shadow standing in the fire. No menacing mass with a gun stitched to the end of its arm. No threat of my safety aside from the sparks that sputtered and spilled from every crack in the wood-paneled walls, the ceiling, the floors.

The floors.

A cold trail of dread crept down my spine as I felt the floorboards shift beneath my feet. I couldn't hear the creaking over the roar of the fire, but I didn't need to. There was no mistaking it. Someone was behind me. This time, I wasn't going to let them overpower me.

I dug my heel into the ground, locked both hands around the base of my gun, and spun back to face my attacker. As I twisted around, I zeroed in on my target, took aim, and fired. The flash of light from the barrel as the bullet burst into the air was the only source of illumination in the shadowy, smoke-filled hallway before me. Between the ringing in my ears from the gunshot and the crackling flames around me, I could barely hear the agony spilling from the lips of the man who had crept up behind me as he lay in a crumpled heap on the floor. My hands tingled from the vibration of the gunfire, adrenaline sending shockwaves trembling all through my body as I blinked away soot and smoke to peer into the face of the man I had shot. As my vision came into focus, I noticed a gun was resting on the floor beside him.

"Don't move!" I coughed out as he started to wriggle on the ground, fearing he would make a move for the firearm and attempt to take me down. "Stay where you are!"

"Goddamn it!" he yelled. My heart leaped to my throat at the sound of his voice. I would recognize that moody, sullen drawl anywhere. Had spent most of my life believing it was the voice of a killer. Had heard it just last week when I stood outside his apartment, still too ashamed to issue the apology he deserved.

"Evan?" I crouched down beside him, rolling him onto his back to assess his wounds. The wounds that I had caused. He groaned in response.

"You fucking shot me," he hissed. "Why the fuck would you do that?"

"I'm sorry," I stammered. "I felt you coming up behind me and I panicked. I thought it was Michael coming to drug me again."

Evan writhed in pain, blood oozing between the webbing of his fingers as he clamped a hand over the bullet hole in his shoulder. I shot him right between the crease of his left shoulder and breast, maybe an inch below the clavicle. It wasn't fatal, but if he didn't get help soon, he might bleed out. I needed to get him out of there fast.

"Evan, I need you to listen to me," I gripped him by his shoulder, the one that I hadn't destroyed with my weapon. "You need to get up. Can you do that for me?"

He yelped in agony as I attempted to lift him into a seated position on the floor, every effort to move him seemingly as painful as it had been to get shot in the first place.

"Stop!" he resisted. "I... fuck, I can't move. Shit, it hurts so bad. I can't... I can't..."

His head rolled back, shaggy locks splaying across the hardwood as he succumbed to shock, the words "I can't" echoing from his lips like a church hymn. No matter how hard I tried to wrestle him upward, he wouldn't budge. As scrawny as he was, his dead weight was too heavy for me to carry on my own. I needed someone stronger. I needed help. I needed—

"RACHEL!" The sound of my name ricocheting through the chaos behind me made my back stiffen at once. I turned to face the familiar voice, straining to see through the blinding combustion still crackling around me. Across the hall on the other side of the room, I could see a distinct silhouette standing in the doorframe, his body like a shadow against the backdrop of the night sky beyond.

"Nick?" I couldn't believe my eyes. He was supposed to be in Charlotte. What was he doing here in Red Rock?

"RACHEL!" he screamed again, louder this time. "ARE YOU IN THERE?!"

"NICK!" I called back, cupping my hands around my mouth so my voice would carry over the roaring flames. "OVER HERE!"

I stood up from the floor and waved my hands, trying to get his attention. He scanned the room from afar and, once his gaze landed on my flailing extremities, proceeded to step through the fire to find me. My heart soared as he approached my side, the sight of him alive and well and most certainly not shot to death on the floor almost too good to be true. I gathered him into my arms, savored the scent of baby powder and aftershave that clung to his skin even in the smoky blaze that surrounded us.

"I've got you, kiddo," he murmured into my hair, "It's okay. I've got you."

"What're you doing here?" The question tumbled from my mouth before I had time to think of something more appropriate to say. Like, *Thank you for saving my life*, or, *I'm so glad you're here*, or, *I love you*.

"I got your text," he answered, the explanation all that was necessary for me to understand. I had sent him the text with my shared location that morning just before I took the exit to get to Matthew Davies' house in Red Rock.

Just in case, you know where to find me, I had said. It seemed like a lifetime ago.

A loud crack ripped through the air as giant, wooden beams careened into the floor from the rafters, tearing a hole through the ceiling so that the stars were visible from the place where we stood inside the crumbling house. Nick grabbed me by the waist, pulling me out of harm's way before the rubble burned into my back.

"Come on!" he hollered. "We have to get out of here. This place is gonna collapse any minute."

He grabbed me by the hand and started to lead me toward the door through which he had just entered, but my feet remained planted on the ground.

"We can't," I protested, using my free hand to point to Evan who was still lying on the floor, motionless and moaning. "He's in shock, but he'll live if we can get him out of here."

Nick wasted no time, springing into action without a moment's hesitation as he stepped around me to make his way to Evan's unmoving body. Placing Evan's uninjured arm around his shoulder, Nick slowly lifted into a standing position, Evan sagging at his side like a ragdoll. I flanked the other side, attempting to ease the load by slinging my arm around Evan's waist as Nick and I staggered through the flames to make our way to safety. We came to a stop as we approached the doorway, the entrance too narrow for us to pass through as a single unit.

"We need to go one at a time," Nick yelled, jabbing his index finger at the entrance. "You go first while I hold onto him."

There was no time to argue about the logistics. I simply did as I was told, untangled myself from Evan, and slipped through the burning doorframe into the velvety darkness beyond. I didn't relish the cool breeze that slid over my skin, frosting over the sheen of sweat that had collected there. I didn't notice how the taste of ash seemed to dissipate immediately as clean air flooded my lungs. I remained focused on the task at hand, turning back toward the burning building as I waited for Nick to hand Evan off to me.

"Ready for him?" he shouted.

"Send him through!" I hollered back. In an instant, Nick pushed Evan through the front door, his limp body crashing into mine, almost sending us both stumbling to the earth. As I struggled beneath his weight, I searched the ground for a spot to lay him down. In the moment it took me to assess my surroundings, that's when it happened. So fast, it almost didn't seem possible. It almost didn't seem real. Like I was living a nightmare.

Only this time, I couldn't wake up.

"No," I heard myself whisper, the sound inaudible over the splintering wood, the crack of support beams crashing in on themselves as the house caved in. The earth tilted beneath my feet, knees turned to gelatin as I watched the building disintegrate before my eyes, nothing but the smoldering imprint of what used to be left in its wake. I blinked in stunned disbelief, willing myself to regain consciousness.

This isn't happening, I told myself. *This isn't real.*

But no matter how many times I tried to convince myself that I was trapped in a terrible dream, I couldn't deny the profound emptiness that consumed me as I was forced to watch my world go up in flames.

It happened.

It was real.

Nick was dead.

"NO!" My knees sank to the grass, tears blurring my vision as I screamed into the burning embers, begging them for mercy. "SOMEBODY HELP! NICK! Oh God, Nick... please. Please, don't die. NICK! PLEASE! NICK! NICK!"

My throat burned as I continued to scream, nothing but the sound of crackling wood greeting me in return. Sharp pains pinched in the center of my sternum as I felt my heart rip open, shattering into a thousand tiny pieces until I was sure there was nothing left to pump the blood through my veins. Clips of our conversation from that morning echoed through my ears, making me queasy with heartache.

I can't lose you, he had said to me. *I don't know what I would do with myself if anything ever happened to you.*

"I can't lose you either," I whimpered into the darkness. "Please... I just got you back. Don't make me live without you again."

But no amount of begging could undo what had happened. It was over. He was gone.

"RACHEL, LOOK OUT!" Evan's screams snapped me out of my torment just in time for me to roll away from the danger I hadn't known was lurking in the shadows, waiting to strike. I scrambled to my feet, wiping the tears from my face and swallowing down my grief so I could focus on what was happening. As I straightened myself, I reached for my gun, keeping a firm grip on the handle as I met the eyes of my attacker. Even in the darkness, I was stricken by those icy irises, like two windows peering into a never-ending snowstorm, threatening to bury any onlooker alive in the squall. I pointed my gun at him, grinding my foot into the ground as I stared down the length of the barrel.

"Don't you fucking move," I spat. "Keep your hands where I can see them."

He took a step forward, the glow from the lingering flames casting eerie shadows over his face, making the slight curl at the corners of his mouth appear even more menacing. Even more out of place.

"I said, *don't move!*" I hollered, cocking my gun for emphasis. As I scanned his body, I noticed for the first time that he was holding a gun of his own. "Drop the weapon!"

A strange gleam twinkled in the corner of his eyes as his lips peeled back around a set of straight, white teeth. He tilted his head back and released a bone-chilling laugh, the spitting image of a wolf howling at the moon.

I wanted to scream.

"*Drop the weapon!*" I repeated. He snapped his head in my direction, not a hint of amusement left on his face as he stared at me through the shadows.

"Maybe in another life," he said, the words instantly raising the hairs on the back of my neck the same way they had each time I had found them scrawled at the top of another "suicide note" that one of his victims had left behind. Rather than discard the weapon as

I had instructed, he raised it higher, pointing it directly at me, his index finger sliding over the trigger, ready to fire.

BANG!

My hands tingled with the vibration of gunfire for the second time that night as my weapon discharged yet another bullet, this time lodging itself inside Michael's body. His gun fell to the ground seconds before he did, a dark maroon stain blossoming across his abdomen in the space where I had shot him. In the distance, the sound of sirens wailed through the night air. It wouldn't be long before the police arrived, but I wasn't going to give them the satisfaction of stealing away the moment I had waited on for fifteen years.

I walked over to the pile of human filth that I had gunned down, kicking his weapon into the rubble as I approached his side. He let out a low grunt as I placed my foot on his chest, fighting the urge to shift the full weight of my body onto his sternum, crush him like the insect he was. Instead, I peered down at him, my gun pointed at his head as the sirens grew louder, drowning out the sound of the sizzling embers from the still-burning wreckage.

"You have the right to remain silent," I began. It didn't matter to me that the words would need to be repeated to hold up in court, that I wasn't a cop, that nothing I said held any weight. All that mattered was that it was over. He was finally going to prison.

And I had been the one to place him there.

EPILOGUE

September 16, 2023

The interior of the car became a sauna the instant Cathryn came to a stop outside the narrow townhouse in Green Valley. It seemed like a decent enough place to live, with clean lines and pristine siding that hinted at its contemporary construction, or at the very least, a vigilant homeowners' association. But compared to the multi-story Victorian farmhouse that towered over a plot of immaculate acreage forty minutes north in the heart of Williamsburg, Cathryn remained unimpressed by the cookie-cutter community of uninspired townhomes that stood before her.

It's just a quick visit, she reminded herself. *You'll be back home before you know it.*

She reached over to the passenger seat to retrieve the bouquet of flowers that were resting there, the pink petals already wilting slightly in response to the relentless heat and humidity. As she exited the car, she did a double take. It appeared she wasn't the only person eager to leave the townhouse community behind—there in the driveway was a bright yellow moving truck that she had somehow overlooked when she parked the car.

Oh no, she groaned inwardly. *Is this the wrong place?*

She scrambled for her phone, tapping at the screen until she found the message with the address she had obtained from her attorney. It had been months since her official release from the county jail and while she no longer had the threat of prosecution looming over her, she still found it difficult to stay focused on the simple things. Like remembering to turn off the television before leaving the house or taking out the trash every Wednesday and Saturday. Or entering the correct address when paying a visit to the person who had saved her life.

Relief washed over her as she located the email from Owen and realized that she was in the right place after all. 732 Mizzen Ave., Green Valley, North Carolina. But if this was the correct address, why was there a moving truck in the driveway? Had someone else moved in? Had she missed her chance to express her gratitude in person?

As Catheryn continued to play guessing games with herself beneath the sizzling sun, the door to the townhouse swung open to reveal a frazzled-looking woman, her thin frame obscured by a tower of cardboard boxes precariously perched in her arms. Before she could stop it from happening, the top box teetered over, crashing onto the concrete slab that comprised the front porch.

"Damnit!" she hissed, bending down to scoop up the mess she had made, tucking loose strands of frizzy hair behind her ear as she did so. Catheryn jogged up to the edge of the porch and knelt at the woman's side, grabbing some of the belongings that were scattered there.

"Let me help," she insisted, throwing the incense burner that had fallen and placing it back into its rightful container.

"Cat?" The woman who had dropped the box blinked away her initial confusion. Catheryn brushed her thick, dark curls over her shoulder, providing an unobstructed view of her face. She smiled back at the woman she had come there to see.

"Hey, Rachel," she answered finally. "Sorry I didn't give you a heads up. I just... wanted to see you. Is it a bad time? I can come back if it—"

"No, no," Rachel interrupted, hoisting herself up into a standing position. "Please, stay. It's fine. It's... wow, it's so good to see you."

The two women embraced, their bodies forming a bridge over the abandoned box still sitting open on the porch. A brief silence fell over them as they pulled away from one another, neither of them sure what to say. Catheryn was the first to speak.

"Are you moving or something?" She motioned at the Penske in the driveway. Sadness crept into Rachel's eyes at the question. She cleared her throat and dabbed the sweat from her brow before answering.

"Yeah, I'm headed back to Arizona," she confessed.

"Arizona?" Catheryn balked. "But what about the department? Don't they need you to—?"

"I was fired," Rachel explained, bending down to pack up the remaining items that had spilled from the box, too embarrassed by her admission to look her visitor in the eyes.

"*Fired?*" The word sounded more like a screech than a question as it left Catheryn's lips. She threw up her hands in frustration. "How can they do that? It doesn't make sense! You single-handedly—"

"—got an officer killed while acting without a badge? Fired the weapon of a suspended police officer at an innocent person?" Rachel finished, effectively bringing an end to Catheryn's tirade. "I'm so sorry about that, by the way. How is Evan doing?"

"He's okay." Catheryn's cheeks flushed pink at the mention of her boyfriend. "He's more than okay, actually. He's three months sober. We both are."

"That's amazing, Cat!" Rachel wrapped her arms around her unexpected visitor, unable to disguise her excitement at the news. "I'm so happy for you both."

"We owe it to you." Catheryn swiped away a stray tear as Rachel released her. "That's why I came here. I wanted to thank you. For everything."

She bent down to retrieve the bouquet that she had tossed to the side in her haste to help Rachel with her boxes.

"Sorry they're a little droopy," Catheryn chuckled at the sorry state of the petals bowing their tired heads over the plastic wrapping. "It's not a representation of our gratitude."

Rachel grinned, bringing the flowers to her nose as she inhaled deeply.

"They're beautiful," she lied. "You didn't have to do that."

"It's the least I could do," Catheryn assured her. "If it weren't for you, I'd still be in jail. I'd still be married to that…"

She trailed off, an involuntary shiver rattling down her spine despite the oppressive heat. Rachel didn't need an explanation. It had been over three months since the night of the fire, but still the embers burned in her mind, the image of the monster she had gunned down forever seared into her retinas, haunting her for all eternity.

"He confessed, you know." Catheryn's voice was small when she spoke, taut with emotion. "I guess I should be grateful for that. Made it easier to dismiss the charges in my case."

"Yeah, I heard about that," Rachel nodded. She didn't mention how Michael's confession had taken the death penalty off the table. Couldn't relive the anguish of knowing that he would never be extinguished the way that he deserved. The way that he had stamped out the light of so many innocent women. The way that he had left his half-brother to die alongside the rotting corpse of their grandfather in that burning farmhouse. The way that he had ripped away the love of her life. She blinked back the tears and swallowed down her rage. If Catheryn had gotten some peace out of it, that's all that mattered. There was no sense in dwelling on the things that couldn't be changed.

"So, when do you leave?" Catheryn attempted to change the subject, her throat dangerously close to closing up around the sobs she wanted to release.

"Today, actually," Rachel admitted. "These were the last boxes I had to carry out before taking off. You caught me at the perfect time. Another ten minutes, and I would have been gone."

"Oh wow, good thing I got to you," Catheryn commented. "Here, let me help you get those into the truck."

Together, the women carried the last of the boxes to the Penske and loaded them into the truck. When they were finished, Catheryn leaned against the metal exterior, folding her dainty arms across her chest as she fixed a pair of somber eyes on Rachel.

"I guess this is goodbye then," she finally acknowledged, the statement sending unexpected tears down her cheeks. Rachel nodded grimly.

"I guess so," she confirmed. Before she knew what was happening, Catheryn had flung her arms around Rachel's neck, pulling her into a tight hug that sent strands of unruly black hair straight into Rachel's mouth.

"Thank you," Catheryn whispered through her tears. "I know we don't know each other very well or anything, but I... I'm going to miss you so much."

Rachel squeezed her a bit tighter. It had been so long since she felt a real connection to another woman, female friendships something she could never bring herself to indulge in after losing her college roommate all those years ago. As she held onto Catheryn in the driveway, it was the first time in fifteen years that she felt anything close to kinship.

"I'm going to miss you, too," she admitted.

"Well," Catheryn pulled away, wiping the tears from Rachel's eyes as she did so, "if you ever get back to North Carolina, you know where to find me."

With that, Rachel watched as Catheryn walked back to her car, slinked into the driver's seat, and pulled away, leaving her standing at the edge of the driveway holding onto the bouquet of flowers. She gave the door on the back of the moving truck a firm tug, ensuring it was closed before giving the townhouse a final walk-through.

She stepped through the empty house, trying not to think about the day she had moved in with Nick. How she thought it had been the start of something everlasting. Something special. Irreplaceable. She tried not to think about the day she returned home from Mia's ten-year celebration of life, or the look in Nick's eyes as he pulled the diamond ring from his pocket and proposed to her in the stairwell. How she would never see those eyes again. Never get to wear the ring that he had picked out for her.

When she was satisfied that the only thing left in the house were the ghosts of her past, she hopped into the moving truck and pulled away from the community that she had called home for so long, stopping only to drop off the house key at the leasing office. As she snaked down the streets of Green Valley and headed toward the interstate, she didn't look in the rearview, just kept her gaze on the open road ahead. If she had bothered to look in the mirror, she would have had a perfect view of the Tar River, plumes of pink and orange glistening along its glassy surface as the sun dipped its golden rays into the horizon. It was so serene, so brilliantly benign, that even the former detective might have forgotten all about its murky past and what happened to Mia Davis along that rocky shoreline.

If only for a moment.

THE END

ABOUT THE AUTHOR

K.T. Carlisle is the pseudonym for a nomadic writer located in the United States. Since early childhood, Carlisle has dedicated her life to the written word. Earning her B.A. in Writing Arts with a concentration in Creative Writing in 2015 from Rowan University, Carlisle received the Excellence in Writing Arts award from the university—an honor reserved for students who exhibit exceptional skill as a writer and teacher of writing.

When she is not busy working on her next novel, Carlisle spends her days exploring the U.S. in her travel trailer with her three crazy dogs. For more information, or to inquire about rights, permissions, speaking engagements, and more please visit www.ktcarlisle.com.

Acknowledgements

To my sister, Sara, this book would not exist without you. Thank you for inspiring me to write something outside of my comfort zone. Your constant cheerleading and encouragement keep me going, even when I feel like giving up completely. I don't know what I would do without you by my side. I love you endlessly.

To my editors, Lauren and Anthony, thank you for investing the time and energy into helping me make this book the best that it can possibly be. Your attention to detail and thoughtful criticism have made me a better writer, and I could not be more thankful for having the two of you in my life. Thank you for being a part of this process and for giving me the tools I need to grow.

To my beta readers, Mike and Heather, thank you for your early feedback and continued support. Your careful reading and enthusiasm for the story make me feel like I might actually be good at this writing thing. I'm so grateful to have you both in my life, and I can't wait to share more of my work with you in the future.

To my publicist, Cat, thank you for helping to make this series the success that it is today. Without your dedication and support, I would not have reached nearly the amount of readers that I have. You have been an absolute dream to work with, and I feel so fortunate to have found someone like you to help amplify my voice when I felt like I was screaming into a void. Thank you for everything you've done and continue to do to make my career a success.

To my father, John, thank you for making me the writer I am. When other parents told their children to pursue careers that were "safe" and "responsible," you never once stopped encouraging me to follow my passion. Wherever you are, I hope I've made you proud. I love you.

And finally, to you, dear reader. Thank you for choosing this book. Thank you for taking a chance on an indie author. Thank you for making all the frustration, the self-doubt, the second-guessing, the suffering all worth it in the end with the simple act of turning each page. Your readership is what makes this dream of mine possible. I hope this is the first of many stories we'll get to share together.

Editing & Publicity

Catherine Kennedy is a public relations professional with more than 18 years of experience planning, managing, and executing successful national and local media campaigns. She started her full-time public relations career at Wiley publishing house, moved onto a position at a boutique PR agency, and then became a freelance publicist helping authors and experts build a successful brand for themselves. She created CK Publicity to continue her work promoting authors and launching books. Kennedy graduated magna cum laude from New York University with a degree in communications. For more information, visit https://www.ckpublicity.com/

Anthony LaFauci is an author of multiple comic books, graphic novels, children's books, and poems. He has written and performed songs in an assortment of genres for various outlets, and has performed as a voice actor in the tabletop role-playing show Critically Stupid. He is best known for making absurd yet relatable jokes on social media and for being the producer and a co-host on a weekly podcast called We Have Issues. For more information, visit https://www.wehaveissuespodcast.com/